I0818308

LET ME LIVE

(An Ashley Hope Suspense Thriller—Book 3)

Kate Bold

Kate Bold

Bestselling author Kate Bold is author of the ALEXA CHASE SUSPENSE THRILLER series, comprising six books (and counting); the ASHLEY HOPE SUSPENSE THRILLER series, comprising six books (and counting); the CAMILLE GRACE FBI SUSPENSE THRILLER series, comprising five books (and counting); and the HARLEY COLE FBI SUSPENSE THRILLER series, comprising three books (and counting).

An avid reader and lifelong fan of the mystery and thriller genres, Kate loves to hear from you, so please feel free to visit www.kateboldauthor.com to learn more and stay in touch.

ISBN: 978-1-0943-9530-2

BOOKS BY KATE BOLD

ALEXA CHASE SUSPENSE THRILLER
THE KILLING GAME (Book #1)
THE KILLING TIDE (Book #2)
THE KILLING HOUR (Book #3)
THE KILLING POINT (Book #4)
THE KILLING FOG (Book #5)
THE KILLING PLACE (Book #6)

ASHLEY HOPE SUSPENSE THRILLER
LET ME GO (Book #1)
LET ME OUT (Book #2)
LET ME LIVE (Book #3)
LET ME BREATHE (Book #4)
LET ME FORGET (Book #5)
LET ME ESCAPE (Book #6)

CAMILLE GRACE FBI SUSPENSE THRILLER
NOT ME (Book #1)
NOT NOW (Book #2)
NOT WELL (Book #3)
NOT HER (Book #4)
NOT NORMAL (Book #5)

HARLEY COLE FBI SUSPENSE THRILLER
NOWHERE SAFE (Book #1)
NOWHERE LEFT (Book #2)
NOWHERE TO RUN (Book #3)

PROLOGUE

Megan Archer struggled to open her eyes, her lids feeling heavy as iron.

Darkness encompassed her like a death shroud.

She blinked once, then twice, in an effort to clear her vision. To discern a shape. To see something – anything. Still the inky blackness pressed against her, refusing to reveal her surroundings.

Where am I?

Pain shot through her left temple as she attempted to lift her head. A wave of nausea hit her and the taste of bile rose in her throat. She swallowed hard – needed to cough – but she couldn't open her mouth. Duct tape covered her face just below her nostrils, winding tight around her cheeks and the back of her neck, trapping several strands of her curly, blonde hair. The adhesive binding had been wrapped in a series of loops around her head, extending all the way underneath her chin.

Fear gripped Megan's heart as she realized her wrists and ankles were bound by duct tape as well.

Twisting her right hand, she fought to break free of her restraints. But each movement sparked a flash of pain in her skull. And she soon realized her struggles were of no use. Several layers of tape encircled her arms. The grip too snug to slip her hands out. The material too strong to tear.

The chill from the concrete floor below her had seeped through her leather trench coat, settling into her bones. But the texture beneath her fingertips suggested there was something between her body and the concrete.

A layer of plastic?

A pungent chemical odor hung in the dank air, almost stealing her breath. She shuddered as another bout of nausea rippled through her stomach.

How did I get here?

A heavy fog filled her brain, clouding her thoughts. She labored to piece together her last memories. To determine what had led her to this horrible fate.

Molly.

Yes, that was right.

Megan had been on her way to rescue her younger sister – again. Molly had fought with her boyfriend, and this time, he'd kicked her out of his apartment. She'd called from Murfreesboro, Tennessee, in the middle of the night, stating she had no money, no automobile, and nowhere to stay. Of course, Megan had agreed to help – the way she always had whenever her sister's life took a U-turn. An event which had occurred on a frequent basis throughout the past two years.

Megan had left Knoxville around ten this morning. At least, she thought it had been this morning. How long had she been unconscious? How many hours had passed?

A noise caught her attention. It sounded as though it was coming from above her. Was she trapped in a basement? She strained her ears, listening.

Muffled voices echoed from the ceiling.

Megan screamed, her cry muted by the duct tape. She forced her tongue between her lips, trying to unseal the adhesive. She cried out a second time, but again, her shout was too weak to be heard.

Tears of frustration sprang to her eyes.

Above, one of the voices grew louder. A man's voice.

A voice she knew.

A slideshow of memories flooded her mind. She'd been driving along a narrow highway – a shortcut from the main road that would shave at least thirty minutes off of her trip. The motivational words of Cecilia Nettle – one of the top real estate agents in the nation – had boomed from her SUV's speakers. Megan had been concentrating on the instructions for *Overcoming Listing Obstacles* when billows of steam had exploded from her vehicle's hood.

Worried she'd inflict even more damage on her SUV's engine if she tried to drive any further, she'd pulled onto the shoulder of the road. She'd grabbed her phone, intent on calling her husband. But then she'd glanced in her rearview mirror.

It was him.

The voice above her.

When he'd first hopped out of his vehicle, she'd been relieved to see a familiar face. Had thought the man she'd met earlier was there to help. But as she'd swung down from the driver's seat of her SUV to greet him, she'd realized something had changed.

He had changed.

His eyes – once feigning kindness – appeared dark and cold. Instead of the pleasant nature he'd displayed before, a distinct hostility seemed to radiate from his soul.

He'd grabbed her wrist. Terrified, she'd jerked her arm, trying to break free. But then she'd caught a swift flicker of movement out of the corner of her eye. Pain had sliced through the side of her skull. He'd hit her with something made of metal. Something heavy. That's where her memories ended.

And now, she was here.

The voices above her faded. She realized the other person she'd heard might be the man's partner. But why had they kidnapped her? For ransom? Money seemed the most plausible answer. The man had met a woman traveling alone, driving a brand new luxury SUV. Megan wore designer clothes, carried a purse that retailed for over five grand. Yes, the kidnappers most likely wanted cash, thinking she would make an easy mark. And she had.

She wondered whether the man had already contacted her husband, Jay. Whether they'd made a deal. She felt certain he would pay whatever sum the kidnappers had demanded.

The squeal of metal scraping concrete split the air above her. A broad shaft of light cut through the blanket of darkness, stinging her eyes. This wasn't a basement. It was a filthy pit. As she'd suspected, a layer of plastic topped the floor beneath her. It appeared to be a shower curtain.

Footsteps clinked down the treads of the aluminum ladder propped against the far wall.

"'Bout time you woke up," the man said, his tone gruff.

A chill ran down her spine as his gaze locked on hers.

"You been out a while. I was starting to worry."

His lips curved into a wicked smile. "You see, it just ain't as much fun when the prey's asleep."

Terror sliced through Megan's heart.

She realized this wasn't about money. This was something far worse.

The man flexed his hand and she caught the glint of silver metal. A large tool. She had no idea what kind. But it was probably the same thing he'd struck her with earlier, when he'd knocked her unconscious.

"We're gonna have a good time, you and me."

The man laughed, the guttural sound bouncing off the walls of the cramped space.

"Yes, ma'am. I'm gonna teach you some respect."

Megan's pulse quickened as he inched toward her.

Hatred radiated from his narrow eyes.

"Let's start with your knees."

No! Please, no!

Silent tears streamed down her face.

As he raised the tool above his head, Megan pressed her eyes closed, bracing herself for the jolt of pain that would follow.

CHAPTER ONE

It was arson.

Ashley Hope's heart sank as she crossed the threshold into the fire-damaged waiting room at her family's automotive repair shop. The acrid scent of smoke lingered in the air, stinging her throat. Black soot coated the concrete block walls that – just a few years prior – she had helped paint a creamy beige. The bare metal frames of the formerly vinyl-upholstered chairs reminded her of skeletons in a tomb. And the sight of the shattered front windows and glass door – now covered by plywood – chilled her to her core.

Sloshing through puddles of water left behind by the Mettler Ridge Fire Department's dousing of the flames, she maneuvered her way past the charred remnants of a pair of vending machines toward the pile of ash where the check-in counter had once stood. The location where the fire had begun.

Although the investigation was still ongoing, according to the fire chief's initial observations, the blaze had erupted inside a trash can filled with oily rags. Her father and Uncle Russ had invested over twenty-five years, building the business from the ground up in their economically-challenged hometown on Tennessee's Cumberland Plateau. Her family members were well aware of the dangers of storing combustible materials. They would never risk throwing dirty shop rags into a garbage can. Ashley knew the fire wasn't an accident.

It was set on purpose.

She jumped as the door leading to the garage bays pushed open behind her. Her older brother, Kyle, met her gaze, his expression grim. Although the room felt cool, sweat had plastered his wheat-blonde hair to his scalp like a helmet. Since their father's retirement – the result of a recent heart attack – her brother had taken over the management of the shop while still maintaining his lead mechanic duties. She could tell the long working hours had taken their toll. And now he had to deal with the fire damage.

"I'm the one who brought this vendetta onto the family, Kyle, and I'm really sorry," she said, her eyes welling with tears.

Ashley felt certain the fire was payback. Working as a consultant, she'd joined forces with the Tennessee Bureau of Investigations in their pursuit of a serial killer. The man had been a local – a deputy with the Laurel County Sheriff's department. When he realized he was trapped, Troy Luckadoo had brandished a hunting knife, intending to plunge the blade into the heart of his fourth victim.

After her pleas for the deputy to drop his weapon had failed, Ashley was left with only one choice. She'd shot Troy. And now, she believed the deputy's backwoods relatives had targeted the auto shop in an act of revenge for the man's death.

A clandestine eye-for-an-eye type practice the Laurel County locals termed *mountain justice*.

Kyle shook his head.

"You done what was right," he told her, sincerity evident in his blue eyes. "You should be proud. You saved Beth's life. And her daddy's mighty grateful. Weren't no way he was gonna let the place burn down."

The father of Troy's would-be fourth victim, Beth, held the rank of captain at the fire department. He'd been on duty when the call from Hope Automotive Repair had gone out. Thanks to the man's quick response, and the fact that the fire department was located only a block away, the blaze had been contained to the waiting area.

Ashley sighed.

"I just wish that Uncle Russ shared your opinion," she stated.

Although the shop had been closed when the fire had started, her uncle's two sons had been working on a customer's car in one of the garage bays. They could have been killed. A point that her uncle had stressed several times since the incident, even stating that Ashley should have refused the request to team up with the TBI – that she should have known that her actions would place her own family in jeopardy. The reality that she had saved a woman's life seemed irrelevant to him.

"It don't matter what Uncle Russ thinks," Kyle said. "You did what you had to. Me, Daddy, and Shane know it. And you didn't go to the police academy for nothing."

She felt grateful that her father and younger brother, Shane, understood – had supported her along with Kyle – but Ashley hated being the source of friction between her family members.

The fire had been set two days earlier – the day of her graduation from Highland Rim Law Enforcement Academy. Up until now, Uncle Russ had never voiced an opposition to her chosen career. It seemed he didn't mind her working as a police officer. He just didn't want her arresting criminals in her own hometown.

As in the days of prohibition when state agents had invaded the mountains searching for moonshine stills, many Laurel County natives viewed law enforcement officials as the enemy. And Uncle Russ feared being on the receiving end of the locals' hostility. He'd warned her father that even more retaliation could follow.

Ashley worried her uncle might be right.

She clenched her bottom lip between her teeth, wondering if she should tell Kyle her plans.

"I drove over to Briarwood early this morning and put in an application for an apartment," she finally said.

For the past few months, Ashley had been staying in an old mobile home on the rear corner of her father's one-hundred-and-fifty-acre property – passed down through the Hope family for generations. Although she loved living on the same plot of land as her father and brothers, she realized it might be best for all of her relatives if she found a place of her own – outside of Laurel County.

"You ain't no city girl," Kyle replied, disappointment clear on his face. "I thought you done figured that out by now."

Ashley had fled her hometown once before – to attend the University of Tennessee in Chattanooga. Just prior to completing her master's in criminal justice, she'd moved to Briarwood with her wealthy former fiancé. Although her brief time in the Nashville suburb had proved challenging as she'd struggled to fit in to an affluent neighborhood, she felt she hadn't given the area a real chance.

This time, she'd strike out on her own. Make new friends. Could possibly meet other people who shared a similar modest background. And if she returned to Briarwood – a two-hour drive away – she wouldn't be present to pose a threat to her family. She hoped the old adage *"out of sight, out of mind"* would hold true in regards to the feud with Troy's relatives.

"If everything goes well with my interview tomorrow and I'm offered an agent position with the TBI, I'll be working out of Briarwood. It just makes more sense for me to live there," she said, hoping her brother would believe her reasoning was that simple.

Kyle stared at her. He didn't seem convinced.

"Don't be leaving on account of the fire," he said. "Me and Shane know how to handle Troy's kin."

Anxiety flooded Ashley's chest. Kyle's words fueled her fear of an all-out war between the opposing families. If her brothers retaliated, the situation would continue to escalate.

She grabbed Kyle's arm.

"I want you to promise me that you and Shane won't do anything to Troy's relatives," she said. "Just let the authorities handle things."

Ashley realized the investigators would likely not be able to collect enough evidence to obtain an arrest warrant for the arson, but at this point, that didn't matter. Her only concern was keeping her family safe. She hoped that if her brothers backed off, if they let the matter drop, the feud would be settled.

Kyle averted his gaze. "Can't make no promises."

She fought the urge to shake her brother, to force him to listen.

"Don't you understand that if you strike back it will only make things worse? One – or maybe even both of you – could get killed."

He pulled his arm from her grasp, brushing her aside.

"We know how to take care of ourselves," he replied as though it irritated him that she might think otherwise.

Kyle's refusal to handle the situation with logic rather than pride cemented her resolution to leave Laurel County. The odds of harm befalling her family increased with every moment she remained. But once she was gone – after Troy's family learned she'd left town for good – the conflict stood a better chance of being resolved.

Ashley heard the door leading to the garage area swing open again.

Her stomach fluttered as a familiar pair of blue eyes locked with her own. Daniel Lansing, a special agent with the Tennessee Bureau of Investigations, strode toward her, a lightweight overcoat topping his athletic frame. His dark brown hair had been trimmed since she'd seen him last. A slight smile danced across his face as he nodded a greeting and then turned toward her brother.

"It's good to see you, Kyle," the agent said, shaking her brother's hand.

Daniel had led the homicide investigation that had resulted in Troy's death. In the process of working with Ashley, he'd come to know her father and brothers as well. Her family seemed to respect the dedicated agent almost as much as she did.

"Same here," Kyle said. "You got any word from the fire investigator?"

On the day of the arson, Daniel had attended Ashley's graduation ceremony at the police academy in the neighboring county. When her family received the news that the shop had caught fire, the agent had rushed to the scene, contacting the TBI's fire investigation division along the way.

Daniel shook his head. "No, not yet. But our team has made your case a priority. They're processing the evidence as fast as they can."

She had assumed the agent had come to share new information regarding the arson. Since that obviously wasn't the case, she wondered what the reason was for his visit.

"We sure appreciate it," Kyle said. He glanced at Ashley with a solemn look in his eyes. "I reckon I best be getting to work, or I won't be leaving till midnight."

As she watched her brother plow back through the door leading to the garage bays, Ashley prayed her warning to stay away from Troy's relatives had sunk into Kyle's thick skull. Stubbornness ran strong in the Hope family line.

She met Daniel's gaze.

"You're not here to tell me that my job interview with the TBI has been canceled, are you?"

The agent had pulled strings with his boss to get Ashley a shot at the position. There was only one job currently open and the competition was fierce. She'd been told that several of the applicants already had years of law enforcement experience under their belt.

He shook his head, his expression bleak.

"No. It's not that."

Apprehension swelled in her chest. Whatever he had to say, she could tell it was bad news.

"It must be something really important for you to make the two-hour drive from Briarwood," she said, bracing herself for his explanation.

"Yeah, it is."

He stepped back and motioned toward the door.

"Why don't you come to the diner with me? We can grab an early dinner, and I'll fill you in."

Although she could tell he was making an attempt to keep his voice light, his body language let her know that something serious had happened. Her only option was to agree.

A cloud of dread hung over Ashley as she led the agent through the garage area and out into the auto repair shop's parking lot. He glanced back at her before hopping into his sedan. She remembered the news that Daniel had delivered the last time she'd seen that look in his eyes.

He'd told her there had been a murder.

CHAPTER TWO

A stiff breeze tousled Ashley's long blonde hair as she slid out from the driver's seat of her silver sedan in the parking lot of the local Laurel County restaurant. Arriving just a few seconds after Daniel, she'd wheeled into the space adjacent to the agent's car. The white TBI-issued Toyota – confiscated to serve as an undercover vehicle – appeared pale amber beneath the glow of the red and yellow sign emblazoned with the name *Mettler Ridge's Finest Diner*. A true moniker due to the fact the establishment was the only one of its kind located in the small town.

Although it was just the first week of November, an unexpected cold front had bombarded the plateau, infusing the early evening air with a frosty chill. Pulling her jacket snug around her, she mounted the sidewalk and headed toward the diner's entrance. A weak smile flashed across Daniel's face as he held open the door and waited for her to walk inside.

Ashley had been surprised by the agent's visit to her family's auto repair shop. She guessed that the news he wanted to share must be serious. Otherwise, he would have related the information over the phone rather than making the long drive from Briarwood. But then she reminded herself that Daniel's assigned territory included Laurel County. It was possible that he could have already been in the area on TBI business.

Had there been another murder in Mettler Ridge?

She pushed the horrible thought aside, not wanting to entertain the notion that someone else may have been killed.

A welcome gust of heat hit her as she crossed the diner's threshold amidst the clacking of plates and the lively chatter of the patrons. Ashley's stomach rumbled as the heavy aroma of fried food wafted through the air. She'd spent the day touring apartment complexes in Briarwood and had skipped lunch. Now at six o'clock, she felt famished.

Greeted by the ever-present floor sign stating *Please Seat Yourself*, she led Daniel past the serving counter lined with customers to a booth in the far right corner. The current hour always proved to be one of the busiest times of day for the diner, so she'd chosen the location farthest from the action. She hoped the spot would afford them a small amount of privacy in case the agent's news involved an ongoing investigation.

Ashley scooted onto the red vinyl bench, feeling her stomach rumble a second time. Daniel plopped onto the seat across from her and grabbed two menus from the wire basket housed at the end of the table next to the window. He slid one of the menus toward her and then flipped open the other.

Anticipation built in her chest as she watched the agent scan the food selections. Although her stomach cried out to be fed, she needed Daniel to reveal the reason for his visit before she could even begin to think about placing an order.

"How much longer do you plan to keep me in suspense before you tell me why you're here?" she asked, struggling to keep her frustration from her tone.

He glanced up at her, his lips pressing into a thin line.

"It concerns Troy Luckadoo," he said, his voice low.

Her exasperation morphed into a sense of alarm. She hoped the higher-ups at the TBI hadn't changed their minds about her well-justified use of deadly force. Was the Luckadoo family pushing for charges to be brought against her?

Before Daniel could utter another word, their server, Lou Ann, approached the table, a harried expression pasted on her face. She appeared to be working the booths alone, leading Ashley to believe the diner must be short staffed for the evening crowd.

Right after high school graduation, Ashley had lived in a trailer park next door to Lou Ann. Almost nine years had passed since that time, but the svelte woman – who was now in her mid-thirties – hadn't seemed to age a day. Not a single line or blemish could be seen on her makeup-free skin. Her long red ponytail bobbed as she whipped out her order pad.

"Hey Ashley," Lou Ann said in a rushed tone. "Y'all know what you want?"

Ashley didn't need to browse the menu; she knew it by heart.

"I'll have the grilled chicken salad and a glass of unsweetened iced tea, please."

"How 'bout you?" the server said, casting a wary eye toward Daniel.

Lou Ann and Daniel had met during the investigation of Deputy Troy Luckadoo. Although the agent should have been deemed a hero for his work in putting an end to the serial murders in Laurel County, like many of the other folks in town, it seemed clear the server still doubted Daniel's trustworthiness.

He closed his menu.

"Give me the double cheeseburger," he said, watching Lou Ann scribble on her pad. "A double order of onion rings. Iced tea – sweet. And a slice of pecan pie."

Based on the quantity and nutritional quality of food Ashley had watched Daniel consume over the past month, she surmised he must either possess the metabolism of a thirteen-year-old track star, or he spent all of his free time at the gym. Maybe both.

Lou Ann stuffed her order pad into the pocket of her apron and headed back toward the counter.

The instant the server was out of earshot, Ashley pounced on Daniel.

"Does the TBI think that I was wrong for shooting Troy – that I screwed up the case?"

The agent shook his head. "You followed protocol. A victim's life was on the line. When you fired, I was already aiming. If you hadn't taken Troy out, I would have."

Although she knew in her gut that she'd made the right move – had saved Beth's life – it was comforting to know that Daniel would have acted in the same manner.

"Then what's going on now that's got you so unnerved?"

The agent glanced behind him as though he was checking to make sure no one was close enough to overhear their conversation.

"I've been in Laurel County since early this morning."

He paused and stared at her a moment.

"We found another body," he finally said.

The news jarred Ashley. "Another body? Where?"

"When our forensics team tossed Troy's trailer, they found something. I'm not at liberty to say what yet. Not even to you. But it led us to an abandoned property in Tucker Hollow. This morning, we searched an old well there."

The thick-forested Tucker Holler provided the backdrop for a number of local legends involving the ghosts of lawmen sent in by the state to shut down the moonshine stills. The men's fate had been sealed the moment they'd entered Laurel County. Their bodies had never been found. Filled with abandoned coal mines and ancient wells from crumbing homesteads, the holler held many hiding spots. And – Ashley ventured to guess – dark secrets.

"Holler," she corrected, supplying the pronunciation that matched the mountain location's spelling.

"What?" He appeared confused, like his mind had gone in a different direction, as though he thought she wanted him to shout.

"It's not important," she said, brushing it off. "Just tell me about the body your team found at the bottom of the well."

Daniel met her gaze. "We think it's Holly."

Troy's ex-girlfriend had disappeared without a trace just a few months before he began his known killing spree. Once his deeds came to light, it was suspected that Holly had been his actual first victim.

The agent continued, "We're keeping it under wraps for now. Until we can get DNA. But the jewelry on the corpse is a match."

Although she wished the outcome had been different – that Holly had simply left the area in search of a more fulfilling life – Ashley was grateful that the woman's family would finally have an answer as to what had become of their loved one.

She caught movement out of the corner of her eye.

"Lou Ann is headed this way," she warned.

The server plucked a glass of iced tea from the tray she carried and placed it in front of Ashley.

"Unsweet, right?" she asked.

Ashley nodded.

Lou Ann placed the other glass in front of Daniel without looking at him.

"Y'all need anything else right now?" she asked, dropping two straws onto the middle of the table.

"I think we're good, Lou Ann; thank you," Ashley said.

The server's ponytail swayed as she turned and made her way toward another booth.

Ashley and Daniel both reached for a straw at the same instant. As the agent's fingertips brushed against hers, Ashley's heart fluttered.

"Sorry," she said, jerking her hand back. She hoped he couldn't see the heat rising in her cheeks.

She'd first met Daniel when she was living in Briarwood with her former fiancé. Their relationship had been nothing but professional – in fact, it still was. But there had come a point during the Troy Luckadoo investigation when her feelings for the agent had shifted. They'd been crossing a creek when Ashley's foot slipped on a stone. Daniel had caught her right before she fell into the water, cradling her in his arms. As they locked eyes, a jolt of electricity had raced through her soul. It was like nothing she had ever experienced before.

Ashley had been both relieved and disappointed that the agent hadn't noticed or that he hadn't shared in the moment. But she knew it was for the best.

Since that day, she'd fought to contain the strong attraction that now drew her to Daniel like a magnet. But no matter how deep she buried her feelings, they kept popping to the surface. She'd reminded herself time and again that a romantic relationship with the agent was out of the question. They worked together. They would be true colleagues if she was offered the job with the TBI. Office romances – which she knew seldom ended well – were especially frowned upon in law enforcement, where lives were on the line.

And she'd built a genuine friendship with Daniel. One she didn't want to risk losing.

Logic would just have to temper her heart. Even though it seemed nearly impossible at the moment, she'd keep shoving her feelings aside until they faded into nothingness.

"You ready for your interview?" he asked, apparently unaware of her discomfort.

"I'm nervous and excited and a whole host of other things, but I don't think ready is one of them."

The change of subject seemed to lighten his mood. He grinned, his dimples showing.

"You'll do well."

"It's good to know that one of us thinks so."

Ashley wondered whether any news of the competition had filtered down to Daniel. No matter how tight the ship, there were always leaks. And she knew that the agent had a friend who worked in the HR department.

"Have you heard how many people they've interviewed for the job so far?"

He nodded. "About a dozen. You're the last applicant."

She didn't know whether that was good or bad.

"Do you know if they're leaning toward any one person yet?"

He stared at her. It seemed as though he was considering his words before he spoke. Although he'd always been quick to give her encouragement, she knew he'd never lie about the situation.

"There's a cop from Nashville," Daniel finally said. "A detective. He's been on the force ten years. I've heard he's in the lead, but that doesn't mean anything. They haven't seen you yet."

Her hopes sank. She'd known they were interviewing people who had law enforcement experience, but to hear that they already had a favorite dampened her spirits.

Lou Ann appeared at their table, her tray loaded with food.

Ashley stared at the plate that had been placed before her, piled high with grilled chicken, cherry tomatoes, sliced cucumbers, and a mix of greens. Only moments ago, she'd felt as though she was on the verge of starvation. Now, her appetite had fled. Replaced by a solid ball of nerves.

She glanced at Daniel as he slathered ketchup onto his burger. The agent had risked his reputation – and his job – by bringing her into Troy's investigation as a local consultant. Then he'd gone out of his way to get her this interview. He had shown tremendous faith in her. She couldn't let him down.

Tomorrow morning she'd march into the TBI office in Briarwood with her head held high. What she lacked in experience, she'd make up for with determination. She'd find a way to outshine the competition. Whatever it took, Ashley resolved to prove to the TBI that she was the right person for the job.

As she watched him chew his food, Ashley noticed a troubled expression drift back onto Daniel's face. Was he still thinking about Holly, or was there another matter that had him rattled?

"Did something else happen that I need to know about?" she asked.

He dropped the burger onto his plate and wiped his fingers with his napkin.

"It's that piece of evidence. The one we found in Troy's trailer. You know I can't discuss the details, but there's something else I need to tell you."

She wondered whether there had been even more murders – more bodies that hadn't yet been discovered.

"What is it?"

He glanced over his shoulder again, checking to make sure Lou Ann was out of earshot.

"Someone else knew about the women Troy killed. We don't know who. It's either a friend or a relative. But we're sure he had help."

Fear wormed its way into Ashley's chest.

Was a murderer still loose in Laurel County?

CHAPTER THREE

Bonner County Sheriff's Deputy Cody Medford wheeled his patrol car off the highway and coasted onto the gravel parking area at the scenic overlook. It seemed as good a location as any to relieve himself. He glanced at the dashboard clock. 3:49 a.m. He still had over three hours left on his graveyard shift. And it hadn't gone well so far.

Just before midnight, he'd responded to a bar brawl and had sprained his wrist in the process of carting two belligerent drunks off to county lockup. After that, he'd been called to a domestic disturbance where he'd barely managed to escape being punched in the face by yet another drunk. And as he'd headed back on patrol, his phone had slipped from his pocket, landing on the pavement, cracking the screen.

What else would the night thrust at him?

Killing his headlights, Cody hopped out of the cruiser into the chilly mountain air. He stood still for a moment, allowing his eyes to adjust to the darkness. The shape of the concrete picnic table – where he'd eaten his home-packed dinner on more than one occasion – materialized before him.

The gravel crunched beneath his boots as he made his way past the table toward the edge of the adjacent forest. He ducked behind a large bush and took care of his business. As he zipped his pants, his radio crackled to life.

"We got a stolen vehicle report," the female dispatcher stated in a flat tone.

He listened to the BOLO (be on the lookout) details – the make, model, color, plate number, and last known location – thankful that he wasn't being called to a scene.

He wandered toward the overlook's barrier – a heavy chain strung along a line of wooden posts – and gazed out at the timbered valley below. In the absence of the moon, the stars sparkled in the inky sky like diamonds.

Like the diamond he'd bought for Tessa.

There were still eighteen months of loan payments left before the engagement and wedding rings would officially be their own. Which wouldn't concern him quite as much if he hadn't been hit by two unforeseen blows. Over the weekend, their landlord had announced he was raising their rent.

And yesterday, Cody had learned he was going to be a father.

Tessa had peed on the sticks from three different brands of home pregnancy tests just to make sure. The results had shocked him so bad his head had spun. It wasn't that he didn't want children; it just felt as though things were happening too fast. They'd only been married five months and he'd only held his job with the sheriff's department for a little over a year.

At twenty-four years old, the thought of raising a child – of being responsible for molding an innocent human being – terrified him. Growing up without his own father for a role model, he feared he would fall short. That he would somehow end up ruining the kid's life.

He slipped the gold band from his left ring finger and slid it back and forth against his palm. He'd known Tessa was the woman for him the minute he'd laid eyes on her. Admittedly, he was first drawn in by her big brown eyes and long dark hair, as well as her perfect hourglass figure. But it was her sweet personality and the fact that she was a fan of *Monty Python* – something the other women he'd dated had never even heard of – that had sealed the deal. He loved her with all of his heart.

But he couldn't help thinking that she deserved more. Deserved a man strong enough to face the future without fear. He needed to be that man.

For Tessa's sake.

For their baby's sake.

He twirled his wedding ring between his thumb and index finger, wondering whether he should try to find a part-time job to supplement their income. His deputy's salary didn't stretch very far and Tessa's cashier position wasn't full-time, so there was no paid maternity leave. And the baby would need things. A crib. A car seat. Clothes. Diapers. And who knew what else.

A high-pitched squeal erupted from his radio and Cody jumped. His thumb flicked against his ring, sending the gold band flying over the barrier chain.

"Shit," he cursed aloud.

Some idiot had keyed their mic too close to their cruiser's radio speaker. When he found out who the culprit was, he'd threaten to wring their neck.

He pulled the Maglite from his belt and switched it on. He had to find his ring. Otherwise, Tessa would kill him. He stepped across the barrier and directed the beam of light into the tall grass. With no idea how far the ring had flown before landing, he dropped to his knees. Moving forward mere inches at a time, he scanned the ground from left to right, parting the grass as he went.

An owl hooted, startling him.

He jerked upright, almost dropping his flashlight. As the beam had bounced upward, he'd caught the glint of metal a few feet in front of him, at the base of a limestone slab. Relief flooded his chest as he lumbered forward and reached for his wedding band.

But as his fingers touched metal, he realized it wasn't his ring after all.

And the dark shape wasn't a slab of rock.

Panic struck Cody as he swept his Maglite across the row of gold buttons, ending at the collar of the leather coat. The beam illuminated what he thought had once been the face of a woman. Dried blood caked her skin and clung to her blonde curls. Her cheeks sunk inward and the cartilage of her nose hung limp. Her mouth gaped open, revealing a dark hollow void of teeth. Her chin and jaws melted into her neck. It looked as though her skull had been pummeled with a hammer.

With a shaky hand, he pressed the button on the radio clipped to his shirt.

Cody didn't need to check for a pulse to know the woman was dead.

CHAPTER FOUR

Ashley struggled to keep from fidgeting as she watched Ted Rayburn, the head of the TBI's human resources department, peck her answer to his most recent question into the laptop lodged on the cherry conference table between them. It seemed clear by his lack of speed that the man was accustomed to having someone else do his typing for him. She wondered why the short, round man didn't just jot her replies down by hand and have them entered into the computer after she left. Or better yet, he could just play the video footage she knew was being captured by the camera housed in the room's upper right corner.

When she'd arrived at the Tennessee Bureau of Investigation's satellite office in Briarwood that morning, Ashley had expected to meet with the deputy director, Brenda Huddleston. But due to an emergency, she'd been informed that Mr. Rayburn would be conducting her interview instead. Which Ashley believed was code for: *you didn't get the job*.

She assumed the position would be – or already had been – offered to the Nashville police detective Daniel had mentioned. And that her interview was merely obligatory. Still, she'd answered each question posed to her with careful thought, as though she had a shot. It was possible another position would become available at a later date, so she wanted to make a good impression.

The interview had fallen into a circular pattern, as though they were rehearsing a dance routine. Mr. Rayburn would read a question from the list on his screen. Then he'd peer at her over the rim of his black reading glasses as she provided an honest response. He'd key in her answer – or perhaps his own version of her answer – at a snail's pace. And then the process would start all over again.

Ashley swiveled in her chair as the door to the small conference room pushed open behind her. An older woman – in her early sixties most likely – wearing a burgundy pantsuit, her salt and pepper hair cut in a short bob, crossed the threshold.

"Ashley, I'm Brenda Huddleston, the deputy director," the woman said as she shook Ashley's hand.

Ashley had recognized Brenda from the pictures she'd seen on the TBI's website.

"I've been looking forward to meeting you," she replied, surprised the woman had actually shown up for the interview.

"Likewise. I'm sure Ted explained the reason for my absence. And by now, he's no doubt filled in all the necessary information on his questionnaire. So what do you say we get down to business?"

Although she wasn't exactly certain what the deputy director meant, it dawned on Ashley that she might still have a chance at landing the job.

"I'm ready." It was the only reply that popped into her mind.

"Good," Brenda said, seeming satisfied with the short answer. "I'm impressed by the work you did in Laurel County last month. According to Special Agent Daniel Lansing's report, you're the person who uncovered the identity of the man responsible for kidnapping and murdering three women. And your actions saved the life of the man's fourth victim."

Ashley hadn't expected to be greeted by praise.

"Agent Lansing is the one who deserves most of the credit," she said. "I was just following a hunch."

"Don't sell yourself short, Ashley," Brenda stated, leaning her hip against the conference table. "The correct instincts are vital in solving the most difficult cases."

Although she guessed that could be true, Ashley knew there was no substitute for hard work.

Brenda continued, "Here at the TBI, we pride ourselves on hiring and maintaining the most competent agents in the state. The top tier of law enforcement. But there seems to be one area where we're lacking."

Ashley wondered what the void could possibly be and whether she would be expected to fill it.

The deputy director folded her arms across her chest. "The crime rate in Tennessee is rising fast, especially in our rural counties along the Cumberland Plateau. I know Daniel explained to you how difficult it was for him to build a rapport with the locals in Laurel County. Every day our agents are faced with roadblocks in obtaining information from the residents in these rural areas. This communication failure has resulted in a backlog of unsolved cases."

Brenda paused, as though giving Ashley time to process the information. But her mind had already skipped ahead. The TBI obviously wanted to add someone born and bred in the backwoods to their team. That desire was probably the only reason she was being considered for the open position.

The deputy director straightened her posture. “We need a special agent who can relate to the people living in these remote locations. A person who can gain their trust. Do you think you have what it takes to be that agent?”

As soon as she’d realized the job would center around the Cumberland Plateau, disappointment had spread throughout Ashley’s veins. She longed to start a new life – away from the mountains. She’d hoped her duties would revolve around the bustling city of Briarwood and the other suburbs of Nashville. She wanted new experiences. To become a better version of herself. To grow to her full potential. And not be stuck in decaying towns like Mettler Ridge where families continued to engage in archaic feuds and clandestine forms of vigilante justice still ruled.

But Ashley’s preferred working territory wasn’t up for debate. The question was whether or not she felt she possessed the ability to communicate with the mountain folk and earn their confidence. The answer was simple.

“Yes, ma’am. I think I do.”

She wasn’t agreeing to accept the position; she was just stating a fact. She’d have time to mull over her decision once a job offer was formally made.

If one was made.

Brenda nodded, a contented expression settling onto her face. “I’m glad to hear you say that.”

The woman leaned against the table once again. “What I have in mind is a bit unorthodox,” she began. “We received a request this morning from the local authorities in Bonner County. Do you know the area?”

Ashley was somewhat familiar with the location – roughly an hour and a half north of Laurel County – but she didn’t know anyone who lived there.

“I’ve driven through Bonner County on my way to Kentucky a few times, but that’s about it.”

The fact that Ashley wasn’t better acquainted with the area didn’t seem to faze Brenda.

"The sheriff has reason to believe that there may be a serial killer stalking the county's roadways. They've found two bodies so far. The only connection the victims seem to share is that they were both killed in the same manner. The district attorney has requested immediate help. And I think it's possible that you might be the best person for the job."

Ashley took a deep breath, trying to digest the situation. It pained her to hear that two people had lost their lives.

"You said that you had something unconventional in mind?"

Brenda nodded. "I'd like to send you in on a trial run. You'll be partnered with a seasoned agent. He'll help you get your bearings and will be there to instruct you in all of our procedures. If things go well, if both you and I are happy with the outcome, then you'll be offered a permanent position."

Although it wasn't what Ashley had expected, the idea seemed to be a fair one.

"How much time do I have to think it over?"

"I need your decision right now," Brenda stated, her voice firm. "And you'll need to be in Bonner County by this evening."

The quick turn of events shocked Ashley. She'd never dreamed that she'd be forced to make a life-altering career decision at the spur of the moment. But in this case, what did she have to lose? She was being offered the assignment on a trial basis. If at any time she decided she hated the work – if being stuck in a small mountain town left her feeling suffocated – she could just walk away.

And if there was even the slightest chance that she could help capture the murderer – that she could prevent them from killing again – how could she refuse?

"Okay," she said, nodding. "I'll take the job."

"Good," Brenda replied, her demeanor reflecting that she'd never entertained the possibility that Ashley would choose otherwise. "Ted will take you upstairs where you'll be issued your credentials and firearm. He'll introduce you to your new partner, and then you'll be on your way to Bonner County."

"Thank you for having faith in me," Ashley said, rising from her chair.

Nervous excitement sprouted in her chest as she watched Brenda head back through the conference room door. Although Ashley wouldn't be fighting crime in the city as she'd hoped, it was finally official. The next phase of her life had begun.

And she couldn't wait to get to work.

But then Daniel's words floated back into her thoughts, as they had several times since the night before. Troy had received some kind of help in the murders of his victims. Maybe from a relative.

Ashley just prayed the Luckadoo clan would stay away from her family while she was gone.

CHAPTER FIVE

Ashley's gaze darted back to her aging mobile home as she climbed into the passenger seat of Special Agent Wyatt Clark's black SUV, plagued by the notion that there was something she'd forgotten to pack. She'd stuffed a week's worth of clothing along with her toothbrush and toiletries into her suitcase at break-neck speed. Except for the silk blouse and black slacks she'd worn for the interview, her wardrobe lacked what she would consider proper TBI business attire. No pantsuits – like the one Brenda Huddleston had sported – or blazers. She'd always assumed that she'd have plenty of time to shop after she received a job offer.

But life just kept throwing her curve balls.

Standing at the door of her bedroom's small closet, it had hit her that for this case, she didn't need to appear professional. In fact, the designer silk blouse – purchased when she'd lived in Briarwood – might prove to be a stumbling block. Her job was to earn the trust of the people living in Bonner County. In order not to alienate the locals right off the bat, she needed to dress like them.

Needed to fit in.

To that end, she'd changed into jeans, a long-sleeved cotton shirt and her trusted hiking boots. And she'd pulled her long hair back into a ponytail, secured with a black scrunchie with her initial, *A*, embroidered in white. Wyatt had cast a wary eye at her as she'd lugged her suitcase down the steps of her trailer's wooden front porch. It seemed clear he preferred her previous outfit.

Her new partner slammed the driver's door shut and started the SUV's engine. His hazel eyes focused on the rearview camera as he backed around her sedan.

"So how long have you been working for the TBI?" she asked.

His name and the fact that he was considered *seasoned* were the only details Ashley knew about the agent. If she had to guess, she'd peg him to be around eight to ten years her senior, which would put him anywhere from thirty-five to thirty-seven years old. He wore his sandy blonde hair parted on the left, in a style that just missed brushing the back of his button-down collar. And he had an air of self-assurance about him, which she hoped stemmed from confidence that they'd be successful in catching Bonner County's murderer and not from arrogance.

"A while," he replied, shifting his gaze toward the long hard-packed dirt driveway that crossed her father's land.

She waited for him to elaborate. He didn't.

In silence, Wyatt steered the SUV along the winding drive through a grove of cedars and past a spring-fed pond. As they approached the Appalachian farmhouse built by her great-grandfather long before she was born, Ashley caught sight of her father's pickup truck pulling into the parking area, a cloud of dust in its wake.

"We need to stop, Wyatt," she said. "That's my father and brother. I have to tell them where I'm heading."

"You know we're pushing the clock," the agent reminded her.

"I promise it'll only take me a few minutes to explain everything. And they'll probably come after you with guns blazing – thinking I've been kidnapped – if we keep going."

The look Wyatt flashed her said that he was debating whether or not she was serious. She was.

With a sigh, the agent circled the SUV around and stopped in front of the farmhouse. Ashley hopped out of the passenger seat as her father strode toward her, confusion clouding his blue eyes. Although he was still weak from the heart attack that had hit him in the spring, she knew he wouldn't hesitate to draw the Smith & Wesson he kept holstered in his waistband if he thought his daughter was in danger.

"Daddy, this is Special Agent Wyatt Clark with the TBI," she said, stepping between her father and newly-assigned partner. "And this is my father, Spencer Hope."

The two men shook hands, but the guarded expression remained on her father's weathered face.

"It's nice meeting you," Wyatt said, as though he was being sincere.

Spencer nodded, the late afternoon sun highlighting the streaks of gray in his auburn hair. "Weren't expecting company, or we would of stayed home."

"Wyatt didn't come here for a visit, Daddy," she said. "We're working together on a homicide investigation."

The explanation seemed to catch her father off guard just as much as finding a stranger's SUV in his driveway had. He'd known about her interview that morning, but like Ashley, he'd probably never anticipated that she'd begin work the same day.

The passenger door of Spencer's pickup slammed shut, drawing Ashley's attention. Her younger brother, Shane, maneuvered his wheeled walker around a rut in the dusty red clay, his steps calculated.

Shane had suffered a spinal injury several months earlier at the hands of the serial killer, Ethan Barrett – who also happened to be Ashley's ex-husband. Although her brother's recovery was going well, it pained her to see him relying on the walker. And Ashley knew the guilt she felt from bringing her ex into her family members' lives would haunt her until the day she died.

"Does that mean you done got the job?" her brother asked, a smile spreading across his face.

Since her position with the TBI wasn't yet permanent, Ashley wasn't quite sure how to answer. She glanced at Wyatt.

"This is my brother, Shane," she stated, deciding to avoid explaining the details of her employment for the moment.

"You be sure to take care of my sister," Shane instructed, gripping the agent's outstretched hand.

"I have it on good authority that Ashley can take care of herself," Wyatt said, surprising her.

"You got that right." A hint of pride infused her brother's words.

Shane adjusted the camouflage ball cap that covered his auburn hair and then turned his gaze toward Ashley.

"Has there done been another killing in Laurel County?"

Her thoughts switched to the skeleton that Daniel's team had found at the bottom of the well in Tucker Holler. Although the TBI had the area sealed off from the locals, she knew it wouldn't be long before news of the recovered bones leaked out. But she would keep the knowledge to herself until after Holly's remains were identified and the woman's family informed.

"We're investigating two murders that took place up in Bonner County," she told her brother.

Wyatt cut his eyes at her, as though he was warning her not to spill too much information. The gesture insulted Ashley. She wasn't stupid enough to risk jeopardizing the case.

Spencer motioned toward the farmhouse. "We got some fresh lemonade inside. Y'all come in and sit a spell."

Her father probably wanted to find out more about Wyatt before he allowed the man to take off with his daughter.

"I'm sorry, Daddy, but we're already running late as it is."

He nodded, stepping toward her. She realized the look of concern was still etched on his face. Instinct told her it wasn't because Wyatt was a stranger.

Something was wrong.

"What's going on?" she asked as a knot of anxiety formed in her chest.

A second ticked by before her father answered. "I reckon it's best you get out of town for a while."

"Has something else happened – is Kyle okay?"

She prayed Troy Luckadoo's relatives hadn't returned to the auto repair shop.

"Kyle's fine. Don't you worry about us none."

Telling her not to worry about her family was equivalent to telling the sun not to shine.

Shane interjected, "The Luckadoo clan's done put out word that they ain't finished. They're looking to mess with you, Ashley."

The fact that Troy's relatives had singled her out specifically might mean that they were shifting their focus away from her father and brothers. At least, she hoped that's what it meant.

"Shane, I want you to send out a message from me," she said. "I want you to tell everyone who will listen that I'm leaving Laurel County for good."

Spencer touched her arm. "Hopes don't run. We stand our ground," he reminded her, his voice firm.

"I'm not running, Daddy," she assured him. "I've just decided that it's time to get on with my life."

She could see in her father's eyes that her absence – the fact that he'd miss her – troubled him more than a dent in their family's pride.

"Alright then," Spencer said, pulling her into a hug. "You best call me when you get to Bonner County."

Although she was an adult – and had proven capable of handling herself on more than one occasion – Ashley knew her father continued to worry about her as though she was still a little girl. And that would never change.

"Be careful, Ash," Shane called as she climbed back into Wyatt's SUV.

The agent shifted the transmission into reverse.

She realized she should explain the fallout of her last case to her new partner. Let him know the reason she was being targeted.

"I killed a man – a sheriff's deputy – named Troy Luckadoo," she said, studying Wyatt's face for a reaction.

He remained stoic.

"I've been briefed on the case, and I know about the fire at the auto shop," the agent stated, his tone flat.

It made sense that the TBI would inform Wyatt. From his nonchalant attitude, it seemed the fact that his partner might be in the crosshairs of a band of mountain vigilantes didn't faze him.

And Ashley knew she needed to push her troubles aside and focus on the murders in Bonner County. But she couldn't shake the feeling that the person who had helped Troy Luckadoo kill his victims was leading the drive for revenge against her.

Were they watching her now?

Would they follow her to Bonner County?

Peering back through the SUV's rear window, she prayed that her family would remain safe. The images of her father and brother faded into the swirls of dust kicked up by the vehicle's tires as the agent sped down the drive.

CHAPTER SIX

Ashley pulled her attention away from the rear window of Wyatt's SUV and settled into the passenger seat. The warning look the agent had thrown her when she'd told Shane about the murders in Bonner County still stung. Did he really believe that she was stupid enough to let privileged information slip out?

The drive from her father's home to the Bonner County Sheriff's Department would span at least an hour and a half. She didn't relish the idea of spending the entire time dwelling on the insult. She needed to set Wyatt straight. Now.

"You do know that I would never divulge the details of an investigation to my family – or anyone else, right?" she asked him.

Wyatt tapped the steering wheel as though he was thinking the matter through.

"I hope not," he finally said.

His answer infuriated her.

"Just because I don't have much experience in law enforcement doesn't mean that I don't know the rules of the game. In fact, I mastered the skill of keeping secrets a long time ago."

Ashley had kept her past with her ex-husband hidden from her friends – and her former fiancé – for years. But that was a subject she didn't plan to discuss with Wyatt.

The agent didn't respond.

Ashley shot her partner a furtive glance. He appeared to be lost in thought. Or maybe he was just ignoring her.

Why hadn't the TBI teamed her up with Daniel again? She guessed that Bonner County was already part of Wyatt's territory. Anyway, the reason didn't matter. She was stuck with him.

As the notion of her partner's implied lack of trust stewed in her mind, her irritation with the agent continued to build. She pressed her eyes closed and counted to ten. This investigation was her one and only chance to prove herself to Deputy Director Brenda Huddleston. If she screwed up – if she allowed a rift to form between herself and Wyatt – she could kiss her job with the TBI goodbye.

And what was worse, if she didn't forge a good working relationship with her new partner, they might not be able to find the person responsible for the murders. Other lives could be on the line. Ashley didn't want that on her conscience. And she owed it to the families of the two victims to do everything in her power to solve the case. To bring the killer to justice.

Ashley realized she needed to smooth things over with Wyatt.

She decided to start again. To clear the slate, pushing her initial impression of him aside, as though they had just met. Maybe he would afford her the same consideration.

"Did you grow up in Briarwood?" she asked the agent in an attempt to break the ice.

"Newberry," he said in a clipped tone, as though he wished to avoid any small talk.

Wyatt motioned toward the seat behind him. "Why don't you break out the file? You can read over the details of the case."

Did he want the two of them to run through the fine points together? Or did he want her to read silently to herself – to get her to shut up?

As the agent wheeled the SUV onto the main highway leading to Ormond, the largest town in Bonner County, Ashley unsnapped her seatbelt and stretched between the two front seats. She grabbed the manila file folder resting on top of Wyatt's leather briefcase. She noticed his initials embossed near the handle of the case. *WEC*. She wondered what his middle name could be. For his sake, she hoped it wasn't *Earp*.

After strapping herself back into her seat, she flipped open the file. She'd been told at the TBI office that, so far, they'd only been given the preliminary information. A color copy of a Kentucky driver's license greeted her.

"Okay, the first victim was a forty-five-year-old male from Lexington, Kentucky, named Ian Driscoll. Marital status: single. Occupation … that line's been left blank."

Wyatt remained silent, keeping his attention focused on the road ahead. At least he hadn't rolled his eyes or growled at her.

Ashley flipped the page.

"His car was found abandoned – with the hood raised – on the shoulder of a road called Linley Pass on Wednesday evening," she continued. "Then on Friday, a farmer discovered Ian's body dumped near a cattle pasture roughly ten miles away. His wallet was in his pocket – no cash inside – but his ID and credit cards were still there."

She skimmed through the responding officer's notes. The deputy assumed – as had Ashley – that Ian had been targeted after having car trouble. She skipped to the next page.

"It says here that the medical examiner suspects that the cause of death was blunt force trauma."

There were no notes identifying the type of weapon that had been used.

She thumbed ahead, tilting the folder toward the light from the west – the driver's side of the SUV. The sun had waded into the horizon, casting shadows into the cab, making it more difficult for her to read.

"I don't see an autopsy report."

"It's not in there," Wyatt volunteered.

So he hadn't lost his voice after all. "Do you know whether or not the autopsy has already been done?"

"Yeah, it has, but I haven't seen it yet. The sheriff's office didn't send it over. Hopefully they'll give us the complete file when we get there."

It sounded as though the Bonner County Sheriff's Department was even more disorganized than the sheriff's department in Laurel County. If such a thing was possible.

Wyatt glanced at her. "We don't even have the basic stats on the second victim."

She was hit by the feeling that there was something he wasn't telling her.

"It doesn't make sense for the sheriff to make us wait to get the information when he knows that the killer could strike again," she stated.

"It's because we're stepping on his toes. The District Attorney made the call to bring us in. And that was probably due to pressure from the victims' families. I'm expecting nothing but flak from Sheriff Powell."

Sighing, Ashley closed the file folder.

So it seemed it wasn't a lack of organization or even incompetence that had stalled the beginning of their investigation. The sheriff's office was withholding the details on purpose. They obviously thought the TBI was stealing their case – along with the glory they felt would come from catching the killer.

Ashley had known that gaining the cooperation of Bonner County's residents might prove difficult, but she'd never imagined that members of local law enforcement would hinder their search for the murderer. How could the sheriff abandon his oath to protect and serve the public?

A familiar chime echoed from her pocket. An incoming text. She pulled out her phone and checked the screen. An uncontrollable smile tugged at her lips when she saw the message was from Daniel.

Congrats! Just heard u were hired.

Let me know if u need anything.

Talk soon.

D.

What she needed was for Daniel to kick Wyatt to the curb and take his place.

Her new partner must have noticed the silly grin plastered on her face.

"Your father?" he asked.

It was the first time Wyatt had shown any curiosity about her at all. Did that mean their relationship was improving? Or was it simply the sudden shift in her mood that intrigued him?

"No, it's just a message from a friend – a good friend," she said as she typed in a reply of thanks to Daniel.

She stuffed her phone back into her pocket as her thoughts drifted to the murder of Ian Driscoll. Since there was no information regarding the second victim included in the file, she wondered whether the woman's body had been discovered in the same location as Ian's.

"You told me that Brenda wants us to check out the area where the second body was found at first light in the morning, right?"

"Right."

"So did anyone give you directions to the location?"

An exasperated chuckle escaped his lips.

"No," the agent admitted. "We'll probably have to pry the information loose with a crowbar."

With local law enforcement pitted against them, Ashley feared that the killer might remain free. That more lives would be put in danger. They had to figure out a way to sooth the sheriff's bruised ego. To make him realize that his department's reputation wasn't the most important thing at stake.

At least her new partner had stopped ignoring her. For the moment, anyway.

She peered out the passenger window as they flew past a crossroads marked by a sign reading: Ormond – 62 miles. The town really wasn't all that far from Mettler Ridge. The local law enforcement probably functioned in a similar way as the Laurel County Sheriff's Department. Many of the deputies were likely related by blood.

Ashley's stomach clenched as a thought struck her.

Maybe it wasn't Sheriff Powell's ego that was preventing him from giving up the details on the case.

What if the sheriff was covering for the murderer?

CHAPTER SEVEN

Ashley cursed under her breath as she flung aside the plastic curtain and stepped out of the dingy motel shower. It had finally dawned on her what the item was that she'd forgotten to pack. Her hair dryer. Unlike the majority of hotels located in the metropolitan areas of Tennessee, she doubted the rustic Pine Cone Inn supplied the necessary appliance. But it wouldn't hurt to look. Wrapping a towel tight around her, she searched the two rickety drawers in the vanity area and the shelf above the hanger bar in the small closet. There was no dryer to be found.

Irritated, she unplugged her phone from the charger and checked the weather app. The time flashed 5:14 a.m. The current temperature in Ormond hovered at thirty-eight degrees with an expected daytime high of fifty. If she went outside this morning with her long hair wet, she'd likely catch her death of cold. She'd just have to wring the water out with a towel the best that she could.

The odor of stale cigarette smoke – which seemed to be baked into the pale green walls and stained brown carpeting – hung in the air as she applied a light sprinkling of makeup to her skin and a soft gloss to her lips. The motel room, with its dim lighting and weak water pressure, left a lot to be desired. At least she hadn't spotted any roaches. Not yet, anyway.

Just as she finished dressing, Ashley heard a knock on her room's door.

The thought that the Luckadoos had followed her to Bonner County flashed through her mind. She'd had an uneasy feeling as she and Wyatt had checked into the motel the night before – like someone was watching her – but she'd brushed it off as nerves. And she realized she was probably overreacting now. If Troy's relatives had followed her, they wouldn't knock. But they might send someone else to her door to lure her outside.

As a precaution, she peered through the tiny fish-eye lens to identify the person on the other side. It was Wyatt.

Her new partner carried two large Styrofoam coffee cups stamped with the logo of the convenience store located down the street. She was thankful he'd thought to bring caffeine.

As he walked through the opened door, Wyatt surveyed her with a critical eye – like he was assessing all of her flaws at once.

"You need more time to get ready?" he asked, handing her one of the cups.

The veiled insult stirred Ashley's ire. Her partner was obviously displeased with her continued choice of jeans and hiking boots and wanted her to change into something he felt was more fitting for a special agent. He apparently failed to understand that his navy blazer, pinstripe tie, chinos, and penny loafers wouldn't win him any points with the locals. His attire simply reinforced the fact that he was a stranger to the mountains.

An outsider.

Reminding herself that she needed to build a good working relationship with her partner, she decided to ignore his question.

Ashley tamped down her anger and replied, "What time do you think Sheriff Powell will show up at his office?"

When they'd arrived in Ormond the previous evening, the Bonner County Sheriff's department had been their first stop. The deputy on desk duty had turned Wyatt away, claiming he was unauthorized to provide them with any information regarding the murders. He'd instructed them to come back this morning, at the beginning of the first shift.

"I think Powell's expecting us at seven," Wyatt stated. "He'll probably come in early, issue his orders for the day, and then sneak out before first shift starts."

Ashley had made the same assumption. The sheriff would avoid meeting with them for as long as possible.

"Then I guess it might be a good idea for us to head over there now," she said.

After slipping into her jacket, she followed the agent into the parking lot. The crisp morning breeze cut through her damp hair, chilling her to the bone. She struggled to keep her teeth from chattering as she slid into the passenger seat of Wyatt's SUV.

As she took a sip of the hot coffee, she noticed the agent was staring at her.

"What?" she asked, in a tone designed to mask her irritation.

She wondered whether she was sipping too loud.

He shook his head as though it was nothing, and then backed his vehicle out of the parking space. Ashley could tell that Wyatt had something on his mind, but she wasn't in the mood to play games. She wouldn't beg him to talk. If he had something to say, he needed to spit it out.

"Thank you for bringing me a cup of coffee," she said, thinking that he might have been waiting for Ashley to voice her gratitude for the caffeine.

Her partner nodded, shifting his focus toward the road.

As they neared the sheriff's office, a thought struck Ashley.

"Sheriff Powell's deputy most likely gave him a description of your SUV," she told Wyatt. "He'll never stop if he sees us sitting in the parking lot."

"I'm way ahead of you."

A used car dealership occupied the corner across from the sheriff's department. Wyatt steered his SUV onto the lot, parking in the second row from the street. Tucked among the vehicles for sale, the agent's car would likely go unnoticed.

He killed his headlights.

Ashley shivered as she scanned the aging brick building across the street. Only one county patrol car rested in the parking lot, and it was situated too far from the entrance to belong to the sheriff. He had a reserved spot next to the required handicap space.

She felt her partner's eyes on her again.

"Is there something that you feel you need to tell me, Wyatt?" she asked, preparing herself for a lecture on professionalism.

"We had time for you to dry your hair." His tone sounded flat.

So that's what was bothering him. She wondered whether he was concerned that she was freezing, of if he only cared about her appearance.

"I accidentally left my hair dryer at home."

The look the agent shot her made Ashley feel like an idiot, as though it was as serious as forgetting her underwear or firearm. She sighed and turned her attention back toward the department's building.

A Ford Interceptor with the words *Bonner County Sheriff* emblazoned on the side appeared on the street in front of them, inching along at a snail's pace.

"That's him," Wyatt said.

"And he seems to be scouring the area looking for your car."

With their vantage point shrouded in the early morning shadows, Ashley doubted Sheriff Powell would be able to spot them. She watched as the Ford turned into the department's parking lot and rolled to a stop in the sheriff's designated space.

"Do you think we should ambush him now?" she asked. "Or should we wait until he gets inside the station?"

"Now. So he can't slip out the back."

At a faster speed than Ashley had expected, Wyatt veered around the used cars and then rocketed across the street into the department's parking lot. The SUV's tires screeched as the agent hit the brakes, parking at a right angle behind the Ford, blocking the sheriff's escape.

"What in the hell do you think you're doing, boy?" Sheriff Fenton Powell shouted as he jumped from the driver's seat of his Interceptor, his dark eyes filled with rage.

Although the sheriff appeared around twenty years older than Wyatt, it was obvious his use of the term *boy* was meant as an insult.

"I'm Special Agent Wyatt Clark with the TBI," her partner stated, shoving his credentials in the sheriff's face. "I need the complete file on the two roadside murders."

Powell straightened his lanky frame. "Well, I'm the law in this county," he barked. "And what you need is to get your damn vehicle out of my way."

It was clear Wyatt's tactics had only served to make matters worse with the sheriff. Intimidation wasn't the key to gaining the man's cooperation.

In a dismissive manner, Sheriff Powell turned on his heel and strode toward the entrance of the station. Ashley glanced at her partner, sending him a look that said, *let me try*, and then took off after the sheriff.

Stepping inside the Bonner County Sheriff's department felt like walking onto a movie set from the nineteen-sixties. Light wood paneling covered the walls and a pebble-patterned tile graced the floor. The waiting area to her right featured orange chairs Ashley felt would best be described as mid-century modern – originals, not replicas. She flashed her badge as she followed Powell past the wooden reception desk, catching up to him just as he reached his office door.

"Sheriff Powell, I'm Ashley Hope," she blurted out. "Could I please speak to you for just a moment?"

The man eyed her in a similar fashion as Wyatt had that morning.

"You sure as hell don't look like no state agent," he said.

Although his tone was gruff, she could tell by his expression that he felt that was a positive.

"No, sir, I don't. That's because I'm not from the city. I was born and raised in Laurel County."

"Good for you," he stated, reaching for the doorknob.

She needed to get through to him before he barricaded himself inside his office.

"Sir, please just hear me out. It will only take a few minutes of your time, I promise."

He hesitated. "Why should I let you stick your nose in my case?"

"Because you care about the people who live in this county and you don't want to see anyone else die."

She could tell that what she'd stated was true. Sheriff Powell wanted justice for the victims, but it was obvious he also wanted control.

Ashley continued, "I realize that it had to be a blow when the district attorney called us in to help with the case. But if we work together – hand in hand – we can catch the killer and put them behind bars."

"My department don't need your help."

Sheriff Powell didn't have a choice in the matter – and he knew it. But he could make the investigation a lot more difficult than it had to be. She needed to appeal to his ego. Find a way for the department to save face.

"Do you know Sheriff Hiram Vance from Laurel County?"

"We've met."

Ashley was glad to hear that the two were acquainted. She knew that Sheriff Vance –who'd tried to talk her into joining his department – would vouch for her.

"I recently worked with him and another TBI agent to catch a serial killer in the county."

"That no good deputy?"

"Yes, sir."

Sheriff Powell was obviously familiar with the Troy Luckadoo case. She hoped that would make her argument carry more weight.

She continued, "We managed to save the life of the deputy's fourth victim, and the whole town of Mettler Ridge is singing Sheriff Vance's praises right now. But I guarantee you that none of the Laurel County locals can even remember the TBI agent's name."

Aside from Ashley's family, she knew her assertion was most likely true. And even if one of the locals – perhaps Lou Ann – did happen to remember Daniel's name, it was probably because they still didn't trust him.

"What's that got to do with me?"

"If you – and your department – will work with us to catch the roadside killer, it will be you who the locals will all thank, not two TBI agents who they don't even know."

Powell stared at the floor as though he was thinking the matter through.

"I got work to do," he finally said, stepping across the threshold into his office. "Come back after lunch."

Every minute was precious in a murder investigation. They couldn't afford to wait.

"But, sir –"

The sheriff slammed his office door in her face.

Ashley chewed her bottom lip, unsure of her next move. Maybe Wyatt's hardnosed method was the best way after all. They could call the district attorney and have him come down to the station. Or at least, they could threaten to.

Determination flooded her chest as she marched back to the reception desk.

"I'm Ashley Hope, TBI," she stated, flashing her badge a second time.

The red-haired male deputy on duty nodded, as though he already knew who she was.

"I need the phone number for the district attorney's office." Ashley kept her voice firm, her jaw set.

The deputy stared at her. "The DA?"

He sounded surprised, but she could tell he was trying to think of an excuse to stall her. She decided to up the ante.

"That's right. And I also need the phone number for the closest television news station. I think it would do the residents of Bonner County a world of good to find out just how hard their sheriff is working to find Ian Driscoll's killer."

The deputy's face turned pale.

A young female deputy seated at a desk behind the counter stood up.

"I can help you, Agent Hope," she said, her dark brown ponytail swinging over her shoulder. "Just give me a minute."

The deputy's name tag read: Halsey. As the woman disappeared through a doorway to her right, Ashley wondered exactly what type of help Halsey planned to offer. Would it just be more of a run around?

With a sigh, Ashley crossed her arms and waited.

After a few minutes, Halsey reappeared, carrying a thick manila file folder.

"Here," the deputy said, sliding the folder across the reception counter. "There's a copy of everything in this file. All the info we have on the murders."

The fact that the woman would risk losing her job in order to help catch the killer astonished Ashley. She guessed that, like herself, Deputy Halsey cared more about the victims and preventing future murders than she did about politics. Or maybe she was just afraid of having to dodge the questions of a TV news reporter.

"Thank you," Ashley replied. "And I'm sure the DA and the citizens of Bonner County would thank you as well. I just hope Sheriff Powell doesn't fire you for giving us the file."

"He won't fire me," Deputy Halsey said with a grin. "I'm his daughter."

Ashley felt a smile spread across her face. She just wished she could be a fly on the wall when Powell found out his own flesh and blood had given them the case file.

A gust of wind hit her as the front door of the sheriff's department swung open. Wyatt walked toward her, his cell phone perched next to his ear. Although she couldn't make out the actual words coming from the other end of the conversation, she recognized the voice.

Deputy Director Brenda Huddleston.

And the woman sounded angry.

Ashley held up the file folder just as Wyatt ended the call. She met the agent's gaze.

"Let's go, partner," she said, feeling like she'd just scored the winning touchdown with only a second remaining on the game clock. "It's finally time for us to get to work."

With a look of astonishment crossing his face, Wyatt followed her back out to the parking lot.

CHAPTER EIGHT

The wary stares Wyatt had received when they'd stopped for gas on the way to the scenic overlook hadn't surprised Ashley. Although he was a seasoned agent, he'd never worked a case in Bonner County before and didn't seem to realize that wearing his badge in open view on his belt would provoke the locals' suspicions. She could almost hear the whispers of warning that had likely echoed throughout the area. Before her partner had exited the SUV, she'd mentioned that he might want to reposition his shield underneath his jacket, but he'd brushed the idea aside. She guessed he'd have to learn the hard way.

The rolling timbered valley – crowded with dormant oaks, hickories, maples, and a few species of evergreens – that stretched below the scenic bluff reminded Ashley of the mountain landscape of Laurel County. In fact, the topography was almost identical. It appeared that the attitudes of the residents living in the two rural counties were similar as well. Both groups of locals seemed to harbor a distrust of strangers – especially outsiders who worked in state law enforcement.

Ashley's boots kicked up a cloud of dust as she crossed the gravel parking area and headed toward the overlook's chain barricade. Yellow flags, indicting the location where the second victim's body – a female – had been found, rippled in the morning breeze. She stepped over the chain and knelt on the rocky slope next to the flag noting the position where the woman's head had lain.

Wyatt stopped at the barrier, the file in his hand. He'd asked Ashley to drive to the scene so he could spend the twenty minute ride studying the details of the case. Most of his reading had been done in silence, so she still wasn't completely clued in.

"Victim number two was a real estate agent," he said. "Megan Archer. Thirty-four years old. Married. She lived in Knoxville. Suspected cause of death: blunt-force trauma to the skull."

The woman seemed to have nothing in common with the first victim, Ian Driscoll, a forty-five-year-old single male from Kentucky.

"Do they have Ian's occupation listed anywhere in the file?" she asked.

"Yeah, I think I saw it." The agent thumbed back through the pages. "He was a pharmacist."

So there was still no clear connection between the two deceased individuals. Ashley knew that serial killers tended to have a certain type that they targeted. But here, there seemed to be no common ground. What had been the killer's motivation?

"Were any valuables – credit cards, jewelry, or anything – stolen from Megan?"

Wyatt shook his head. "Her purse was underneath her body. There was no cash in her wallet, but her credit cards were still there."

Ashley watched the agent flip through the file again.

He continued, "She was wearing a diamond wedding set, a Cartier watch, gold earrings, and a gold necklace."

Robbery obviously was not one of the killer's motives. It seemed illogical to murder someone only for the cash they carried and not take a watch that was likely worth a small fortune. As she recalled, nothing seemed to have been stolen from Ian either.

Ashley stood, turning her gaze toward the narrow highway that ran west of Ormond. "How far away from here was her car found? Is that in the file?"

"Twelve and a half miles. Her abandoned SUV was found on Sunday, and Megan was found Monday night. The road where her car was located doesn't get a lot of traffic. The same goes for the location of Ian's car."

She remembered reading that Ian's vehicle had been discovered ten miles away, and almost two days before his body had been found.

"So we have a murderer who stalks the backroads looking for people with car trouble," she stated. "The killer kidnaps the victims, takes them somewhere, kills them, and then dumps their body miles from their car."

But what was the reason behind the murders? Were they searching for someone who killed simply for the thrill of it?

"I think it was opportunity," Wyatt said. "I think the killer just happened upon the stalled cars by accident. He found Ian first, and maybe he pulled over to offer help. They got into an argument over something. The guy snapped. He decided to kill Ian. When he found Megan, he'd already killed once, so it was easier to do it a second time. Maybe he made a sexual advance and she refused."

Ashley shook her head. She wasn't buying her partner's version of the events.

"If these were simply crimes of opportunity then why didn't the murderer just kill Ian and Megan right where he found them?"

The look Wyatt shot her said he didn't have an answer.

She crossed back over the chain barrier. Although the entire overlook area had been cordoned off with crime scene tape, no other evidence markers had been placed.

"I'm guessing that nothing was found here that could indicate who the murderer might be," she said, motioning toward the file.

Her partner shook his head. "Just the body. No tire tracks. No footprints."

Ashley glanced back at the limestone-dotted slope where Megan's body had been discarded. While located quite a distance from town, the picturesque overlook – complete with a picnic table – was sure to draw at least a few visitors. Even though clumps of tall grass had surrounded the corpse, in the daylight, anyone standing as far as five feet from the barrier chain would have spotted it.

One swift kick would have been all that was required to send Megan tumbling over the edge of the drop off and into the dense valley below. Her body would likely have remained hidden for years, if not forever. And yet, the murderer had chosen to leave her out in the open.

The killer obviously wanted someone to find Megan.

Along with the kidnapping, that action screamed that the murder had been cold and calculated. People who committed crimes of opportunity usually fled the scene as fast as possible, leaving their victims in the spot where they were murdered. Where time wasn't an issue, opportunity killers most often resorted to great lengths to hide the body in order to avoid being caught.

Megan's death just didn't fit Wyatt's hypothesis.

"I still think that both of the victims were targeted for some reason rather than just being in the wrong place at the wrong time," Ashley said. "Serial killers are usually always stalkers first."

"It takes three murders to make a serial. We only have two."

Wyatt was right about that. But although Ashley hoped the killings had come to an end, she had the unnerving feeling that the body count would continue to rise.

"So are you telling me that you don't think the killer will strike again?" she asked.

He seemed to ponder the question. “No. I think the odds are good that he’s finished.”

She wondered what had led Wyatt to that conclusion.

“What makes you so confident that we’re dealing with a person motivated by anger – who just snapped – and not a serial killer?”

“Number one: the first victim is male, and the second is female. Unless a serial’s a health care worker, or killing for financial gain, that’s unusual. Number two: there’s no hint of sexual assault. That’s often a serial’s prime motive. Number three: the only thing Ian and Megan have in common is that their cars broke down. They don’t fit a specific type. The victims are as different as night and day. There’s no pattern here.”

While it was true that serial killers usually confined their murders to one gender, there had been exceptions in the past. And there were a vast number of serials whose hallmarks didn’t include a sexual motivation. Although Ashley had no idea what connected Ian and Megan, she felt certain there was a common thread somewhere.

Wyatt continued, “This case reminds me of one I worked before. We had two bodies dumped in out-of-the-way locations. The victims had nothing in common except their dozens of stab wounds. The guy who killed them acted on the spur-of-the-moment. Out of anger. It was several months before we caught him, but he never killed again.”

So Wyatt was basing his beliefs on past experiences. Ashley understood that he would draw parallels between cases and expect the same kind of outcome. But just because Wyatt’s previous killer had stopped at two victims didn’t mean that this murderer would.

She sighed. Other than the view, there was nothing remaining for them to see at the bluff.

“Are you ready to head over to the impound lot and check out Megan’s SUV?” she asked, wondering whether any clues as to the identity of the killer had been left in – or on – the vehicle.

According to the partial file she’d read the evening before, Ian’s car had already been processed and released to his nineteen-year-old son.

Wyatt nodded. “Yeah. You can drive. I want to go through the file again.”

Somehow, she suspected her partner would say that.

As Ashley hopped into the driver’s seat of Wyatt’s SUV, a strange feeling gnawed at her. A feeling that they were overlooking something.

Something hiding in plain sight.

CHAPTER NINE

Dodging a pothole the diameter of a hula hoop, Ashley steered Wyatt's SUV into the gravel parking lot of the Bonner County Sheriff Department's impound facility. The pewter-colored metal building with its light gray roof appeared only a few square feet larger than Ashley's single-wide trailer. And judging by the spots of rust dotting the exterior, she guessed the structure was just as old.

A tall, galvanized steel fence, resembling one that might surround a prison, encircled the impound area behind the building. From her vantage point, Ashley could see that several dozen automobiles had been seized. But with their dusty hulls, it looked as though most of the vehicles had been there for quite a while – maybe years.

Pulling into a space beside a white hatchback, she shifted the transmission into park and killed the engine.

The twenty-five minute drive from the scenic overlook had passed in silence. Wyatt had kept his nose stuck in the case file the entire time, only uttering an occasional grunt. Even when he wasn't studying the details of the investigation, her partner seemed reluctant to join her in a conversation. His quiet demeanor might just be a quirk of his personality. Or it could mean – as Ashley suspected – that he wasn't all that fond of her.

The feeling was mutual.

As she unbuckled her seatbelt, she glanced at Wyatt. He hadn't budged an inch in the passenger seat. He was still reading.

"Do you want to wait here in the car while I go check out Megan's SUV?" she asked.

They'd already suffered a late start with the investigation and she didn't want to waste another second. Contrary to her partner's theory, Ashley believed the person responsible for the murders of Ian and Megan would strike again. That the killer was probably searching for his next target.

And it was likely the agents would be forced to jump through several hoops just to gain access to the vehicle. As with the case file, the sheriff had probably issued strict orders to keep the TBI far away from Megan's SUV.

The agent tore his gaze from the file.

"No. I'm ready."

Seeming eager to prove his statement, Wyatt snapped the folder shut and barreled out of the passenger side of his vehicle. He held open the glass front door of the impound office, letting Ashley enter first. The interior décor of the county buildings appeared to share a common theme – light-colored wood paneling and decades-old furnishings.

A plump young woman – her wavy brown hair cut short – greeted them from behind a steel tanker desk topped by a computer monitor, keyboard, and a wire basket containing a stack of yellow forms.

"Can I help y'all?" she asked in a hesitant voice.

Ashley noticed the woman's gaze had darted to the TBI badge prominent on Wyatt's belt.

Her partner glided up to the desk, his entire demeanor and body language changing before her eyes.

"Why, yes. I'm sure you can," he said, in a syrupy tone that Ashley had never heard him use before. "I'll bet it's *your* hard work that keeps this place running."

Knowing the motivation for his sudden charm, Ashley was stunned by how genuine the agent sounded. Apparently, the man possessed the talent of a chameleon. Which could prove to be either a good or bad trait, depending on the situation.

He tilted his head to the side. "I'm Special Agent Wyatt Clark with the Tennessee Bureau of Investigations. And what's your name?"

"Bonnie. Bonnie Childers."

Wyatt circled around the end of the desk, leaning his hip on the corner next to the woman's chair.

"Well, I could have guessed," he replied, flashing a perfect smile. "Did you know that in Scottish, the name Bonnie means beautiful?"

Ashley almost gagged.

But the agent's words seemed to have hit their mark as a slight blush spread across Bonnie's cheeks.

"My mama told me that," the woman said, obviously enamored with Wyatt.

Although the agent wasn't her type – not by a longshot – Ashley couldn't deny the fact that he was an attractive man, with his sandy blonde hair, chiseled jaw, and broad shoulders. Still, she couldn't stomach the fact that her partner's manipulative ploy might actually stand a chance of working in this day and age.

But this was Bonner County. And like Laurel County, the mind frames of the residents seemed stuck in a time warp.

The agent nodded. "Well, she sure picked the perfect name."

Ashley fought the urge to roll her eyes.

"That's awful nice of you to say," Bonnie replied, clearly enchanted by the compliment.

A murderer remained on the loose, and the clock was ticking. Ashley wondered how long it would take her partner to get to the point of their visit.

Wyatt leaned closer to the woman, as though he was about to share a secret.

"Bonnie, we're working a homicide case," he said. "And the clue that could solve it might be right here at the impound."

It surprised Ashley to hear him use the term "*we're*" since she was pretty sure that both Wyatt and Bonnie had forgotten that she was still in the room with them.

The woman's eyes widened. "Really?"

He nodded. "You've got an SUV that belonged to Megan Archer. We just need to take a quick look at it."

"Um … let me check."

Bonnie's fingers raced across her computer keyboard. As her eyes scanned the screen, her expression shifted from a desire to be helpful to one of guarded suspicion. She grabbed the edge of her monitor, swiveling it so that Wyatt wouldn't be able to read the displayed information.

"The car's here … but I can't let you see it."

The agent's sweet talk had failed to serve its purpose.

Wyatt feigned a hurt look. "Why not?"

Bonnie sighed. "Unless you've got papers, like a court order. Or you can prove you're the owner, then you're not allowed to see the car."

Ashley knew they'd have no problem obtaining a warrant to search the SUV, but it would add at least a few hours to the already stalled investigation. Wasting time was a luxury they couldn't afford.

Now that Wyatt's attempt at flirting his way onto the impound lot had proven unsuccessful, she decided to break into the conversation.

"We haven't been introduced," she said stepping closer to the desk. "I'm Special Agent Ashley Hope."

"You're an agent, too?" Bonnie said, her tone skeptical.

The woman must have assumed that Ashley worked as Wyatt's administrative assistant.

"Yes." She flashed her credentials so that Bonnie would know she wasn't lying. "I'm guessing that you just read on your computer that the Sheriff ordered Megan Archer's SUV off limits to the TBI."

The sheepish expression that crossed the woman's face let Ashley know that her assumption was correct.

Ashley met Bonnie's gaze. "I know that you're just trying to do your job – and I respect you for that. But you need to think about the consequences of your actions."

"Consequences?"

Ashley nodded. "Every second that we waste on this case gives whoever killed Megan Archer extra time to go after someone else. Megan was married. She had two small children. Now, her kids will be forced to grow up without their mother's love to guide them. She won't be there at their high school graduations or their weddings. How would you feel if it was your mother who'd been murdered?"

Bonnie broke eye contact, her gaze dropping toward her desk.

Ashley continued, "There could be another woman out there just like Megan. A woman who the killer is stalking, who he plans to take away from her family – her children. Wyatt and I can get a warrant to search the SUV, but with all the paperwork involved, it could take hours. And by then – for that woman – it might be too late."

When Bonnie looked up again, her eyes appeared moist. She rose from her chair and headed to a metal cabinet hanging on the wall adjacent to the desk. Unlocking the door, she scoured the contents. A moment later, she handed Ashley a key fob.

"It's the red SUV in row B, spot 14," Bonnie told her. She motioned to the back entrance of the building. "You can get onto the lot through that door."

Wyatt motioned for Ashley to lead the way and then followed her out of the rear of the building.

Once they were outside he said, "That was some speech."

Ashley shrugged. "I was just letting my heart do the talking. Thankfully, Bonnie listened."

It only took them a few minutes to locate Megan Archer's red SUV. Black dusting powder, a remnant from collecting fingerprints, still marred the exterior of the vehicle in the areas an assailant would likely touch. But since the victim had worked as a real estate agent, carting clients from one property to another, there were bound to be a hoard of unknown prints.

After pulling on a pair of latex gloves, Wyatt opened the driver's side door. "According to the file, nothing unusual was found in the car. But we're dealing with a small sheriff's department, so …"

Ashley realized that Bonner County most likely lacked the funds to educate their deputies on the finer points of forensic evidence collection. Snapping on her own pair of gloves, she dove into the back floorboard of the vehicle. She inched the beam of her Maglite along the tan carpeting, searching for the tiniest clue that may have been overlooked during the first inspection.

"Anything?" Wyatt called from the front seat.

"No, it looks like they did a pretty good job of vacuuming everything up back here."

She checked the seats, doors, and the various pockets. They'd all been emptied. Their contents likely sent off to the lab in Briarwood. Ashley decided to move to the cargo area. Wyatt joined her. Together, they scoured every millimeter. The deputies with the sheriff's department had left nothing behind.

Although she knew that searching the SUV could have produced a vital clue, Ashley was hit again by the feeling that they were wasting valuable time.

With a sigh, Wyatt slammed the cargo door closed.

Ashley moved back around the vehicle. As she pushed the rear driver's side door shut, her Maglite slipped from her fingers, landing on the gravel below. Squatting down to pick up the flashlight, something caught her eye.

Three tiny rust-colored spots on the vehicle's running board.

"Hey, come here and look at this, Wyatt" she said, her gut telling her that the stains were significant.

He peered at the spots beneath the beam of his Maglite.

"Yeah. I think it's blood spatter," he told her. "And it's not noted in the file. I'll call Brenda and have her send our forensics team over."

Before he could pull out his cell phone, it rang.

He glanced at the screen "Guess who?" he asked Ashley.

She didn't have to guess. She knew Brenda was likely wondering what was taking them so long to report on their findings.

"Yeah," Wyatt said into the phone.

Ashley studied the agent's face as he listened to the deputy director on the other end of the line. His expression didn't give anything away, but as it had earlier, Brenda's tone sounded angry.

Wyatt's voice faded from Ashley's mind as an unsettling feeling overtook her. It was a feeling she'd experienced before, when her ex-husband, Ethan Barrett, had escaped from prison.

Eyes were watching her. She was certain.

Fear gnawed at Ashley's heart.

She scanned the impound lot, searching for Bonnie or another employee. No one was there. At least no one she could see. But she knew what it felt like to be watched.

She'd been stalked by Ethan Barrett.

"Ashley," Wyatt said, as though he'd been trying to get her attention for some time.

She noticed the agent was no longer on the phone.

"We need to get back to the sheriff's office," he told her.

A knot of apprehension formed in her chest. She hoped the killer hadn't claimed a third victim.

"Please don't tell me that they've found another body."

Her partner shook his head. "No. But Megan's husband is there. Brenda thinks he may know who killed his wife."

CHAPTER TEN

The enraged expression on Jay Archer's face forced Ashley's stomach to drop as she walked into the tiny windowless conference room at the Bonner County Sheriff's Department. In the majority of murder cases, the spouse or significant other of the deceased is most often considered the prime suspect. However, when it came to the death of Megan Archer, it appeared her husband had no involvement in the crime.

According to what Wyatt had told Ashley on the drive to the station, Jay had been in Knoxville at the time of the murder. And he had a solid alibi to prove it. While there was still the possibility that the man could have hired another party to kill his wife, with the similar murder of Ian Driscoll in the mix, the odds seemed unlikely.

Her partner attempted to make the introductions, but Megan's husband ignored Wyatt's outstretched hand.

"What in the hell have you been doing to find my wife's killer?" Jay shouted. "Not a damn thing that I can see."

Dressed in a charcoal gray suit, the man's auburn hair matched both his tie and the current shade of his face.

When Brenda had phoned Wyatt earlier, she'd informed him that Megan's husband was responsible for forcing the district attorney to call in the TBI. Ashley doubted that Jay was aware of the sheriff's reluctance to hand over his control of the case, and she wasn't about to bring the law enforcement politics to his attention. Apparently, Wyatt shared her thoughts.

Her partner remained calm.

"I know it feels like things are moving slowly," he said. "And they have been. But we just took the case. We'll do everything necessary to find out what happened."

"All I've seen so far is incompetence. Sheriff Powell can't – or won't – tell me anything. And today, I found out that Megan was the second person murdered. Why didn't you stop the man the first time?"

"Sir, like I said, we were just asked to join the case."

Jay stared at Wyatt like that fact didn't matter.

Her partner motioned toward the battered wooden conference table. "Please," he said. "Let's sit down."

After exchanging a glance with Wyatt, Ashley took the chair directly across from Jay. The man's righteous indignation hung in the air like a thick blanket of smoke. It was a palpable feeling, too intense to be faked. At least as far as she was concerned. But she realized that Wyatt might possess a different opinion. Her partner might believe that Jay was somehow involved in the murders.

She decided to start the interview.

"I'm Ashley Hope, Mr. Archer," she said. "And like my partner, Wyatt, finding your wife's killer is my first priority. I promise you that I will do everything in my power to make sure the person responsible is brought to justice."

Jay grunted as though he doubted her sincerity. And until the murderer was caught, she realized that, to Megan's husband, their best efforts would never be enough.

Ashley continued, "Can you tell us why Megan came to Bonner County?"

"She was on her way to Murfreesboro to meet her sister, Molly," Jay stated. "She drove down from Knoxville on Saturday morning. I don't understand why she decided to stop here. Megan always sticks to the main highways when she travels. But today I was told – by the district attorney, not the sheriff – that her SUV was found on one of the backroads, not the highway like I'd assumed."

The fact that she had veered from the main thoroughfare did seem puzzling. Unless she'd known the area well and had decided to make an unplanned stop at a location off the beaten path.

"Did Megan drive through Bonner County on a regular basis?"

Jay shook his head. "Her sister just moved to Murfreesboro a few months ago. We haven't driven across this area in years."

A thought struck Ashley. It was possible that Megan's car had begun showing signs of trouble and she'd pulled off the highway heading toward a repair shop. But if that had been the case, why hadn't she notified her husband?

"Did Megan call you or send you a text after she left your home on Saturday?"

Jay pressed his lips into a thin line. Ashley's question seemed to have hit a nerve.

"We were arguing," he confessed. "I didn't approve of her decision to allow her sister to move in with us. Molly … well, I didn't feel like she would be a good influence on our two children. When Megan left home Saturday, we weren't exactly speaking."

If the couple wasn't on speaking terms, then the idea that Megan might have been looking for a repair shop – without calling her husband first – seemed plausible.

"Do you know whether Megan's SUV had given her any trouble before she began her trip?"

"On Friday, she told me a warning light had flashed on, but it turned back off by itself. She'd planned to take it to the dealership on Monday. We thought it might just be a sensor malfunction."

Ashley didn't know what had been wrong with the SUV, but she thought the details might be listed in the case file. She looked at Wyatt. He seemed to understand her silent question.

"There was a problem with the radiator," he told Jay. "It overheated. Which would have caused Megan to pull off the road."

Ashley added, "And maybe the warning light had come on again while she was on the highway. She could have turned onto the backroads, driving to a repair shop."

Jay's gaze sank to the table. He opened his mouth as though he was about to speak, but then closed it again. His rock-hard veneer had finally begun to crack. The silent tears that slipped from his eyes pained Ashley's heart.

The man cleared his throat, bringing back his stone face.

"When Molly called … when she told me late Saturday evening that Megan never made it to Murfreesboro, I knew something terrible had happened," Jay said. "I retraced Megan's path. I drove all night long looking for her. And then I received a call on Sunday afternoon notifying me that her SUV had been found."

Ashley knew that a sheriff's deputy had discovered Megan's body at the overlook on Monday night. Which meant that the killer had likely held her hostage for two days. Ashley hoped the woman's death had been swift – that she had not been subjected to torture during those hours.

Wyatt leaned toward Jay. "Do you know whether your wife had any enemies?" he asked.

The man shrugged. "Real estate is a cutthroat business. The agents all act like they're friends, but deep down, they hate each other.

Especially the females. But I don't really think another agent would kill her."

Not unless the agent also knew Ian Driscoll. It was difficult for Ashley to believe that the two murders were unrelated.

Her partner hesitated. "This is a delicate question, but I have to ask. Do you think Megan could have been having an affair?"

A new wave of anger seemed to flow through Jay's body. It took him a moment to answer.

"I don't know," he finally said.

"But you suspect that she was?"

The man sighed. "She had an affair a few years ago, but that's been over for a long time. Lately, I've been noticing some of the same signs. I confronted her about it, but she denied that she was seeing anyone else."

Could Megan have been meeting up with a lover when she'd decided to take the backroad? Ashley guessed that was the theory behind Wyatt's current line of questioning.

"When you thought she might be cheating, did you have a person in mind?" her partner asked.

Jay shook his head, fire returning to his eyes. "No. But finding out who might have wanted her dead is your job. You need to be out on the streets of this hillbilly town right now, asking the locals questions. Megan was killed here in Bonner County, not Knoxville."

Wyatt's held his poker face. He wasn't letting the man get to him.

"Yes, sir, that's true. She was killed here. But we have to question everyone who might have a motive."

Ashley wondered whether her partner's words were a dig at Jay. Was Wyatt insinuating that the man may have had a motive to kill his wife?

Jay bolted straight up from his chair. He'd apparently had the same thought.

"You'd better get out there and find my wife's killer fast. I happen to be a personal friend of the governor's son. If you screw this up – or try to blame the murder on me – I'll have you fired so fast your head will spin."

The man strode back across the conference room and jerked open the door.

As Ashley watched Jay march down the hallway, she heard Wyatt's cell phone chime behind her. She'd become familiar with the sound of her partner's ringtones. He'd received a text message.

Wyatt's expression remained neutral as he scanned the screen of his phone. If Brenda had sent the text, maybe her partner's demeanor meant that the deputy director had calmed down a bit.

"They just finished Megan's autopsy," he informed her.

According to Tennessee state law, all autopsies ordered by a district attorney had to be performed by a board-certified forensic pathologist at one of the seven regional forensic centers.

"Did they send her body to the morgue in Loganville?"

The forensic center in Loganville – at least a two-hour drive away – was the nearest facility to Bonner County.

He nodded. "Yeah. And Brenda wants us there asap."

"Am I still the designated chauffeur, or do you want to take over?" she asked, turning back toward the conference room door.

"I'll drive. You study the file."

As she headed down the hallway toward the exit of the sheriff's department, Ashley wondered what Megan's body would tell them.

CHAPTER ELEVEN

The fancy red convertible popped into view as the killer steered his car around the bend on the tree-lined road. Sweet anticipation swelled in his stomach and he felt a smile spread across his face. The stalled vehicle hugged the narrow shoulder, the hood raised.

The sports car was right where he knew it would be.

He didn't see the man – not yet. The convertible's top was raised. The bigshot from the city was probably tucked in his leather seat, eyes glued to his phone, trying to call for help. But there was no cell service in this part of the low-lying valley.

The city man's expensive gadgets couldn't save him. Not this time.

Crushing the last of his cigarette in the car's ashtray, the killer lifted his foot from the gas pedal and coasted in behind the convertible. He couldn't wait to see the look on the bigshot's face. The smugness would be gone – that was for sure. Knowing he was helpless, the stranger would be quick to offer money – might even utter the word *please*.

Who held all the cards now?

There was nobody else the man from the city could turn to. Nobody for miles. The road that snaked through the dense-forested valley saw little traffic. And if any of the local riffraff happened by, the only reason they would stop for the stranger would be to steal his little red sports car so they could chop it into parts.

Later, when the bigshot was gagged and bound, he would wish he'd fallen into the hands of the chop-shop crew. At least then, he would have escaped with his life. And even if the riffraff had stumbled upon the city man first, and had decided to knock him off, they'd have done it fast.

But the stranger deserved to suffer.

As the killer shifted his car's transmission into park, he chuckled. He couldn't believe how easy it had been to get the bigshot to fall for his lie. Unlike the other two city slickers that had gone before him – who had been hesitant to veer from their planned route – Mr. Sports Car had swallowed the bait – hook, line, and sinker.

"There's been a big wreck up on the highway," he'd told the city man. *"A pileup. Road's gonna be closed for hours. You best take a detour."*

Now, who was the idiot?

The rich city folk were all the same. Looking down their noses, all high and mighty. Flaunting their power. Playing their games. Just waiting for the chance to trip him up. To prove to him that they were smarter. To try to make him feel like he was nothing more than a dimwitted, redneck hick.

But he wasn't stupid.

It was just that when he tried to read a sentence, the letters became jumbled. They rearranged themselves in a way that made no sense. Like they were taunting him. But if he held his finger steady beneath a line of words, he could almost always make them behave. If he took his time, he could decipher their meaning.

And he was good with numbers.

He could add, subtract, multiply, and divide in an instant. Numbers didn't set out to confuse him in the way that the fickle letters did. Numbers held their place. They were solid. Dependable.

The fact that he had command over the digits – even fractions and decimals – proved he wasn't dumb. Despite what the city folk thought.

Despite what his father had told him.

Adjusting the bill of his hat, pulling it down closer to his eyes, the killer pushed open the driver's door of the car. As his boots hit the gravel shoulder, the distant hum of an engine rumbled through the air.

Apprehension flooded his chest.

He froze, straining his ears.

But then a second later, a stream of confidence flowed back into his heart. He recognized the unique sound. It wasn't a vehicle heading toward them, it was a tractor. The wind had carried the roar of the machinery from the farm that lay to the east, perched on the hill of a parallel highway, at least a mile away.

Nobody would interrupt his plans.

The driver's door of the red sports car popped open as he strode along the shoulder of the road. The heavy machinery from the distant farm continued to sing on the breeze. The steady hum was like a death knell, urging the killer forward. His hand flew to the bulge in the cargo pocket on the leg of his pants. His weapon was ready.

He was ready.

The bigshot slid out from the driver's seat of the convertible, an expression of relief on his face. The man in the blue jacket adorned with an embroidered polo pony had no idea what fate had in store for him. No hint of the danger approaching.

"You don't know how thankful I am to see you," the city man said as he walked along the side of the snazzy red vehicle.

The killer knew the bigshot's feeling of gratitude would soon turn to regret.

"Car broke down, huh?"

It was important that the killer acted surprised. Vital to pretend that it was coincidence that had led him down that very road at just the right time.

The city man nodded. "Yes." He raked his hand through his perfect light-brown hair. "Can you believe my luck? This car has had one issue after another since the day I first drove it off the lot."

If the bigshot had been smart – half as smart as he thought he was – he would have picked a cheaper, more dependable model. Instead, the man had chosen something flashy. Like his ego.

"Let me take a look."

The city man pivoted and headed back toward the front end of the sports car.

Following close behind, the killer's fingers clenched the handle of hardened alloy steel protruding from the top of his cargo pocket. His pulse quickened. Sweat broke out along his palm, but his grip on the weapon remained firm.

The bigshot pointed beneath the raised hood of the vehicle as a cloud of steam swirled in the cool breeze.

"A hose must have ruptured, or pulled loose, or something," the city man guessed.

Keeping his outward expression neutral, the killer smiled inside. The bigshot probably didn't know the difference between a spark plug and an alternator. And the city man fancied himself intelligent.

"Naw, it ain't no hose."

"How can you tell?" the bigshot asked, a puzzled look crossing his face.

The killer's heart began to pound as he motioned under the hood with his left hand.

"Look right down there," he said, tightening the fingers of his right hand around the thick steel.

The city man tilted his head – his untrained eyes focused on the inner workings of the vehicle.

Without making a sound, the killer drew the heavy weapon from his cargo pocket.

Using just the right amount of force – practiced to perfection – he slammed the steel end into the side of the bigshot's head.

The blow caught the city man off guard. With likely no time to think or even scream out in pain, the man's body jerked to the side, and then crashed onto the gravel below.

Slipping the tool back into his pocket, the killer stepped toward the bigshot's crumpled form. A bloody gash dented the man's right temple. The stranger's mouth gaped open, though his eyes were closed.

The killer knelt on the road's shoulder and checked the city man's pulse.

The bigshot was still alive. But to the killer's delight, the man was out cold.

CHAPTER TWELVE

An unexpected chill ran down Ashley's spine as she crossed through the automatic glass doors leading into the Eggleston Forensic Center in Loganville. It was the first time she'd ever visited a morgue, and the anticipation of the experience had set her nerves on edge.

The soles of her hiking boots squeaked against the highly-polished, onyx-colored floor tiles as she followed Wyatt to the glass-enclosed reception desk. The stoic expression on her partner's face led her to believe that he'd become accustomed to attending victim's autopsies. Although she knew there would come a day when she'd be forced to witness the procedure, she felt grateful that the pathologist had already completed his work on Megan Archer.

"I'm Special Agent Wyatt Clark with the TBI, and this is Special Agent Ashley Hope. We're here to see Dr. Northcutt," Wyatt told the elderly woman stationed behind the reception window.

Ashley winced at the name of the forensic pathologist. Ironically, it reminded her of the Y-shaped incision – running north to south on the chest of the deceased – required to perform an autopsy. But if Wyatt had noticed the strange coincidence with the doctor's last name, he wasn't letting it show.

The elderly woman typed something into her computer.

"Dr. Northcutt's office is on level B1," she said. "Room 12."

Of course the pathologist's office would have to be in the basement. Why did the deceased need to be housed in the dark bowels of the building? It was like a cliché from a horror movie. She'd hoped to be directed to a nice multi-windowed office on the second floor with a view of the manicured grounds below. Had wished for a serene landscape to gaze upon that would distract her from the morbid nature of their business here.

Wyatt motioned for her to take the lead. After rounding the corner to the left of the reception desk, she pressed the *down* button located between the two elevators. She glanced at her partner. He was still wearing his poker face. As she had expected, their conversation had been sparse during the drive from Bonner County. At least she'd had the chance to familiarize herself with the case file – to review the evidence collected so far in the murders of Ian and Megan. At this point, they didn't have much to go on.

The elevator to her right chimed and the doors slid open.

As Ashley stepped inside and hit the button for level B1, she felt Wyatt's eyes grazing her.

"Are you okay?" her partner asked.

Two people had been murdered and the killer remained on the loose; the face of Megan's husband – when he'd cracked and had let the tears slip out – kept haunting her thoughts; the sheriff who was supposed to be helping in the investigation was instead blocking them at every turn; her partner acted as though he hated having a conversation with her; and now she was headed to a location that was sure to give her nightmares – the basement of a morgue. What could possibly be wrong?

"I'm fine," she replied, unwilling to let Wyatt know that traveling to the basement rattled her.

"You look a little pale."

It didn't surprise her that her partner was again focused on her appearance. But despite her discomfort, she was far too strong to let a bout of squeamishness hinder her from performing her job. She'd suck it up and behave like a professional.

Ashley was no stranger to dead bodies; she'd justifiably killed two men. The serial killer – who was also her ex-husband – Ethan Barrett, along with serial killer, Deputy Troy Luckadoo. And she'd studied countless crime-scene photos of the deceased, both during her coursework to obtain her master's degree in criminal justice and during her classes at the police academy. She just didn't enjoy thinking about a doctor dissecting the corpses.

"There's no need for you to be worried about me, Wyatt. I can handle anything – and everything – this case throws at me with no problem."

The elevator jerked to a halt and the doors opened. The placard posted on the wall indicated that room 12 was located to their right. Ashley strode down the wide hallway with Wyatt at her side. The unusual width, she assumed, was to allow for the easy passage of medical gurneys.

When they reached room 12, Wyatt tapped on the closed door.

"Come in," a male voice called from inside the room.

Ashley entered first. The dozens of framed photos lining the walls of the office captured her attention. Obviously taken at various dog shows throughout the years, each of the pictures featured Dr. Northcutt standing alongside one of several different Afghan hounds, their silky black coats brushed to a high sheen and their curved tails held high. In every shot, the doctor lovingly stroked his hound as the judge displayed the dog's trophy and prize ribbon – the majority of which were blue, representing a first-place win.

"I see that you've taken notice of my champions," Dr. Northcutt said to her, a hint of pride in his tone. "I've been breeding and showing Afghans for the better part of twenty years."

Except for his silvery gray hair, the doctor's physical features – his narrow face, long neck, and lean frame – resembled the characteristics of the dogs he cherished.

"They're beautiful animals," Ashley stated. "Each and every one."

Although she didn't have the time to care for a dog of her own, she'd always been fond of them.

With nothing more than a polite glance at the photos of the hounds, Wyatt introduced himself and Ashley. His abrupt manner indicated that he was eager to conduct their business.

"We'd like to take a look at Megan Archer. And get your thoughts on her murder," he told the doctor.

Ashley knew they had to view the body; that's the reason they were here. However, the task sparked a flame of apprehension in the pit of her stomach. She steeled herself for the worst possible damage to the woman's body, and for the likely pungent odor. She had discovered a decaying corpse once. The smell of rotting flesh was one she'd never forget.

"Of course," Dr. Northcutt said, rising from his chair.

The pathologist led them down the hallway, through another set of automatic doors, and into a room lined on both sides with rows of stainless steel refrigerated drawers. Each drawer was numbered, and the ones that were occupied featured a rectangle of white paper – with the decedent's name – wedged into a small frame-type holder.

Without taking a moment to ask whether they were ready, the doctor flipped the handle on the door labeled *Archer* and pulled it open.

Ashley resisted the powerful urge to flee from the room.

The woman's feet were visible, sticking out from beneath a white sheet. Black and purple bruises marred the skin, and the bones of each foot hung in an unusual fashion, as though they were deformed. A tag listing Megan's name, date of birth, height, weight, hair and eye color, as well as the morgue's case number, dangled from the woman's right big toe.

Dr. Northcutt grabbed the stainless tray on which the body lay, pulling it forward, out of the darkness of the refrigerator unit. He lifted the sheet, folding it just beneath Megan's shoulders. The Y incision that Ashley had dreaded seeing was clearly visible. But the incision wasn't nearly as disturbing as the dark bruising that covered almost every inch of the woman's skin.

And even more frightening than the bruising was the condition of Megan's skull.

The woman's face was almost unrecognizable as being human. It appeared that the killer had struck her repeatedly, crushing the bones in her cheeks and nose, and knocking out all of her teeth.

For the first time since Ashley had met him, Wyatt looked shaken. The sight of Megan's body had obviously jarred him as well.

"What exactly happened to her, Doctor?" he asked, a hint of sadness in his voice.

"I can only tell you of her physical injuries," the pathologist replied. "Anything else would be supposition."

Ashley had expected the doctor's revelations to be limited to the facts alone. But the woman's injuries should tell them almost everything they needed to know about her story – except for the name of her killer.

Her partner nodded. "Yes, I understand."

"Mrs. Archer died from a blow to her skull. But prior to her death, she sustained a number of injuries – an estimated two hundred blows. Almost every bone in her body suffered at least one fracture."

As Ashley had feared, it appeared as though the woman had been tortured. The pain she'd endured must have been horrific.

"Do you have an estimated time of death?" Wyatt wanted to know.

"She passed between the hours of six and nine p.m. on Monday."

Megan had disappeared on Saturday. The killer had held her hostage for two days.

Ashley asked, "Did all of her injuries occur at the same time – just before her death?"

Dr. Northcutt shook his head, his expression grim. "Unfortunately, no. The injuries were inflicted over a period of several hours – as many as fifty."

Although she'd already guessed as much, it pained Ashley to hear that the woman's death had been slow.

"Have you been able to determine the kind of weapon that was used in the murder?" she asked.

"Based on several of the marks left behind, it appears to have been a metal object, but we haven't pinpointed the exact type."

With the way Megan's body looked, Ashley had been expecting to hear that the murderer had bludgeoned the woman with a sledgehammer.

Wyatt chewed his bottom lip. "Did you find any fibers, hairs, or any other foreign material?"

The doctor nodded. "There was an adhesive – consistent with duct tape – found in her hair, on her face, and on her wrists and ankles."

The woman had evidently been bound and gagged with the tape.

Dr. Northcutt continued, "We also collected several long white hairs from her clothing. They've been sent to the lab for DNA testing."

Wyatt looked intrigued. "White hairs?"

The doctor nodded. "I'm expecting the DNA analysis to confirm that the hairs are from an animal."

Ashley wondered whether Megan owned a white pet. If not, the hairs might prove to be a valuable clue as to the identity of the murderer.

Her partner asked, "Did you perform a rape test?"

"Yes. That's standard procedure, but there's no indication that the woman was sexually assaulted."

Although it seemed a small consolation, at least Megan hadn't suffered that trauma. Ashley knew that a murder victim's fingernails were always scraped during the autopsy. Since there was no semen for analysis, she just hoped that the skin collected from beneath the woman's fingernails would include foreign DNA – genetic material from the killer.

Wyatt rubbed his chin as though he was thinking.

"I understand you also conducted the autopsy on Ian Driscoll," he stated.

"Yes, that's correct. Mr. Driscoll was killed in the same manner, and his injuries were comparable to Mrs. Archer's injuries."

"Most of his bones were broken?"

Dr. Northcutt nodded. "Yes. And we also collected duct tape residue and long white hairs from his body. I would allow you to view him, but Mr. Driscoll has already been sent back to his family."

That meant the pet that had shed the hairs belonged to the killer, not Megan.

Wyatt glanced at what had once been the murdered woman's face, and then stepped away from the body.

"Thank you for your time, Doctor," he said, his tone somber.

"I'm always glad to help."

The doctor pushed the stainless tray holding Megan back into the refrigerator. As he closed the compartment's door, a vision of Jay Archer's face flashed in Ashley's mind once again. She wondered whether Megan's husband had been forced to identify the body in person, or whether they'd used some other method of identification. For Jay's sake, she hoped it was the latter.

Her footsteps plagued by a strange heaviness, Ashley followed Wyatt back to the elevator rather than walking by his side.

"Cat or dog?" her partner asked as they traveled back to the ground floor.

She knew he was referring to the white hairs found on both victims' bodies.

"I guess it could be either – the hairs could even be from a rabbit for that matter – but I was thinking they were likely from a cat. Cats always seem to want to rub up against you. The friendly ones, anyway."

"I figured they were from a dog. Dogs can sense when people are in trouble. They try to help."

It was no surprise to Ashley that Wyatt would disagree with her opinion. But he did have a good point regarding the behavior of dogs.

She climbed into the passenger seat of her partner's SUV and made herself comfortable for the two-hour ride back to Ormond. As she stared out the side window at the manicured shrubs, the image of Megan's battered and broken body popped into her mind.

The killer was even more diabolical than she'd previously imagined. What could possess someone to break every bone in a person's body, one at a time, over a period of days? The pain inflicted would have been so intense, it may have driven both Ian and Megan insane.

The murderer was obviously as evil as the devil himself. And Ashley feared he'd already taken another victim.

CHAPTER THIRTEEN

The odor of stale cigarette smoke hit Ashley once again, almost making her gag, as she crossed the threshold into her dreary motel room at the Pine Cone Inn. If it wasn't November – with the temperature stuck in the forties – she'd pry open the windows and let the evening breeze wash away the rancid scent. But since bringing in fresh air wasn't an option, she'd try to remember to pick up a can of disinfectant spray tomorrow, which would at least mask the stench. Then she realized that adding a layer of fragrance might just make matters worse.

Maybe she'd ask to switch rooms.

As she picked up her cell to call the front desk, it rang. She smiled as she read the caller ID.

"Hi, Daniel," she said into the phone.

She was both surprised and happy that he'd decided to call.

"Hey. How's your first case going?"

Ashley hesitated. She didn't feel it would be right to complain about a fellow TBI agent – namely Wyatt – so she decided to stick to the details of the investigation.

"Well, we were sent to Bonner County to investigate the abduction and murder of two out-of-towners. The only problem is that the local sheriff's not happy that we're taking over his case. He doesn't want to share any information with us and keeps putting roadblocks in our way. Other than that – everything's great."

She could sense Daniel smiling on the other end.

"Yeah, get used to hostility from local cops," he said. "It happens all the time."

Although she'd had an idea that the jealous competitiveness the sheriff had displayed might turn out to be common with other law enforcement agencies, she had hoped it was a rare occurrence.

"I was afraid that you were going to tell me that."

"Sorry, but that's the way it goes. Who did they partner you with?"

Ashley wished he hadn't asked that question. She knew it would be hard to hide her dislike of Wyatt from Daniel. But she needed to put her personal feelings aside and act professional. All three of them were on the same team.

"Wyatt Clark," she said, working hard to keep her tone neutral.

Daniel paused. She wondered whether he was struggling to remember Wyatt. With all the meetings the TBI routinely held, the two must have met at least once.

"Is he there with you now?" the agent finally asked.

There was a strange note in his voice. Something she couldn't quite discern.

"No, I'm alone in my motel room right now. Why – is something wrong?"

Maybe Daniel wasn't very fond of Wyatt either, but didn't want to divulge the information if there was a chance the other agent might overhear it.

"I wish Brenda had picked someone else," he stated, almost sounding as though he was angry.

Maybe the two agents had gotten into a disagreement in the past. Something Daniel didn't feel comfortable sharing. Should she tell him that she had the same wish? Or should she remain diplomatic? Perhaps, she could do both.

"Well, I would rather that she had paired me with you again, but I didn't have a say in the matter."

"Yeah. I know." Daniel's words came out clipped. "Just be careful around him. Watch yourself."

The warning – and the tone in which it was given – made Ashley realize that the root of the agent's concern extended beyond a simple disagreement. Were there rumors floating around that Wyatt was a dirty cop? Was he on the take?

"Daniel, what is it about my new partner that you're not telling me?"

The agent hesitated again, as though he was choosing his words.

"Wyatt has a reputation," he finally spat out. "And it's not because of the high number of cases he's solved."

It was definitely anger she heard in Daniel's voice.

"What do you mean – what kind of reputation does Wyatt have?"

The agent sighed. "He's a player, Ashley."

A player?

Was he referring to the term in a romantic sense? Daniel couldn't be jealous, could he? He'd never given her the slightest hint that he was interested in anything more than a platonic friendship in addition to their professional relationship. Romance and the business of law enforcement didn't mix well. Not when people's lives were at stake.

"Are you saying that you think Wyatt might try to hit on me or something?"

She heard the agent sigh again.

"I'm sure of it," Daniel stated.

The idea that Wyatt would even consider Ashley to be a viable target for a sexual advance seemed ridiculous. Her partner's general attitude toward her had screamed that she was not the type of woman he would find interesting. And as to her opinion of him … if he even looked at her the wrong way, she'd cut him down to size.

"I don't even consider Wyatt to be my friend, Daniel, let alone anything else. And I'm pretty positive that he's well aware of that fact."

The agent remained silent for a moment.

He responded, "You two don't get along?"

Daniel almost sounded pleased by the possibility of friction between Ashley and Wyatt.

"We haven't had any arguments – nothing like that – it's just that our personalities don't seem to mesh very well. But we've managed to work together so far with no problems."

"Oh."

She'd expected more than the short, one-word reply. Was Daniel disappointed that she and her new partner hadn't declared war against each other? He obviously knew that the pair had to maintain a good working relationship in order to solve the case. Catching the roadside killer was the number-one priority.

"Would you prefer it if Wyatt and I were constantly arguing?"

"No. Of course not," Daniel said, though he still sounded upset.

She had to make the agent understand that she had no personal interest in Wyatt – romantic or otherwise.

"The only thing that I'm focused on is finding the person who murdered the two out-of-towners. That means that I'll have to do my best to get along with my new partner – no matter what kind of reputation he has. I don't care the least bit about Wyatt's love life."

"I just don't want you to get hurt, Ashley."

Daniel was her friend. A good friend. It made sense that he wouldn't want to see her make the mistake of falling for Wyatt, only to get her heart broken. Daniel had personally witnessed the destruction of her former engagement. It was obvious that he didn't want her to suffer that kind of pain again.

"Okay, I appreciate the fact that you let me know about Wyatt's reputation. But there's really no reason at all for you to worry."

She heard background noises on the other end of the line. A male voice talking to Daniel. She couldn't make out the man's words, but his tone sounded urgent.

"Ash, I'm working a case right now," Daniel said. "I'll have to call you back later."

As she told him goodbye, a feeling of longing flooded Ashley's heart. She couldn't help it; she missed Daniel. And it shamed her to realize that for a split second, the thought that the agent might be jealous had actually made her happy.

But the truth remained: because they would likely be partnered together on another case, she and Daniel could never be anything more than friends. She'd heard too many horror stories of the things that had gone wrong when partnered cops had allowed their personal and professional lives to mesh. Unchecked emotions on the job could get you killed.

Pushing her thoughts of the agent aside, Ashley decided to bury herself in the case at hand. They had two victims – one male and one female – who lived in different cities, had different occupations, and were traveling to different locations. And yet somehow, both of the deceased had caught the attention of the same killer. Were the murders random, as Wyatt supposed?

Ashley still couldn't shake the feeling that Ian and Megan must have a common link.

Propping pillows behind her on top of the dingy room's double bed, she pulled her laptop from its carrying case and booted it up. She logged onto the motel's sluggish Wi-Fi network and clicked on her browser.

The search for Megan Archer returned a seemingly endless supply of real estate related hits: houses currently on the market, houses that had recently been sold, news articles touting the various sales awards Megan had won, tips the real estate agent had written on how to prepare a home for sale, and thousands of other mentions. There were pages and pages of documents. It was a lot to wade through.

Deciding to try and narrow the results, Ashley typed in *"Megan Archer" "Bonner County"* and pressed enter. A social media post the woman had written popped up on the screen. It was a review of a restaurant located in the nearby town of Stewartville. The post was dated the very same day Megan had disappeared.

I made the unfortunate decision to eat lunch at South Bend Grill in Bonner County. After waiting for ten minutes, a server finally took my order. Despite the place being half-empty, which should have been a warning sign, it took another twenty-five minutes for my food to arrive. I wish I had just walked out.
The chicken tenders had an unusual smell and tasted like they had spoiled. The French fries that came with the meal were cold and rubbery. Needless to say, I left the uneatable stuff they called food on the table and went elsewhere.

The owner of the restaurant had replied to Megan's comment:

Lies! All lies! This woman owns another restaurant and is trying to put me out of business! She will regret it!

As far as Ashley knew, Megan and her husband didn't own any restaurants. But it was possible that the South Bend Grill's owner had mistaken the real estate agent for someone else. Could the man have been angry enough to follow Megan to Ormond? It seemed like a stretch.

Ashley scanned the remaining search results, but didn't find anything else of interest.

Next, she typed in Ian Driscoll's name and limited the search results to include Bonner County. To her surprise, another social media post appeared. Ian had reviewed the same restaurant just before he disappeared.

Take my advice. If you're in Bonner County, don't eat at South Bend Grill. I ordered the meatloaf. It arrived at my table cold and had a strange green tint to it. I was afraid to even taste it. When I complained to my server, she acted as though I had no idea what meatloaf should look like. She didn't even offer me a different meal. Unless you want food poisoning, stay away from this place.

The owner had replied to Ian's comment as well.

This man lies! Don't believe him! He is with a group who wants to put me out of business! But he will be sorry!

It seemed the owner of South Bend Grill believed there was a conspiracy against his restaurant. Was that enough of a motive to commit murder? Ashley reminded herself that innocent people had been killed for even stranger reasons. And the bad reviews were the one common denominator that tied the two victims together.

What kind of man was Dennis Linton, South Bend Grill's owner?

Ashley logged onto the TBI database and ran a criminal background search. His sheet appeared clean except for a single entry. Twenty years prior, Linton had been arrested for assault, but the charge had never been prosecuted.

Although the man wasn't a hardened criminal, he'd had at least one violent outburst.

Ashley packed up her laptop. She needed to share the information with Wyatt.

CHAPTER FOURTEEN

Ashley could hear Wyatt's muffled voice leaking through the cracks around the double-wide window of his motel room. An awkward feeling swept over her as she realized he might have a guest inside. If that were true, the agent wouldn't be happy to see her. He'd likely tell her to come back later, which – she decided – she'd refuse to do. Interrupting his date might damage her working relationship with her partner, but it was a risk she had to take. Solving the murders of Ian and Megan was far more important than Wyatt's social life.

Bracing herself for an irate response, Ashley knocked on the motel room door.

Seconds later, her partner pulled the door open, his cell phone glued to his ear. He motioned for her to come inside.

A soft chuckle escaped Wyatt's lips. "You and me both, sweetheart," he said into the phone.

He was speaking in the same syrupy tone he'd used on Bonnie at the sheriff department's impound lot.

"Listen, I'm going to have to call you back. You know what they say: a lawman's work is never done."

Ashley rolled her eyes. Wyatt apparently didn't notice.

"Yeah, you too," he cooed before ending the call.

She guessed that her partner's reputation for being a player wasn't based on mere rumors.

"What's up?" he asked Ashley. His professional voice had returned.

"I ran a search on the internet and found a link between Ian Driscoll and Megan Archer."

A surprised expression crossed Wyatt's face. It was almost as if he didn't believe her.

"I searched too," he said. "I didn't see anything."

Ashley dropped her computer case on the end of the agent's bed and zipped it open.

"Did you limit the results to only the documents that included Bonner County?"

With all the hits that had come up for Megan, it was easy for the important one to become lost. She could tell by the blank look the agent shot her that the idea of limiting the search by location had never occurred to him.

Turning her laptop toward Wyatt, she flipped up the screen. She still had two browser tabs open – Megan's review on the first, Ian's review on the second.

"Ian and Megan both ate at the same restaurant over in Stewartville on the very day that they disappeared. Each of them wrote a bad review and posted it on social media. And the restaurant's owner, Dennis Linton, was arrested twenty years ago for assault."

"Does Linton have any criminal convictions?"

"Well … no. He was never prosecuted for the assault charge."

Her partner knelt beside the bed. She waited while he read through the posts.

When he finished, he stood and shook his head.

"So they both hated South Bend Grill," he said. "That's not really that strong of a lead."

Ashley couldn't believe what she was hearing. Other than the fact that both victims had suffered car trouble, the bad reviews were the only thing that tied them together. How could Wyatt discount that connection?

"Did you not read the owner's replies that said Ian and Megan would be sorry for posting their reviews?"

"Yeah, I saw it," he told her. "But if what Megan and Ian wrote is true, that restaurant probably gets tons of bad reviews. We only have two dead bodies. If there were similar murders in Stewartville, we would have received an alert."

Ashley knew that the TBI monitored all the crimes in the state. The database checked for patterns and notified agents of any similarities to the cases they were working. However, the fact that no roadside murders had occurred yet in Stewartville didn't mean that South Bend Grill's owner was innocent.

"But what if Ian's review was the one that pushed the restaurant owner over the edge and made him decide to retaliate? He has that assault arrest on his record."

Wyatt rubbed his chin as though he was considering her theory.

"I don't think so," he said.

They'd finally discovered a probable lead on the case and her *seasoned* partner refused to take it seriously. Ashley might be a rookie, but she knew that when it came to murder, coincidences were few and far between.

"Well, I think that there's a possibility – although it might be a slim one – that South Bend Grill's owner could be the killer. And even if I'm way off base, we can't just ignore the fact that eating at the same restaurant is the only thing our victims have in common. Something else could have happened there that led to their deaths."

"Like what?"

What difference did it make? Couldn't he just agree that she had a valid point?

"They could have met the person who killed them when they were at the restaurant. Maybe an employee will remember if Megan or Ian got into an argument with another customer or someone who works there. I just think we need to follow up on this lead."

"I think it would be a waste of time."

Wyatt obviously felt that she had no idea how to work a case. And she wasn't going to beg him to change his mind.

"Okay, fine," she said. "Just let me borrow your car for a couple of hours and I'll leave you in peace."

He stared at her. "You're going to drive to Stewartville? Alone?"

Anger rumbled in Ashley's chest. Did Wyatt not believe what he had told her brother, Shane, when he'd said that she was capable of taking care of herself? Did the big, tough agent think that she needed his protection?

"I don't care if you're not willing to lend me your SUV – that's okay, too. I'll just find another way to get there."

Ashley closed her laptop and stuffed it back into the carrying case.

"Just hold on a minute," Wyatt said.

Hold on?

Didn't he realize that every second counted?

"I'm not really sure how long it will take me to get to South Bend Grill and they close at nine o'clock tonight. I don't have time to wait."

Wyatt walked to the small motel room closet and slid back the mirrored door.

"I never said that I wouldn't go with you," he stated.

He slipped on his sports jacket and then his overcoat. "But I need to tell you the reasons it might be a waste of time."

"Okay, enlighten me."

Was he going to tell her about another case he'd solved?

"I've worked a lot of murder cases," he began.

She turned her head and rolled her eyes.

He continued, "It's been my experience that people feel emboldened when they can hide behind their computer screen. They post about things they would never do in real life. And Linton's assault charge is from twenty years ago. It wasn't serious enough to prosecute, and he's been clean since. Let's look at some of the guy's other comments."

Wyatt plopped down on the end of the bed, pulled out Ashley's laptop, and opened her browser. He clicked on the avatar for Dennis Linton. A sea of posts popped up.

Her partner scrolled to a comment several months old.

"Look, starting last year, everything this guy has posted has a hint of a threat to it," Wyatt said as he continued to scroll through the page. "There are dozens of angry comments. If he'd killed all the people he was mad at, we'd know about it."

She stared at her partner.

He sighed. "I'm not saying it's impossible. Anything's possible. And you did a good job finding a link between the two victims. But it's not likely the owner is the killer. If he'd murdered Ian and Megan, he would have deleted his comments to them."

Ashley didn't want to admit that Wyatt was right about the posts not being deleted. It would be stupid for the killer to leave his threats on the internet for everyone to read. Especially the police.

Wyatt closed her laptop. "I just don't want you to get your hopes up," he said.

Although her partner had a few good points, Ashley still wanted to visit the restaurant. If there was a possibility that a drive to Stewartville would provide them with information that could prevent another murder, then it was well worth the trouble.

Leaving her laptop on the end of the bed, she marched out of Wyatt's motel room, stood next to his SUV, and counted down the seconds, waiting for him to unlock the vehicle's passenger door.

CHAPTER FIFTEEN

As Wyatt steered his SUV into the parking lot of South Bend Grill, Ashley noticed there were less than half a dozen cars outside the Stewartville restaurant. She wondered whether that was due to the late hour – 8:07 p.m. in a town that rolled up its sidewalks at nine – or if the negative reviews had scared off the customers. Maybe it was the terrible food that had driven them away. One bad meal – or a night of bad service – was all it took for some people to refuse to return to a restaurant.

Ashley didn't wait for Wyatt to switch off the vehicle's engine. She jumped from the passenger seat as soon as she felt the transmission shift into park. Although her partner doubted that the reviews Megan and Ian had posted on social media were related to their murders, Ashley was eager to speak with the establishment's owner.

In the darkness, the old brick building exuded a sense of foreboding. Ashley thought the structure might have functioned as a small warehouse years earlier. Narrow windows lined a stretch of wall that had once featured a loading door. The bricks surrounding the bottom and sides of the glass panes measured a different size, and registered a few shades deeper, than the originals. The patchwork renovation reminded her of teeth shining inside a gaping mouth.

What had led Ian and Megan to choose this particular restaurant? Maybe it was because the establishment fronted the main highway. The restaurant also sat right next door to a gas station, so it was possible both victims had originally stopped to fill up their vehicle's tanks. And she realized that in the light of day, the building wouldn't appear quite so ominous.

She pushed through the heavy wooden door into a dim foyer. A sign instructed: *Please Wait To Be Seated*, but she didn't see a host on duty. She spotted the bar area just ahead on her left. With a slew of empty tables in the dining room to her right, it seemed the bar had drawn the handful of current customers. She guessed the quality of the alcohol ranked higher than that of the food.

Hearing the door open behind her, she glanced back to see Wyatt. The slow pace at which he entered reinforced his reluctance to believe Ashley's theory. Rather than being an active member of this leg of the investigation, it seemed he was merely tagging along. She didn't care. Ashley had made a promise to Megan's husband that she would do everything in her power to bring the killer to justice. That meant following up on every single lead.

Pushing her irritation at Wyatt aside, she plowed ahead into the bar. A solemn cloud seemed to hang over the middle-aged patrons as they sipped their drinks. Their conversations droned in low tones with no laughter to be heard. The only cheerful voice came from the announcer recapping various sports scores on the large-screened television bolted to the wall, but no one appeared to be watching.

"What's it gonna be?" the bartender asked her.

The thin man with dark balding hair seemed bored and ready to go home.

"I need to speak with the owner, Dennis Linton."

The bartender's eyes grew wide as Ashley pulled out her TBI badge. At least he no longer seemed bored.

"Uh, he's in the back. I'll have to go get him."

The man disappeared through a door behind the bar. Ashley was glad the owner was still on the premises. She'd expected to be told that Mr. Linton had already left for the day.

Glancing over her shoulder, she noticed Wyatt draped across a bench at one of the small booths in the bar area. He seemed content to let her question the restaurant's owner on her own. And she was more than happy to oblige.

A low whirring sound caught her attention. She looked to her left as a motorized wheelchair rounded the corner. A man who appeared to be somewhere in his early forties with short brown hair and a trimmed beard piloted the chair. Both of the man's limbs had been severed at the knee. She recognized his face from the social media posts. It was South Bend Grill's owner, Dennis Linton.

"You want to see me?" the man barked.

It seemed that Wyatt had been right. In his condition, it would have been next to impossible for Mr. Linton to have kidnapped and killed Ian and Megan. At least, not without help. Still, the man might have information relative to the case.

“Yes, sir. I’d like to talk with you about two of your recent customers.”

Ashley handed the man a picture of Megan Archer. “Do you remember this woman?”

Mr. Linton brushed the photo aside after just a quick glance.

“I don’t know her,” he said, aggravation clear in his tone.

She wondered how the man had forgotten Megan so fast after having replied to her review only a few days prior.

“The woman’s name is Megan Archer. She wrote a post on social media criticizing your restaurant, to which you responded, ‘She will regret it.’ Do you remember her, now?”

“You’re one of them!” the man shouted. “You’re trying to run me out of business!”

It wasn’t the reply she had expected. In addition to his physical impairment, Mr. Linton’s mental status appeared to be questionable.

“Daddy, is everything all right?” a female voice called from behind Ashley.

A teenager with long brown hair tied up in a French braid rushed to the man’s side. Petite and slim, the girl looked like she would weigh no more than one-hundred pounds soaking wet.

“Ruby, get this woman out of here,” Mr. Linton ordered.

“I’ll take care of it, Daddy. You go back and play your video game, okay?”

The man scowled at Ashley before steering his wheelchair back around the corner.

“Can I help you, ma’am?” Ruby asked, her voice apologetic.

From the expression on the teen’s face, it was clear that her father’s behavior had embarrassed her.

“My name is Ashley Hope and I’m a special agent with the Tennessee Bureau of Investigations. I was just asking your father about one of your recent customers – a woman named Megan Archer.”

As Ruby scanned the victim’s photo, recognition flooded her dark eyes.

“I waited on her,” the teen stated in a hushed tone. “She didn’t like the food. Said it wasn’t up to her standards. She left without paying.”

Ruby motioned for Ashley to move toward the hallway where her father had disappeared, out of earshot of the bar patrons. There was an air of sadness in the girl’s demeanor that tugged at Ashley’s heart.

“How old are you?” she asked the teen.

"I'll be nineteen next month."

Ruby appeared much younger than her years. Ashley would have guessed her to be no more than sixteen.

"Does your mother work here at the restaurant too?"

The young woman shook her head. "She passed away last year."

The revelation hit Ashley in her core. Having lost her own mother to cancer many years before, she knew the pain Ruby had suffered. And from the lack of customers in the restaurant, it appeared that the family might be on the road to losing their business as well.

"Were you aware that Megan Archer wrote a bad review of your restaurant on social media?"

"No. But it don't surprise me none."

As bad as Ashley hated to admit it, Wyatt had probably been correct when he'd guessed that South Bend Grill had likely garnered a high number of critical reviews.

"Would it be true to say that you've gotten used to receiving a lot of negative posts on the restaurant's page?"

Ruby nodded. "But it weren't always this way. Business was good before the car crash last year. That's how we lost my mama. And how Daddy lost his legs. His mind's not so good anymore. We've had a hard time keeping a manager. Daddy just seems so angry all the time. He runs the help away."

Ashley's heart broke as the young woman explained her situation. Ruby had a lot of weight on her shoulders.

"Did you notice whether or not Mrs. Archer spoke with anyone while she was here – another customer or one of your employees?"

"I didn't see her talking to nobody. She was real stuck up. And kind of mean."

"In what way was she mean?"

Ruby sighed. "She made fun of the way I talk. But in a backhanded kind of way. She said I needed to improve my grammar if I wanted to work with the public."

The idea that Megan had been cruel to Ruby sparked a flame of anger in Ashley's soul. The young woman had enough problems. She didn't need to feel belittled on top of everything else.

Ashley pulled out the photo of Ian Driscoll.

"Do you recognize this man?" she asked.

“Yeah.” Ruby nodded. “I waited on him too. He weren’t very nice either. He said that the hillbillies around here were cooking up roadkill and calling it meatloaf.”

How could Ian and Megan have justified their rude behavior? Their words sounded like the taunts of spoiled children, not the type of conversation expected from professional adults.

“Do you remember whether or not this man spoke with anyone else while he was here?”

“I don’t rightly know.”

The idea that the killer could have been at the restaurant and had overheard Ian and Megan demean their server crossed Ashley’s mind. It seemed unlikely that the two victims had been murdered because of their haughty attitudes, but not impossible.

However, Ashley felt one thing for certain: neither Dennis Linton nor his daughter had committed the murders.

“Thank you for answering my questions, Ruby,” she said, slipping the photos back into her coat pocket.

“Can I ask you something, ma’am?”

Ashley nodded. “Of course you can.”

“What did those people do?”

The young woman obviously thought that Ian and Megan were criminals. There was no use hiding the truth from her.

“I’m trying to find the person who murdered them.”

The color drained from Ruby’s face. Maybe it would have been better if Ashley had kept the information to herself.

Apparently realizing that she had completed the interview, Wyatt slid out from the booth and motioned for Ashley to proceed with him out of the bar area. Although the owner of South Bend Grill appeared innocent – as her partner had assumed – the trip to Stewartville had not resulted in a loss. Not by Ashley’s standards.

She now knew that both Ian and Megan seemed to share a disdain for the mountain locals. It wasn’t a lot to go on, but it was something.

As she climbed back into the passenger seat of Wyatt’s SUV, Ashley realized that her partner had most likely not been able to hear everything Ruby had told her. She wondered whether it would make a difference to him. It didn’t matter. The more she mulled over the out-of-towners’ attitude toward the Bonner County residents, the more she felt it was important to the case.

Ashley had a gut feeling that this clue might just prove pivotal in solving the murders.

CHAPTER SIXTEEN

Nick Weaver forced his eyes open. He had no idea of the time, whether it was day or night, or how long he'd been drifting in and out of consciousness on the cold, hard floor. The pain that throbbed in his skull felt so intense that he had trouble stringing his thoughts together. But he knew he needed to get up on his feet – to find a way out of this dank pit.

Dizziness hit him as he raised his head. Nausea threatened his stomach. His vision blurry, he struggled to focus on the stained concrete-block walls that surrounded him. Fought to erase the dark spots that plagued his sight. But one image burned clear in his mind. The face of the person who'd attacked him. Even now he could see the man's dark narrow eyes and the wicked grin twisting the man's lips.

He should have known not to trust the Bonner County local.

Nick had heard rumors about the chop shops that littered the mountain region, but he'd never imagined that he'd fall into one of the criminal gang's traps. The man – who he'd once thought was a pillar of the small community – must actually reign at the top the gang. The local had obviously taken one look at the red sports car and had calculated the worth of its parts. Each piece sold separately would likely fetch a higher total price than what the vehicle was worth.

And the man had pegged Nick as an easy mark.

The ruse concocted by the Bonner County local had worked like a charm. He'd told Nick that there had been a major wreck on the main highway and that the road would be closed for hours. Taking a detour seemed like Nick's only option if he wanted to make it to Loganville before dusk. At the time, the change in plans had only seemed like a minor inconvenience. One he could take in stride.

After giving Nick directions for an alternate route that ran through a deep valley with no cell phone service, the Bonner County local had followed him from town. The man had probably planned to run him off the road. The fact that the sports car had overheated had been a lucky break for the gang. The lack of damage to the vehicle's body would garner the criminals an even sweeter payday than they had anticipated.

How could Nick have allowed himself to become so gullible?

Choking back the bile that rose in his throat, he yanked his arms for the hundredth time, fighting to free his hands from behind his back. But it was no use. Duct tape bound his wrists and ankles in a manner that was so tight, he was surprised it hadn't cut off his circulation. The man had also wound tape around Nick's head, covering his mouth and chin. The first time he'd awoken inside the narrow pit, he'd cried out for help. But his voice had been muffled by the adhesive gag.

Who would help him anyway? Nick was a hostage in a criminal's den.

He twisted his legs, trying to loosen the bonds around his ankles. As he struggled, he realized that there was a plastic sheet stretched beneath him on the hard concrete floor. He peered down the length of his body, past his feet. From what he could tell from the narrow shaft of light that streamed through an opening in the ceiling, it appeared as though there was a series of flimsy metal rings embedded into the plastic. The kind of rings that would slip over a shower rod.

A wave of fear hit Nick.

Why had the man dumped him on top of a shower curtain? He knew it wasn't to keep the grime from marring his clothes. Was it to prevent his DNA from being discovered in the pit?

Since he'd first come to, Nick had told himself several times that if the gang wanted to kill him, he'd already be dead. That the man would have shot him on the roadside. Now, he wasn't so sure.

He pressed his eyes closed and forced the thought that the gang might murder him from his mind. Instead, he conjured up a vision of Valerie. He imagined her wearing the blue dress she'd donned the night he'd asked her to marry him. He pictured her warm smile lighting up her big brown eyes and her long chestnut hair draped across her shoulders.

It had been his love for Valerie that had led him through Bonner County. He'd been on his way to pick up a gift to surprise her. He knew the Yorkshire terrier puppy he'd chosen from a breeder in Loganville wouldn't replace the dog Valerie had lost two months prior, but it would definitely make her happy. And all that mattered to him was her happiness.

Hearing a noise above him, Nick opened his eyes. An aluminum ladder dropped down from the opening in the ceiling, a couple of yards from his feet. The man's boots clinked against the metal treads as he descended into the pit.

It was the same man who had attacked him on the roadside.

As his abductor approached, Nick jerked his legs and kicked out at the man. But the Bonner County local dodged the blow.

"You better watch yourself, boy," the man yelled.

The threat echoed off the walls of the cramped space.

"You don't wanna make me any madder."

Nick scooted in the opposite direction, away from his abductor, but his head butted the concrete-block wall behind him. Fresh pain sliced through his skull, followed by another wave of dizziness.

"You done crossed the wrong man."

Crossed?

What was he talking about? Nick hadn't done anything that could be construed as crossing the man. He hadn't cheated the local or wronged him in any way. Not that he could remember.

Did the man have another motive for Nick's abduction? Was it more than just the sports car?

"I'm gonna teach you some manners."

The man's teeth glowed like fangs as his lips curled into a smile.

"We're gonna have a lot of fun."

Panic stirred in Nick's chest. He squirmed, twisting his body from side to side. If he tried to kick out with his feet, the force would knock his head back against the wall again. He had no way to defend himself.

The local chuckled.

"You ain't getting loose. You might as well take your medicine like a man. And I'm gonna give it to you one spoonful at a time."

Nick caught the flash of metal in his abductor's right hand.

A gun? No, it was some type of pneumatic tool.

The man seemed almost euphoric as he inched toward Nick.

"Let's get this party started!" the local shouted.

Evil radiated from the man's dark eyes as he raised the metal tool above his head.

Terror raced through Nick's heart. He now knew for certain that he was going to die. He would never see Valerie again. They would never be married. Never have children.

The man slammed the end of the steel tool into Nick's right leg.

A muffled scream escaped his lips as his kneecap shattered.

Excruciating pain shot up Nick's thigh and rushed through his abdomen. He thought he might lose consciousness again.

"That was your first dose of medicine," the man taunted.

The local moved to the other side, toward Nick's left leg.

"A couple of days from now, I'll give you your last."

Tears flooded Nick's eyes as his abductor raised the tool a second time.

CHAPTER SEVENTEEN

The blaring tone from the alarm on Ashley's cell phone jostled her from a deep sleep. Her drowsy brain screamed for her to tap the snooze option – to roll over and drift back to dream land. If only for a few more minutes. But it was five a.m., and she had work to do.

Throwing back the flimsy blanket, Ashley forced herself from the cocoon she'd made on top of the hard motel mattress. Just as her feet touched the floor, she heard a knock on the door of her room. She grabbed her robe and slipped it on.

Wyatt stood on the other side of the fish-eye lens peephole.

A bolt of dread hit Ashley. Why would her partner show up at her motel room door so early? Had local law enforcement found another body?

Bracing herself for the worst, she jerked open the door.

"What's going on, Wyatt? Has something happened?"

"Everything's okay," he said, still standing at the threshold. "I thought you might want to borrow this."

He handed her a dark-blue oblong box with the name *Dyson* embossed on the top.

"You got up early so you could bring me your hair dryer?"

She couldn't believe he'd woken up, showered, and dressed, all before five. She guessed he didn't want to be seen with her again if her hair wasn't perfect.

Wyatt shrugged. "I don't want you to get sick. Yesterday, I was worried you'd catch the flu."

Her partner's words stunned Ashley. She had stewed the whole day prior, thinking he was displeased with her appearance when she'd left the motel with her hair damp. But in reality, he'd been concerned with her health.

Had she been reading Wyatt wrong since the day they'd met?

Shame filled her heart. She'd been quick to jump to conclusions. Never once stopping to consider the different motivations Wyatt might have for his actions. It was clear that his mind worked in a unique way. Had she even given her new partner a chance?

“I really appreciate this, Wyatt; thank you.”

“No problem.”

He nodded and stepped away from the door.

Ashley placed the Dyson on the counter in the motel room’s vanity area. As far as she knew, Wyatt was the only man she’d ever met who had paid five-hundred-dollars for a hair dryer. Even though she’d decided to start over again with her new partner, to listen to him with an open mind, and give him the benefit of the doubt from now on, the expensive appliance said a lot about where Wyatt’s priorities lay. But he was a single guy, and had to spend his money on something.

No matter how busy her day turned out to be, Ashley vowed to stop at a drugstore and pick up a travel dryer. She didn’t want to risk damaging Wyatt’s. And she didn’t want to be the reason he cut his sleep time short.

As she adjusted the water temperature in the shower, her thoughts jumped to Ruby Linton. She wondered what would happen to the young woman if South Bend Grill closed down. Like Ashley’s hometown, it appeared as though the employment opportunities in Bonner County ran slim.

Her heart broke for Ruby. On sight, she’d felt a connection with the sad young woman. Ashley had lived through a similar situation, losing her own mother as a child. And her father’s auto repair business had struggled for years before making its first profit. Even then, as the sole source of income for not only her family, but her uncle’s family as well, the shop had only provided for the necessities. It was only in recent times that her father’s business had earned a little extra.

Ashley had been fortunate to land a partial scholarship to the University of Tennessee at Chattanooga. Along with the financial support of student loans and a job waiting tables, she’d managed to earn a bachelor’s degree and then a master’s. With her education as the vehicle, she’d escaped the economic drought in Laurel County.

Would Ruby ever have that kind of opportunity?

Anger swelled in Ashley’s chest as she thought about the rude comments Megan had made to Ruby. She remembered how it had felt to be looked down upon by city dwellers as they passed through her hometown. Those who believed in the stereotypes played out in movies and television shows. Who thought that people born and raised in the mountains possessed little more than the mental abilities of a five-year-old.

But a lack of education didn't mean a person suffered from a low IQ. Although her older brother, Kyle, had quit high school to work at the auto shop, he was one of the brightest people she'd ever met. But making a living – putting food on her family's table – had ranked first on Kyle's priority list.

She unpacked the Dyson from the padded box with a black velvet-type lining. As the blast of hot air hit her scalp, she realized the reason she'd been so hasty in interpreting Wyatt's behavior. His apparent scrutiny of her jeans and hiking boots – while he wore a jacket and tie – had made her feel inferior. Just like the city folk had made her feel when she was a child, dressed in hand-me-down clothing from the town church's donation bin.

However, she had no idea of her partner's true thoughts. It was possible he hadn't been judging her at all. It was her past experiences that had sparked her feelings of inadequacy. The same way that legends of the harassment, imprisonment, and seizure of their ancestors' assets, passed down through the generations, fueled the mountain locals' distrust of law enforcement.

As Ashley switched off the hair dryer, her cell phone chimed. It was a text message from Daniel.

Working undercover. Can't call.
Will text again later. Stay safe.
– D.

The fact that the agent had taken time out of his morning to send her a message – that he was thinking of her – made Ashley smile. He would likely be using a burner phone for his assignment and would be leaving his own cell at home in case he was frisked. It was his safety that was on the line.

Reminding herself that Daniel knew what he was doing and that he had the support of a professional team behind him, she pushed away the fear that nagged at her. Fear that the agent would run into trouble. That he'd get hurt.

She'd seen Daniel's intense dedication to his job first hand. And she hoped to one day be just as fine an agent. Even if Brenda only assigned her cases in rural mountain areas.

Stuffing her phone back into the pocket of her jacket, draped across the bed, a thought hit her.

It wasn't her casual mode of dress, or her – sometimes heavy – southern accent that allowed her to fit in with the locals. It was something deep inside of her that the mountain folk recognized. She had lived their lives. And no matter what town – or city – she decided to call home in the future, she would always be one of them.

Having decided that she'd pull her hair back into a ponytail for the day, she walked to the bedside table to get her scrunchie.

Ashley stopped short.

The black hairband with the initial *A* stitched in white wasn't there.

She'd fished the scrunchie out of her suitcase yesterday, but had chosen not to wear it because her hair had been wet. She was sure she'd left it on the table. Dropping down on her knees, she searched underneath the bed. All she found were dust bunnies.

Ashley scoured the motel room. The vanity area, the dresser, the bathroom. She even dumped out the contents of her purse and checked her suitcase again. The scrunchie was nowhere to be found. The personalized hairband, purchased at a craft fair in Briarwood, didn't seem like an item a housekeeper would steal. So where did it go?

Fear rushed through her.

Had one of Troy's relatives been in her room? The one who'd helped him with the murders?

She thought about telling Wyatt about her feelings of being watched. Would he think she was crazy? Probably. And he'd likely think she just misplaced her scrunchie.

Maybe she had. Or maybe the housekeeping staff had thrown it away by mistake.

Telling herself that she was being paranoid, Ashley packed the Dyson back inside its case and slung her laptop bag over her shoulder. As she headed across the threshold of her motel room, she caught sight of a gray, four-door pickup idling in the parking lot.

Ashley froze.

The truck's bed angled toward her. The tint of the rear window made it impossible for her to see into the extended cab, but the familiar eerie feeling hit Ashley again. The feeling that the people inside were watching her.

Studying her.

Goosebumps broke out on her arms as her attention jerked toward the vehicle's license plate. A large swath of mud obscured the tag number and issuing county. As she took a step forward, the driver of the pickup slammed on the gas. The tires squealed as the vehicle swerved out of the motel parking lot and onto the highway.

It had to be the Luckadoos.

CHAPTER EIGHTEEN

The layer of dust on the motel laundry room's decades-old, coin-operated washers and dryers proved to Ashley that it had been quite a while since the appliances had housed a load of clothing. She wondered whether they even still worked. But what she found unsettling about the coating of grime was that it also indicated a lack of attention by the motel's housekeeping service. As she navigated her way past the machines to the laminate-topped table in the back, Ashley hoped that the guest rooms ranked higher on the cleaning staff's roster.

She dropped her laptop case on the table and searched for an electrical outlet. The closest one was located at least ten feet away. She shoved the table to the right, butting it against the pale yellow wall.

Since Sheriff Powell had attempted to sabotage their investigation, Wyatt had suggested they meet in the laundry room to work on the case, rather than driving to the Bonner County Sheriff's department. Judging by the condition of the surroundings, they'd definitely have plenty of privacy here. And they wouldn't have to put up with the dirty looks thrown at them by the majority of the deputies.

As Ashley booted up her laptop, she heard the laundry room door push open. It was Wyatt. Along with the computer case that was slung over his shoulder, a plastic bag hung from his left wrist, and he carried two large foam coffee cups in his hands. She was grateful that he'd made a trip to the convenience store down the street.

Although their partnership had suffered a rocky start, she had to admit that Wyatt could be thoughtful. This was the second time he'd included her in his coffee run.

"Thank you for taking the time to bring caffeine," she told him.

"Not a problem."

He dumped the contents of the plastic bag onto the table. Two packages of cinnamon buns, two packages of crackers with peanut butter, two packages of crackers with cheese, and two packages of beef jerky.

"I circled the town twice," he said. "You know there's not a single fast food joint here?"

She wasn't surprised.

"There are no fast food restaurants located back in Mettler Ridge either. I think a town has to have a certain number of residents before the big companies will issue a franchise license."

"That makes sense. Anyway, I hope there's something here you'll eat. The minimart has a deli counter, but the food looked iffy."

Ashley wasn't that picky. She opted for the peanut butter crackers. She ripped open the package while Wyatt set up his laptop.

"Do you still think that the two murders were crimes of opportunity?" she asked.

Wyatt stared at the ceiling as though he was gathering his thoughts.

"Yeah," he said.

"Even knowing that Ian and Megan were beaten so badly that almost all their bones were broken?"

"The guy has a lot of anger inside. The victims said or did something that set him off. He snapped, and beat them to death. The killings were an outlet for his rage. But I don't think he's looking for anyone else to murder. I think it's over."

Ashley stared at him. She feared he was wrong.

Wyatt could obviously tell by her expression that she doubted his opinion on the events of the crime.

"You still think we've got a serial killer?" he asked.

She nodded. "I just have trouble believing that a murderer who made a spur-of-the-moment decision to kill someone would take the time to abduct them, torture them for days, and then dump their body miles away. I think the killer chose and stalked Ian and Megan for a particular reason."

"And that reason would be?"

Despite the fact that it sounded like a stretch, she decided to fill him in on what she'd learned from Ruby.

"The server at South Bend Grill said that both Ian and Megan had a judgmental attitude toward the Bonner County locals. What if the killer was in the restaurant and overheard the rude comments they each made and decided to go after them?"

Now, he stared at her.

"That's all you've got?"

Wyatt was starting to grate on her nerves again.

Although she didn't have an inkling as to the motive, Ashley was convinced the person responsible for the murders already had another victim in their sights. Not just because of the details she'd listed. It was a gut feeling. Something she couldn't put into words.

Deciding to end the conversation for the time being, she focused her attention on her laptop. She searched the TBI database just to make sure no similar murders had been logged during the night. There were no matches. And other than the restaurant reviews, they still had no evidence linking Ian and Megan together. She knew the lack of a common denominator was likely one of the main reasons Wyatt didn't buy into her serial killer theory.

Her partner's cell phone rang, startling her.

He glanced at the screen. "It's Brenda."

Ashley hoped the deputy director wasn't on the warpath this morning.

"Hello," Wyatt said into the phone.

Although she couldn't make out Brenda's words, Ashley didn't hear any anger in their boss's tone. Not this time.

After listening to the deputy director speak, and then voicing several affirmations, Wyatt ended the call. A somber look tainted his hazel eyes.

"You know the spots we found on Megan's SUV?" he asked Ashley. "We got the results back. It's blood spatter. And it's a match for Megan's type."

As soon as she'd seen the rust-colored specks on the running board of the vehicle, Ashley had known it was the victim's blood.

"So the killer must have hit her with something – probably the murder weapon – and knocked her out," Ashley stated.

"That's how it looks."

"But I still can't help wondering that if your theory is right, then why didn't the murderer just kill her on the roadside?"

If the agent couldn't come up with a plausible answer this time, then maybe he'd change his mind. Maybe he'd see things Ashley's way.

"The guy was probably afraid another car would drive by. So he put Megan in his vehicle and carried her home. Or to a place where he knew he wouldn't be interrupted. And he killed her there."

Even though Wyatt's answer might sound logical, she still believed the murders had been planned in advance. Only time would tell who was right. And for once, Ashley hoped it was her theory that was wrong. She prayed the killer wouldn't strike again.

Wyatt tapped his fingers on the tabletop.

"The guy probably lives near where the cars were found," he said.

This time she agreed with her partner. His assumption made sense, even if the murderer was a stalker.

She pulled up a map of Bonner County on her laptop. It took her a few minutes to locate Linley Pass, where Ian's car had been discovered. She zoomed in on the area and searched for the road where Megan's abandoned SUV had been located. She was surprised at how close in proximity the two roads were.

On a hunch, she activated the 3D topography layer to get a lay of the land.

"Both Linley Pass and Bat Creek Road are located in the same valley," she told Wyatt. "And I'll bet you that there's no cell phone service in that area. The signal would most likely be blocked by the mountains on each side."

"Which would explain why they didn't call for help."

Ashley noticed that there seemed to be one continuous parcel of land wedged between the two roads. She switched to the satellite view. She could see a large barn, several outbuildings, a pond, and tiny black figures she felt certain were cows.

"I think I may have found the place where the killer might live," she said. "There's a large farm that just happens to be bordered by both roads."

Wyatt rose from his chair and peered over Ashley's shoulder.

"Switch over to the property records and get the owner's name."

With just a few clicks, the information popped up: Warren Shipley. As she searched the TBI database for a criminal history of the farmer, Wyatt began packing up his laptop.

"Warren Shipley doesn't have any criminal convictions on his record," she told her partner, "but he's been arrested twice and each time the charges were dropped. Both arrests were for pulling a shotgun on someone who was trespassing on his land."

"Ian and Megan could have tried to get help. Maybe Shipley saw them, flew into a rage, and knocked them out. He tied them up in one of the sheds. And then ..."

The scenario sounded plausible. The farmer could have chased Megan back to her SUV where he hit her in the head with something, maybe the butt of his shotgun.

"How long do you think it will take us to get to Shipley's place?" she asked.

"If you'll hurry and pack your stuff, I can have us there in thirty minutes."

Ashley closed her laptop and shoved it back into the carrying case.

A rush of adrenaline hit her. Maybe they'd finally found their killer.

CHAPTER NINETEEN

As Wyatt's SUV veered right onto Bat Creek Road, Ashley pulled her cell phone from her jacket pocket and checked the screen.

"It's just like I thought," she told her partner. "There's no cell phone service out here in the valley."

Although Megan and her husband, Jay, hadn't been on speaking terms the day the woman had been abducted, she couldn't have called him even if she'd wanted to. She couldn't have phoned anyone for help. Not with her cell. But she might have ventured up to Shipley's farm. A mistake she may have paid for with her life.

"Not much of anything out here," Wyatt replied.

He was right. After leaving the main highway, Ashley noted that the signs of civilization faded fast. No businesses were located along the narrow tree-lined road and the few farmhouses that dotted the landscape rested miles apart. There was nothing she could see that would entice an out-of-tower to drive into the valley. Why did Megan choose to travel this route?

At the beginning of the investigation, Ashley had surmised that a warning light on Megan's dashboard had flashed on again, and that the woman had left the highway in search of a repair shop. But now, that scenario appeared to make no sense.

"Do you have any ideas as to where Megan could have been heading?" she asked.

Her partner seemed to be giving the matter some thought.

"Maybe there's land for sale out here," he said. "She might have seen an ad in town. Thought it fit one of her buyers, and decided to check it out."

Although Ashley hadn't observed any real estate directional signs anywhere along the way, she supposed Megan could have been scouting property. If the locals in Bonner County were as similar to those in Laurel County as Ashley believed, they may not have allowed markers to be placed. Rural residents often policed the ditches that bordered their land, pulling up and throwing away real estate, political, and other advertising signs.

Wyatt slowed the SUV as they neared Warren Shipley's farm. Ashley noticed that a wire fence with metal posts surrounded the property. A red and white mailbox, shaped like a miniature barn, marked the hard-packed dirt driveway. The same quaint postal boxes were a common sight in her hometown as well.

As the SUV's tires left the asphalt and hit dirt, Ashley spotted a double metal gate stretched across the drive up ahead. A padlock dangled from the heavy chain that secured the gate to the fence. Wyatt glanced at her as though he was reading her thoughts: they had to leave the vehicle behind. They'd be forced to walk up to Shipley's farmhouse, hidden somewhere beyond a grove of pine trees. Her partner shifted the transmission into park and killed the engine.

Thunder rumbled in the distance as Ashley hopped down from the passenger seat. The sky above them had morphed from baby blue to steel gray. A stiff wind tousled her hair as she made her way toward the metal barrier. She hoped they wouldn't be struck by lightning.

Just before Ashley reached the gate, Wyatt motioned for her to stop.

"Mr. Shipley?" he yelled, his hands cupped around his mouth. "TBI!"

Her eyes scanned the trees while they waited for a reply. The man could be inside his home, parked in front of the television. Or any number of other places on the property that were out of earshot. But she knew that it was better to announce their arrival before they went any further.

Receiving no response, Wyatt shouted out a second time.

A few moments later, the agent shrugged.

"After you," he said, gesturing toward the gate.

Ashley grasped the metal fence post and hoisted herself over. On the other side, she paused and waited for her partner, half expecting to hear gunshots ring out. Once Wyatt had maneuvered his way across the gate, she glanced at his belt, making sure that his TBI badge was visible. She doubted the farmer would be reckless enough to shoot at law enforcement agents.

But then she reminded herself that this was Bonner County. And many of the mountain people felt they had a right to fire at trespassers – even if the trespassers wore a badge.

Warren Shipley probably viewed the TBI as his enemy.

With the low growl of thunder moving closer, they trudged up the hard-packed red-clay drive, side by side. As they topped a slight rise,

Ashley heard the clanking of cowbells. A small herd of white Saanen goats grazed beneath the trees to their right. The bells dangled from collars fastened around their necks. Her cousins raised the same affectionate breed, known for their superior milk production.

Three of the goats trotted toward them, likely looking for a treat.

As the largest of the goats nudged its nose against Ashley's leg, she met Wyatt's gaze.

"White hairs," they both said in unison.

Although the majority of the Saanen's coat grew short and fine, longer hairs sprang from their hips. Were these the same hairs found on the bodies of Ian and Megan?

Apprehension fluttered in Ashley's chest. What were they walking into?

"Do you think we should head back into town and get a few of the sheriff's deputies to come out here with us?" she asked.

Wyatt tilted his head, shooting her a look of incredulity.

"You really think the sheriff would give us backup?" he asked as one of the friendly goats brushed against him.

He had a point. And she knew it would take a TBI team a few hours to get to Bonner County. If they turned back now, they'd lose valuable time. And although they hadn't yet seen Warren Shipley, he might be aware that they were on his property. The farmer could already be destroying evidence that linked him to the murders.

As a precaution, she drew her Glock from its holster in the waistband of her jeans. With a nod, her partner followed suit. They couldn't be too careful.

Realizing there was no food to be had, the goats lost interest and wandered back to their herd.

Wyatt motioned for Ashley to stay behind him as they continued up the drive. Walking a slight distance to his right, she scanned the property on both sides, watching for an ambush. As they rounded a bend, a clearing opened up before them. A white farmhouse with a long, narrow front porch rested in the center. The blue pickup parked on the right led her to believe there was a good possibility Mr. Shipley was at home.

She stopped next to the porch as Wyatt mounted the steps.

Her partner pounded on the front door.

"Mr. Shipley," he shouted. "It's the TBI. Open the door."

Ashley stepped up onto the porch and inched toward a window, listening for movement inside. She heard nothing. The closed shade blocked her view of the interior of the home.

Wyatt banged on the door again. "TBI! Open the door!"

Backing down off the porch, she gestured to her partner, letting him know that she was heading to the rear of the house. It was possible Mr. Shipley had already sneaked out the back door.

She crept along the left side of the farmhouse, her back to the wall. Keeping her Glock raised, she rounded the rear corner. There was no one in sight. A clap of thunder jarred the ground, and cold rain drops needled her face. Driven at an angle by the wind, the sudden downpour made it difficult for her to see.

Hopping onto the covered back porch, she peered through the window in the door. A dark kitchen appeared on the other side. She could make out a round table in the eating area, but she didn't catch any movement or see any signs of life.

Leaving the porch, she continued along the rear of the farmhouse. Lightning streaked across the sky and rain pummeled her head. She blinked, struggling to keep her vision clear, as she neared the next corner.

The crack of a rifle split the air just ahead of her.

Panic surged in Ashley's chest.

The return fire of her partner's Glock echoed a moment later. At least that meant Wyatt was still alive. She peeked around the corner. A man wearing a camouflage jacket and cap knelt behind the blue pickup, his rifle aimed toward the front yard. He appeared to be lining up his sights.

The rifle blasted a second time.

Again, Wyatt returned the fire.

With the roar of the driving rain and the crashing thunder masking her approach, Ashley circled around the farmhouse. She hoped Wyatt could see her. She would hate to be killed by her own partner.

Keeping her footsteps light, she slunk toward the man. Halfway between the house and the truck, she slipped on the wet grass. Ashley caught herself just before she hit the ground.

With her pulse racing, she took a silent deep breath and steadied her feet. She couldn't risk drawing the man's attention. If she landed on her butt, he'd be sure to hear her.

The man appeared to be lining up his sights again. Another blast rang out as he squeezed the rifle's trigger.

This time, there was no return fire. That could only mean one of two things: either Wyatt was afraid he'd hit Ashley if he fired back, or her partner had been shot. She prayed it was the former.

Afraid to even breathe, she tiptoed forward, careful where her feet landed. Her heart pounded in her ears, blocking out the drumming sound of the rain. As she took her final step, lightning ripped across the sky, striking the ground somewhere behind the farmhouse.

Shipley swerved around facing her, his eyes wide.

With too little distance between them to aim his rifle, he lunged toward Ashley, swinging the butt of his weapon.

On instinct, Ashley jumped to the side. Pain sliced through her arm as the rifle clipped her shoulder. She stumbled backward, but managed to regain her balance. Her grip on her Glock firm.

Ashley trained the pistol on the farmer's chest.

"TBI!" she shouted. "Drop your weapon, or I'll shoot!"

The man stared at her for a moment, as if debating whether or not she'd really kill him. She would.

The farmer let go of the rifle and it fell to the ground.

"Hands behind your head!" Ashley ordered. "Now!"

As she slammed a pair of handcuffs around the farmer's wrists, Wyatt appeared at her side.

"What took you so long?" he asked.

Blinking back the rain, she cut her eyes at him. With his poker face and flat tone, she couldn't tell whether the question was lighthearted or if it was a serious complaint. For all she knew, her partner despised her – hated her theories, her lack of experience, and the way she dressed.

She was sick and tired of trying to figure out Wyatt.

With her shoulder throbbing, anger bubbled in her chest.

"Maybe next time I'll just sit back and watch the gunfight play out," she spat. "How would you like that?"

As soon as the words left her mouth, Ashley regretted saying them.

A stunned look crossed her partner's face, as though she'd cut him to his core.

She shook her head. "I didn't mean that, Wyatt. I'm sorry."

He seemed to ignore her apology.

"Let's get him to the station," he said, his eyes cold.

Wyatt yanked the man up off of his knees and pushed him forward. As another bolt of lightning split the sky, they headed back down the driveway toward the SUV, which she hoped was still parked on the other side of the gate.

Mud caked the soles of Ashley's hiking boots as she followed behind the prisoner and her partner. She chided herself for not giving Wyatt the benefit of the doubt – for taking his words as a criticism – when it was now clear to her that he'd been kidding. She wouldn't be surprised if he called Brenda and asked for a new partner.

She vowed to learn to read Wyatt better. As soon as they reached the sheriff's department, she'd pull him aside and apologize again. Make sure that he understood that she would never do anything that would put his life in danger. Maybe he would forgive her.

And then again, maybe not.

CHAPTER TWENTY

Inside the ladies' room at the sheriff's department, Ashley slung her right foot up onto the chipped porcelain sink and scraped the mud off the sole of her hiking boot with a wad of paper towels. Since they'd arrived at the station, she'd attempted to speak with Wyatt in private several times, but he'd brushed her aside. It was obvious he wasn't interested in hearing her apologize again.

Ashley just wished she'd taken a moment to mull over her partner's words before she'd opened her big mouth. She could have at least asked him whether he was kidding or not when he'd questioned why it had taken her so long to sneak up behind the rifle-shooting farmer. And of course, she now knew Wyatt's query had been nothing more than a lighthearted rib.

The way things stood, he likely thought that she wouldn't care if he died. Which couldn't be further from the truth. Even though their relationship had been rocky thus far, she knew she'd be upset if something bad happened to him.

With her right shoe cleaned as well as it could be, she tossed the muddy paper towels into the trash and switched to the other foot. She needed to have a heart-to-heart talk with her partner and explain that she was having trouble reading him. It seemed the only way they could get their differences ironed out. If that didn't fix the problem, she'd likely be pulled from the case and fired from her job with the TBI.

She stared at her reflection in the mirror. The rain had hammered away her mascara and had plastered her hair to her head. She had peeled off her wet fleece jacket and had hung it over a heating vent next to Deputy Halsey's desk in an attempt to dry it out a bit. But her jeans were still soaked. She grabbed another handful of paper towels and squeezed the water from her long hair and then combed out the tangles. She still looked like a mess, but it was the best she could do.

As she trudged out of the bathroom, she heard Sheriff Fenton Powell's angry voice echoing down the hallway. Turning the corner, she caught sight of Powell and Wyatt standing on the other side of the open door of the sheriff's private office.

“Warren Shipley ain’t no killer,” Sheriff Powell shouted.

“He fired a rifle at a TBI agent,” Wyatt countered. “That’s attempted murder.”

The sheriff shook his head. “Must have been some kind of misunderstanding. He probably thought y’all were about to rob him. Or kill him. You was on his property. We got a stand-your-ground law in this state, you know.”

To Ashley, it seemed like the sheriff’s defense of Mr. Shipley sprang from a desire to push back against Wyatt rather than from his belief in the farmer’s innocence. She moved closer to the door, careful not to make a sound.

“I identified myself as a law enforcement agent before he started shooting,” her partner said. “He realized exactly what he was doing.”

“Shipley don’t know you. He probably thought you was lying. Just pretending to be a cop.”

“The charge still stands. And I expect you to hold him in the county jail until his arraignment.”

Wyatt glanced at Ashley as he marched past her, heading down the hallway. She guessed he was almost as angry at her as he was at the sheriff. She caught up with him just as he reached the door to the interrogation room. She touched his arm.

“Wyatt, I really need to talk to you.”

“Not now, Ashley.”

He pushed his way into the department’s small interrogation room. She followed, taking a seat next to him at the metal table. Mr. Shipley hadn’t been brought into the room yet. The deputies were likely stringing out the booking process, looking for any excuse they could find to slow down the TBI’s investigation.

“Did Brenda tell you how long it will take to get a warrant to search Shipley’s farm?”

He sighed, as though it irritated him to speak to Ashley.

“We’ll have it by the time the team reaches Bonner County,” he said.

She resisted the urge to ask him when he thought that would be. She knew that once the forensics team descended on the farm, they’d likely be able to determine whether or not the murders had taken place in one of the out buildings – or inside Shipley’s home – in a reasonable amount of time. They could test blood spatter in a matter of minutes, identifying it as either human or animal.

Hearing a noise in the hallway, she turned her attention toward the door. A deputy led Mr. Shipley into the interrogation room and cuffed him to the metal ring bolted to the table. The man sneered at Wyatt, his bald head reflecting the florescent lighting.

Her partner crossed his arms. "Why did you shoot at me, Mr. Shipley?"

"Cause I knew you meant to do me harm," he said in a defiant tone. "I got a right to protect myself."

"You saw my badge and heard me tell you that I'm an agent with the TBI."

The farmer snorted. "That don't mean shit. People can say anything. It don't make it true."

The man's response seemed a little too familiar. Ashley felt certain that Sheriff Powell had coached Mr. Shipley.

"Okay. Fair enough," her partner said.

Ashley knew Wyatt wasn't letting the man off the hook. Shipley would still face an attempted murder charge, but appearing to dismiss the shooting seemed like a good strategy in getting the real answers they sought.

Wyatt uncrossed his arms and leaned forward.

"Tell me about Megan Archer."

A confused expression crossed the farmer's face. "Who?"

"A thirty-four-year-old real estate agent from Knoxville. Curly, shoulder-length blonde hair. Pretty face. You remember her," Wyatt stated, his voice firm.

Shipley shook his head. "No, I don't."

Based on his body language, the man was either an expert liar, or he was telling the truth.

"She had car trouble on Bat Creek Road," Wyatt continued. "She walked onto your property, looking for help. She was trespassing on your farm. Things got out of hand."

"You're talking crazy. Ain't no woman asked me for no help with her car."

Her partner stared at the farmer. Both Wyatt's expression and his tone softened. "I know it's hard to talk about. There's something deep inside you that you can't control. But it's not your fault."

Wyatt had switched roles midstream. He was playing both sides – tough cop and sympathetic cop – by himself. He was obviously too angry at Ashley to allow her to join him in interrogating their suspect.

She wondered what the agent had told Brenda. Had he already requested a new partner?

As she realized that she might have let Jay Archer down, her heart sank. It was possible that she wouldn't be able to fulfill her promise to Megan's husband. Her promise to bring the killer to justice. Wyatt would likely have to keep it for her.

The farmer seemed even more puzzled. "What ain't my fault?"

"I know you're not a bad person, Warren. Can I call you Warren?"

The man glanced at Ashley like he thought Wyatt was insane.

"I guess so," Mr. Shipley said.

"Good. And you can call me Wyatt."

The farmer shrugged. At least her partner had diffused some of the man's initial hostility.

Wyatt rested his arms on the table.

Kindness in his voice, he said, "Warren, I understand. I really do. I know you didn't want to hurt her."

"Now wait just a damn minute," Mr. Shipley replied, anger in his tone. "I ain't hurt nobody."

Ashley studied the man's face. She almost believed him. But there was still a lingering doubt in her mind. The two roads where the victims' vehicles had been found bordered his farm. He'd been arrested twice for threatening trespassers. And the hairs shed from the goats on his property would likely match the white hairs found on the murder victims' bodies. It all seemed too coincidental to deny at this point.

Her partner pressed on. "Warren –"

"Stop saying my name," the farmer barked.

Wyatt raised his palms. "Everything's okay. There's no need to get upset. We can talk this out."

She feared her partner had pushed the man too far.

"Ain't nothing to talk about. You're trying to pin something on me, and I ain't having it."

"I'm not –"

"I want a lawyer!" Shipley yelled. "Right now."

And with that, Ashley knew the interview was over. Once a suspect invoked his legal privilege, the questions stopped.

Wyatt nodded, rising from his chair. "Okay. You'll get your attorney."

Ashley followed her partner from the room. She could feel the heat of anger radiating from his body. His mood was likely the reason he'd rushed things – had botched the interrogation. If he'd just let her help, maybe they could have uncovered some information.

"Wyatt –"

He stopped short, turning around to face her in the hallway.

"Ashley, I know you want to talk, and we will. But I need a minute. Alone."

He held out his key fob. "It's already after two o'clock. You should go eat lunch. Maybe you can run some errands. You said you wanted to pick up a hair dryer."

She realized it might take an hour or two – maybe more – for the forensic team to arrive. And now that Mr. Shipley had requested an attorney, there was really nothing left to do here but sit and wait.

"Do you want me to bring you back some food?"

He shook his head. "I'll grab something from the vending machine, for now."

"I guess I'll be back in a little while then."

"Take your time."

It wasn't just a polite phrase. She knew he wanted her gone as long as possible.

Ashley headed out the front entrance of the sheriff's department and into the parking lot, littered with puddles. A gray sky still stretched above her, but at least the rain had ended. Since she had the time, she'd head back to the motel and change clothes before stopping at the diner.

And it might be a good idea to try and find out more about Warren Shipley.

Ashley decided she'd drive out to the exact location where Megan's SUV had been abandoned and poke around a little, while she still had her badge.

As she climbed into the driver's seat of Wyatt's SUV, she feared this was her final day as his partner. And with the TBI.

CHAPTER TWENTY ONE

A burst of adrenaline flooded Ashley's body as a black pickup crossed into her lane and barreled straight toward her on the narrow highway that led to Warren Shipley's farm.

That truck's going to hit me head-on!

She jerked the steering wheel of Wyatt's SUV and swerved to the right. The tires bit into the gravel on the road's shoulder as she yanked her foot from the accelerator. It wasn't the first time she'd noticed a driver in Bonner County ignoring the yellow dividing line that striped the center of the asphalt.

And she'd thought Laurel County's drivers were bad. At least in her hometown, people knew to stick to their own lane.

The SUV idled on the road's shoulder while Ashley caught her breath.

As she eased back onto the highway, her cell phone rang. Not wanting to pull her eyes away from the road for any longer than necessary, she slid her phone from her jacket pocket and held it near the top of the steering wheel before glancing at the screen.

The caller ID had been blocked. Maybe it was Daniel calling from a burner phone. She put the call on speaker.

"Hello?"

There was only silence on the line.

Guessing the caller was a telemarketer, she was about to hang up when she heard a faint noise echoing over the phone.

It sounded like laughter.

A split second later, three beeps signaled the call had dropped.

How odd.

Ashley was about to shove the phone back into her pocket when it rang a second time. The caller ID displayed the number this time, but it was one she didn't recognize. She debated answering, but the possibility that she might miss a call from Daniel outweighed any annoyance a telemarketer would bring. Again, she answered on speaker.

"Hello?" she said, her tone tentative.

"Hey."

This time she was right. It was Daniel.

"It's so good to hear your voice."

The words spilled out before she could stop them.

"Yours too," the agent replied.

Ashley smiled. "I see by the number you're calling from that you're still working undercover."

"Yeah. But we've hit a snag. The good news is: that gave me time to call. How's your case going?"

She wondered whether she should tell Daniel that it was possible Wyatt hated her. That her partner likely believed that Ashley was reckless enough to put his life in danger.

"Well, there's a good chance that we may have caught our roadside killer."

"That's great news."

She sighed. "But there's also the chance that I may have screwed up – big time."

"How so?"

Hoping Daniel wouldn't think she was a terrible person, Ashley struggled to find the best way to explain the situation.

"I said something to Wyatt that I didn't really mean and it's driven a wedge between us. But I realize now that I've been reading him wrong since the day we met. I need to figure out a way to smooth things over – to let him know that he can trust me."

The agent remained silent.

Was he still on the line?

"Daniel?"

"I'm here."

She wondered if they had a bad connection.

"Did you hear what I told you about Wyatt?"

"Yeah."

"Well, what do you think I should do?"

She heard the agent sigh. "The last thing you need is to get close to Wyatt Clark."

Daniel's response stunned her. She had no desire to get close to her partner. She just wanted to establish a solid working relationship based on trust.

Up ahead, she caught sight of Bat Creek Road. She zeroed out the trip odometer as she made the turn onto the tree-lined roadway.

"Daniel, I'm about to drive into a deep valley, and in a few seconds, I'll lose the cell signal."

"It's time for me to go, anyway."

"Okay, just please promise me that you'll –"

Three beeps signaled the call had dropped. Did she lose the signal, or did Daniel hang up on her?

"… be careful," she finished the sentence aloud.

The agent's behavior struck her as strange. Like he had during their last conversation regarding Wyatt, Daniel almost sounded jealous. Only this time, it didn't make her happy. Not even a little bit.

Knowing that she still had a job to do, she pushed her thoughts of Daniel aside. She'd talk things out with the agent later.

According to the case file, Megan's SUV had been discovered on Bat Creek Road, six-point-three miles from the highway. As she watched the trip odometer tick up, Ashley recalled the notes from the responding deputy's report in her mind. At the time the Knoxville woman's abandoned vehicle had been found, local law enforcement had no idea the area would turn out to be a crime scene. The SUV had not been reported stolen and Jay Archer had not yet filed his wife's missing person's report. The deputy had assumed that after having car trouble, Megan had secured a ride back into town. As per procedure, he'd had the vehicle towed to the impound lot.

There were no notes indicating that the sheriff's department had found any evidence along the shoulder of the road. Had the deputies even searched the area?

At the six-point-one mile mark, Ashley pulled over. Five days had passed since Megan's abduction. And the rain that had pummeled the countryside that morning had likely washed away any footprints or tire treads that might have once marred the gravel shoulder. But Ashley hoped she'd find something – anything – that could link Warren Shipley to the crime.

To her right, Black Angus cattle grazed on the other side of the wire fence that bordered the farmer's property. It seemed unlikely that Megan would have crossed over into the pasture in an attempt to reach the farmhouse, nestled between the trees on the top of a rise. According to her missing person's report, the woman had been dressed in designer leather pumps when she'd embarked on her trip from Knoxville to Murfreesboro. Dodging cow patties didn't seem like something Megan would have been inclined to do.

Unless she'd seen Mr. Shipley in the pasture.

Maybe she'd called out to him to get his attention. He could have been the one who'd crossed over the fence. With her disdain for the locals, she might have said something that offended the farmer. And Shipley had attacked her.

Ashley inched along the shoulder, her eyes scanning the ground. Decaying leaves, spindly tree branches, and rainwater filled the shallow ditch that lined the road. She walked well past the point where Megan's SUV would have been parked, but didn't find anything. As Ashley had suspected, the rain had scoured away any remnants that would indicate a vehicle had even touched the gravel.

Long shadows grew from the trees, stretching across the roadway, as dusk began to fall. Ashley flipped on her Maglite as she turned around and headed the opposite way down the shoulder. The beam from her flashlight swept back and forth, from the pavement to the water-logged ditch. At almost the exact spot where Megan's vehicle would have rested, something white caught Ashley's eye.

She stopped and knelt next to the edge of the ditch. Stuck to a clump of leaves, she found part of a cigarette.

An odd-looking cigarette.

She pulled a pair of latex gloves out of her coat pocket and snapped them on. Studying the crumpled inch of tobacco-filled paper in the glow from her flashlight, she realized why the cigarette looked strange to her.

There was no filter.

The brand name *Black Panther* inked the side of the white paper. She was surprised that unfiltered cigarettes still existed. Although the cigarette appeared to be fairly fresh, there was no way for her to know how long it had lain by the roadside. Could it belong to the killer?

Using her phone, Ashley shot photos of the crumpled cigarette from various angles. Then she dropped it, along with the clump of leaves, into an evidence bag and sealed the top. She continued to search the roadside, all the way back to Wyatt's SUV. She didn't spot anything else.

Gazing up at Shipley's farmhouse, partially hidden behind the grove of pine trees, she noticed light radiating from every visible window. Had the farmer left the lights on, or was the TBI team already there? She hopped back into Wyatt's SUV.

After rounding the bend in the road, she steered the SUV onto Warren Shipley's driveway. The metal gate had been propped open, held in place by a large rock. Tire tracks cut into the hard-packed dirt, now muddy from the rain. It appeared several vehicles had entered the property.

If the TBI team had already arrived and was conducting their search, it would be customary to have a sheriff's deputy posted at the entrance. However, considering the nonexistent cooperation from local law enforcement, Ashley wasn't surprised that no one was standing guard.

Splashing through puddles, she maneuvered her way along the winding drive. As the clearing opened up, she spotted a TBI mobile crime unit vehicle and two white TBI SUVs parked in front of the farmhouse.

From her current vantage point, she could see light emanating from the outbuilding nearest the house, on the right. If Warren Shipley had tortured and killed Ian and Megan, the large shed seemed to be an optimal location to carry out the deeds.

Ashley slid from the driver's seat of Wyatt's SUV and headed toward the long, narrow porch of the farmhouse. Just before she reached the steps, the front door opened. Piper, a forensic tech Ashley had met during the Troy Luckadoo investigation, greeted her.

"I was hoping Brenda would have the sense to hire you," Piper said as she tucked a wayward strand of auburn hair back underneath the hood of her Tyvek suit.

Ashley felt grateful for the vote of confidence. Although after her misunderstanding with Wyatt that morning, she doubted the deputy director would choose to make her position as a special agent permanent.

"Thanks," she replied, forcing a half smile. "Have you found anything yet that could link Warren Shipley to the murders?"

The tech shook her head. "We've been here over an hour. So far, we've come up empty. Nothing's in the sheds but animal feed and farm equipment. There's no sign that anyone's been held captive, or killed, in the house or barn either. But we'll keep searching."

The way Ian and Megan had been beaten, it was likely the crime scene would be covered in blood spatter. Was Shipley an expert at cleaning up after himself? Or was he innocent?

Ashley held up the evidence bag.

"I found this cigarette on the shoulder of Bat Creek Road, right where Megan Archer's car was abandoned."

Piper squinted at the white paper. "No filter. That's unusual. Maybe we'll get lucky and be able to recover DNA."

Ashley nodded. "Well, I don't want to get in your way here, so I guess I'll head back into town."

"We'll let you and Wyatt know when we're finished."

A brisk wind rustled through the pines surrounding the farmhouse as Ashley climbed into her partner's SUV. She wondered whether Wyatt was ready to see her face again. When she reached the highway, she checked for a cell signal. Two bars. She tapped her partner's contact.

"Hello," Wyatt answered, his tone flat as usual.

Ashley couldn't tell whether he was still upset with her or not.

"I just left the forensic team at Warren Shipley's farm," she told him. "They haven't found anything out of the ordinary yet."

"Yeah, I heard."

One of the techs must have called Wyatt from Shipley's land line or from a satellite phone.

"I'm driving back to the sheriff's department now. Is there anything you want me to pick up for you on the way?"

"No, I'm not there," he replied. "But we've done all we can do, so let's call it a day. You can head back to the motel."

Before Ashley could respond, Wyatt cut the connection.

Where was he? Already at the motel? Or maybe a bar? It didn't really matter. It was obvious her partner had no desire to speak with her at the moment. She'd have to wait until the morning to tell him about the cigarette she'd found.

As she placed her cell on the center console, it rang. Thinking it was Wyatt calling back, she answered without checking caller ID.

"Hello?"

Silence … and then laughter.

Deep guttural laughter.

"Who is this?" she demanded.

A chill raced down Ashley's spine as the line went dead.

CHAPTER TWENTY TWO

The pounding on the motel room's door jarred Ashley awake. She glanced at the clock perched on the bedside table. 4:29 a.m. A sense of panic rushed through her as she ripped back the covers and swung her legs over the edge of the hard mattress.

Something terrible has happened.

The door vibrated as an unseen fist banged against it in rapid succession.

"Ashley, it's Wyatt," her partner's muffled voice called out.

"I'm coming," she answered, her tone heavy with anxiety.

She threw on her robe and jerked open the door. The haunted expression on Wyatt's face sent a chill down her spine.

"You were right," he said. "There's been another murder."

Her stomach sank. This was one instance when she wished her instincts had been wrong. Wished her partner's hunch had been right and that Megan had been the murderer's final victim. But now they knew for certain they were searching for a serial killer.

"When did it happen?"

"Just a few hours ago."

"Okay, give me a minute to get dressed and I'll be right out."

As she pushed the door closed, a realization hit Ashley. Warren Shipley couldn't possibly be the roadside killer. Not unless he'd escaped from the Bonner County jail during the night. Losing their prime suspect hurled the investigation back to square one. Without a single suspect.

Ashley yanked a fresh pair of jeans up over her hips with one hand while she scrubbed a toothbrush across her teeth with the other. She wondered whether the unfiltered Black Panther cigarette she'd discovered on Bat Creek Road would lead to a dead end as well. Wyatt would probably dismiss the find as soon as he heard about it. And she knew it would be days before they received the DNA results. But despite the lack of interest she expected to receive from her partner, something deep in her gut screamed that the cigarette was important. It was the same instinct that had told her the killer would strike again.

Making sure to lock the motel room's door, she hurried out into the parking lot and veered toward her partner's SUV.

"Ashley," Wyatt's voice echoed from behind her.

She turned around and saw him standing next to a Bonner County Sheriff's SUV.

"We're taking the county car," he told her.

Surprised, she doubled back and climbed into the passenger seat of the Ford.

"I can't believe the sheriff actually let you borrow one of their SUVs," she said, snapping her seatbelt into place.

"He didn't have a choice."

She guessed Wyatt must have asserted his authority at the sheriff's department while she was out at the Shipley farm the previous evening. And he'd obviously made at least a small amount of headway. Maybe this meant that they'd finally receive some cooperation from the deputies.

Her partner steered the county vehicle onto the highway. The SUV's flashing blue lights cut through the early morning darkness, casting an eerie reflection in the windows of the convenience store on the corner. Ashley was glad he'd opted to keep the siren turned off.

She stole a glance his way, trying to gauge whether or not he was still upset with her. It was hard to tell. But the fact that he was including her in the investigation of the latest victim seemed to be a good sign. If he wanted her fired, he likely would have let her sleep. She decided it would be best not to invite trouble by bring up the prior day's events, instead keeping the conversation focused on the murder at hand.

"What do you know so far about the person killed last night?" she asked.

"The victim's a male. According to the driver's license in his wallet, he's thirty-two years old and lived in Chattanooga."

Another out-of-towner. Ashley believed it was more than just a coincidence that no locals had been targeted.

Wyatt continued, "One of the deputies found the body during a routine patrol."

"Where?"

"Not too far from here. He was dumped near one of the boat ramps at Iona Lake."

The fingers of Iona Lake lay just outside the city limits of Ormond. The man's body had been left closer to town than the other two. Did this mean the killer was becoming more brazen?

"Where did they find the victim's car?"

She wondered whether the deceased man had been driving through the same valley as Ian and Megan. Anger sizzled within Ashley at the thought that the sheriff had failed to alert them to the discovery of another abandoned vehicle. Vital clues had most likely been overlooked and lost.

Wyatt glanced at her. "They haven't."

"Wait a minute – you're telling me that we have a dead body but no abandoned car?"

"Right."

Serial killers didn't change their MOs midstream. Had the vehicle been left so far from civilization that it hadn't been located yet? Or had someone else – not the roadside murderer – claimed the man's life?

"Then how do you know that we're dealing with the same killer?"

A look of anguish clouded her partner's face.

"By the condition of the body."

She winced, surmising that the latest victim had been subjected to hours of torture. "So most of the man's bones have been broken?"

"Yeah." Although Wyatt wore a mask of distress, his voice was steady. Firm. "I put out an APB on the car registered in his name."

"We'll probably find it in some dense hollow out in the middle of nowhere."

Likely a place where there was no cell service and no one around to offer help.

The bright glow of halogen lights caught Ashley's attention as they pulled off the highway into the parking lot of the boat ramp. The TBI's forensic team had already started work, their efforts focused on a picnic shelter located among the trees, a couple hundred feet to the right of the ramp. Wyatt angled the SUV next to a Bonner County patrol car and cut the engine.

As she slid from the passenger seat, Ashley noticed a group of sheriff's deputies huddled together beneath the bare limbs of an oak. One of them carried a clipboard, and it appeared as though he was recording the names of everyone entering and exiting the cordoned area. The presence of local law enforcement surprised her.

What had Wyatt said to Sheriff Powell that had forced him to allow his deputies to provide support? Had her partner resorted to coercion? Or had the two lawmen come to a peaceful agreement? Either way, she was thankful Wyatt had secured the deputies' help.

She followed her partner across the parking lot and into the radiance of the halogen work lights positioned throughout the grounds surrounding the aging shelter.

Wyatt greeted the mustached officer with the clipboard, introducing himself and Ashley.

"Where can we find Deputy Cody Medford?" he asked.

The name sparked a memory in Ashley's mind. She'd read in the case file that Cody Medford had found Megan's body at the overlook. Had he found this victim as well?

"That's him," the deputy said, pointing to a young man with dark hair, just inside the cordoned area.

Medford had joined the team conducting a grid search for evidence that might have been left behind by the killer. The beam from his flashlight scanned the ground as he inched along the yellow barrier.

Wyatt turned to Ashley. "Let's get a look at the body first," he said. "Then we'll find out what Medford knows."

Despite the heat radiating from the bank of bright halogen lights, a chill raced down Ashley's spine as she stepped onto the concrete slab of the shelter. Two wooden picnic tables rested beneath the weathered roof. The remnants of what had once been a man, in the prime years of his life, topped the table farthest from her.

Ashley's breath caught in her throat as she drew closer to the corpse. Although she had seen the roadside killer's handiwork previously at the morgue, viewing Megan's broken body hadn't even begun to prepare her for the sight she beheld now.

The man that lay before her had no face.

There were no features left. No cheeks or nose or chin. Just a bloody mush of pulverized bone and flesh.

"You were right about one thing, Wyatt," she said. "Whoever did this was obviously full of uncontrollable rage."

Her partner sighed. "Almost like it was personal."

He was right again. It did seem personal. As though there was something about the victims that had spawned an overwhelming hatred in the mind of the killer. And from the condition of the body on the picnic table, it appeared the murderer's loathing had grown more intense.

Wyatt stared at the corpse a moment longer, as if he was trying to figure out what kind of monster could have inflicted so much damage.

"Let's go talk to Medford," he finally said.

She nodded and then trailed behind her partner. Wyatt made the customary introductions, shaking the deputy's hand.

"You found the body?" he asked, motioning toward the picnic shelter several yards away.

"Yes, sir," Medford said, his voice shaky. "I was doing my normal rounds. When I circled the parking lot, my headlights hit the picnic table. I seen the body lying on top and thought it was a drunk, sleeping it off. I was planning on hauling him in. But when I got out of the car and got a closer look … well, I knew he was dead."

Was the fact that the young deputy had discovered two of the roadside killer's victims just a span of bad luck? Or was it something more? Could the murderer in Bonner County be a member of law enforcement? Someone who knew all the stops on the nightly patrol?

It was obvious by the placement of the body that the killer wanted the corpse found. That the murderer was sending some kind of sick message.

"Do you take the same route – around the same time – every night?" Ashley asked.

"Yes, ma'am. More or less."

She glanced at Wyatt, wondering whether he had picked up on her suspicion that a member of local law enforcement might be involved. He didn't return her gaze. Instead his attention was focused on the deputy.

"Did you see any other vehicles?" he asked.

Medford shook his head. "Nobody else was around."

Although the deputy hadn't seen anyone, Ashley wondered whether the killer had been watching from the cover of the forest, waiting for Medford to arrive.

Wyatt pressed on. "Other than the body, did you notice anything else unusual?"

"No, sir," Medford replied. "There was nothing else. Just the man."

She could tell by the deputy's demeanor that he wished he could offer more information. Considering the fact that he'd only been on the force for a little over a year and was obviously light on experience, it was likely he had stayed close to the body while he waited for backup to arrive rather than scouring the woods by himself. Which was actually a smart move on his part. If he had stumbled upon the murderer lurking in the shadows, Medford probably wouldn't be here to tell about it.

"Thanks for your help," Wyatt said, dismissing the deputy. "You can get back to what you were doing."

Ashley gave Medford a polite nod and then fell in beside Wyatt as he headed toward the parking lot. His expression revealed that his mind was racing.

"We should check out the valley near Shipley's farm," he told her. "See if we can find the victim's car."

It seemed like the next logical step. She was glad that for once, they were on the same page. The best way to ensure no evidence was lost was for them to find the vehicle first, before the deputies trampled the scene.

Ashley pulled open the passenger door of the county SUV and then stopped dead in her tracks. The hairs on the back of her neck bristled as a wave of fear swept over her. A hairband rested in the middle of her seat.

A black hairband with the initial A embroidered in white.

Her missing scrunchie.

CHAPTER TWENTY THREE

In rapid motion, Ashley spun around from the passenger door of the county SUV and drew her Glock from the holster in her waistband. Stepping out of the halo of light from the Ford's interior, she scanned the parking lot of the boat ramp. Someone had been inside of her motel room. Had stolen her scrunchie. And that someone was likely still here at Iona Lake, watching her. Gauging her reaction to finding the hairband on the SUV's seat.

There was no movement in the parking lot. Only empty Bonner County police cruisers and vehicles belonging to the TBI agents. The boat ramp lay outside of the cordoned area and therefore wasn't guarded by the deputies. Anyone could have placed her scrunchie inside the SUV. What message were they sending her? Was this just a sick game Troy Luckadoo's relatives were playing in order to scare her?

Or was her life in danger?

The person who had helped Troy commit multiple murders was still roaming free.

Wyatt appeared at her side, his firearm drawn as well.

"Did you see him?" he asked in a hushed tone.

He obviously thought she was aiming for the roadside killer. That she'd seen the murderer lurking in the shadows of the forest.

"No," she replied, her voice strained. "But someone's been following me – watching me."

Wyatt stood silent for a moment, the aim of his weapon sweeping the parking area.

"Are you sure?" he asked.

Realizing that whoever had her in their crosshairs was unlikely to make a move against her with the hoard of TBI agents and Bonner County deputies on the grounds, she raked her eyes across the edge of the forest one last time and then holstered her Glock. Ashley glanced at Wyatt as he mirrored her actions, relaxing his posture. She knew he might be skeptical of the hair-raising feelings she'd experienced, but he couldn't refute the physical evidence.

She motioned toward the county vehicle behind her. “They left a souvenir for me on the seat of the Ford.”

Wyatt moved to the open passenger door.

The bridge of his nose wrinkled. “What is that?”

“It’s a hairband that was stolen from the bedside table in my motel room. I tore the place apart yesterday looking for it.”

She studied his face, wondering whether or not he believed her. He probably thought the scrunchie had been in her pocket the entire time and had just fallen out onto the seat.

After a moment’s hesitation he said, “You think someone broke into your room?”

“I know it.”

He stared at her. “Why didn’t you say something earlier?”

She hadn’t exactly felt as though they were on the same team lately. That she could trust him with her suspicions.

“Because I figured you would accuse me of being paranoid and brush it off.”

Wyatt shook his head. “Don’t keep things from me. It doesn’t matter what I might think.”

And what did he think? That she was indeed paranoid, imagining threats when there were none? As usual, she couldn’t read him.

Ashley sighed as she watched her partner circle around the front of the Ford and slide into the driver’s seat. It seemed he had no interest in letting her know whether or not he believed her allegations. She climbed into the SUV, feeling as though she needed to bolster her claim of being followed.

“A black truck almost ran me off the road when I was on my way to Shipley’s farm yesterday.”

He shot her an alarmed look. “Did you get the plates?”

“No. At the time I thought it was just a reckless driver, eyes off the road, sending a text or something. But then right after that I received two strange phone calls, both from blocked numbers.”

“What did they say?”

“They didn’t speak. I just heard laughter – a deep-voiced, creepy laughter.”

“You think it’s Troy Luckadoo’s family?”

Wyatt knew that Troy wasn’t the only man she’d killed. Her ex-husband, Ethan, also had a slew of relatives who hated her. But since the Luckadoos had made it known that they were actively gunning for her, they seemed like the most obvious suspects.

"That's my best guess."

He didn't respond. At least rather than dismissing her fears outright, he appeared to be pondering the situation.

The first rays of morning sunlight broke over the horizon as Wyatt steered the SUV onto the highway leading into the valley where the vehicles belonging to Ian and Megan had been found. She hoped it wouldn't take long for them to locate the car driven by the most recent victim.

"Do you know the identity of the dead man left at the picnic shelter?" she asked.

"The name on the driver's license is Nick Weaver. He owned a red sports car. A convertible. His girlfriend filed a missing person's report on Wednesday."

Due to the condition of the corpse, a DNA match would be the only way they could be certain the ID actually belonged to the man, but at the moment it seemed a fairly safe bet. An abandoned red sports car would stand out. Should be easy to spot. Nick Weaver must have run into trouble on a seldom-traveled back road. Otherwise, the vehicle would most likely have already been discovered.

About a mile past the Shipley farm, Ashley noticed a gravel road veering off to the right, almost hidden by the tree line. She remembered the area from the satellite map she'd studied. As she recalled, only pastureland butted the single-lane road that cut through the valley, eventually joining a parallel highway. There were no houses along the way.

"Turn here," she said. "This road looks about as remote as it can get."

Wyatt nodded his agreement. Loose gravel flew from beneath the tires as he piloted the SUV down the narrow lane. Ashley's focus darted from the right shoulder to the left, hoping to spot the red convertible. Disappointment weighed on her heart when they reached the opposite highway with no car in sight.

They spent the next two hours scouring the valley, checking every road – even a dirt path that turned out to be a driveway – but they came up empty. Where was Nick's car? Ashley had felt certain the man had been abducted in the same general area as Ian and Megan. Had the killer expanded his territory? If that were the case, it might take days to find the vehicle. Enough time for another victim to be murdered.

As they hit the highway heading back toward Ormond, Ashley's thoughts drifted to the young deputy, Cody Medford.

"Does it seem odd to you that the same deputy found two of the three bodies?" she asked.

Wyatt swung his gaze toward her. "A little. But I don't think he did it."

"I didn't mean to imply that Medford is the killer," she stated, shaking her head. "He doesn't seem like the type to me. But it could be someone else who works at the sheriff's department."

A sly grin crossed her partner's face. "You think it's our buddy, Sheriff Powell?"

She couldn't tell whether he was teasing her, or if he really thought it was possible that the man leading the department was involved.

"I didn't say that, either. But just think about the circumstances for a minute. Whoever killed Ian, Megan, and Nick left their bodies in a place where they would be found right away. We know for certain that two of those locations are stops on the nightly patrol. Is that just a coincidence?"

Ashley had studied enough cases to know that when it came to murder, true coincidences were rare.

He tilted his head. "Maybe. Maybe not."

"So you agree that the killer could be someone on the force who knows the rounds? Who knew that Deputy Medford would spot the bodies?"

He paused, as if in deep thought. "You might be right."

Wyatt's response surprised her, spurring her to continue building her theory.

"If someone – let's say a woman traveling alone like Megan – had car trouble, who would they be the most relieved to see pulling up behind them? Who would they trust the most to help?"

"A cop."

Since all three of the victims were out-of-towners and most likely didn't share the Bonner County locals' suspicion of law enforcement, a badge seemed to be a perfect cover for the killer.

"A person diving through the area from another county would probably let their guard down, thinking they were being saved. They wouldn't be expecting a deputy to turn on them."

“Your idea makes even more sense than you realize.”

His comment brought a smile to her lips. It was the first time he’d ever expressed a genuine interest in one of her theories.

“How so?” she asked, hoping Wyatt wasn’t just leading her on.

“It would explain how the victims were located. A killer prowling the backroads would waste a lot of time. Hours upon hours. But like you said before, deputies have to go on patrol. Riding the highways is their job.”

Wyatt was right. A job in law enforcement would give the killer the perfect opportunity to search for his targets. For once, everything seemed to be clicking into place.

“I guess we need to go find out which one of the deputies is assigned to patrol the valley,” Ashley said.

Wyatt smiled. “I can’t wait to put the screws to Sheriff Powell again.”

CHAPTER TWENTY FOUR

Ashley trailed behind Wyatt as he barreled through the glass door into the lobby of the Bonner County Sheriff's Department. Again, she wondered what leverage her partner had employed to secure the use of the county SUV, not to mention the cooperation of the deputies at Nick Weaver's crime scene. Whatever he'd done or said, it had proven to be a game changer. She realized she might be about to witness Wyatt's method in action, firsthand. And she steeled herself for the anticipated fireworks.

"Is he in?" Wyatt asked the officer behind the reception desk.

Ashley could tell the man knew Wyatt was referring to Sheriff Powell.

"Uh …"

The red-faced deputy seemed unsure of how to respond. He'd obviously missed the morning meeting explaining the current instructions for dealing with the TBI. Were the two agencies foes again?

"Never mind," Wyatt said, heading toward the sheriff's private office. "I'll find out for myself."

Her partner pounded his fist against the closed door. The flimsy wood shuddered with each knock.

"Powell? We need to talk," he called out.

There was no response from inside the office.

Wyatt glanced at Ashley and shrugged. Apparently not willing to give up so easily, he wrenched the knob and shoved open the door.

Sheriff Powell stood behind his desk, his eyes wide. The man appeared shocked that Wyatt would take it upon himself to enter the hallowed domain uninvited.

"What the hell do you think you're doing, boy?" Powell shouted. "Barging in without permission?"

"You should have answered."

"I've got work to do. I ain't got time to babysit you all day."

Ashley realized the sheriff's words were like a match to dry tinder, igniting Wyatt's anger. She surmised her partner had been expecting a less hostile reception this time.

His eyes narrowed. "Who patrols the valley where the abandoned cars were found?"

The vein in the sheriff's temple throbbed. "That ain't none of your business, son."

It was obvious Wyatt was working hard to keep his temper in check, to keep his voice from rising.

"Whether you like it or not, my badge makes it my business."

"Naw, that's where you're wrong," the sheriff barked. "This is my department. And I say that information's classified."

The two men glared at each other, the hatred so thick it crowded the room. Ashley fought the urge to shrink into the corner. Instead, she'd claim ground of her own. She checked to make sure the office door was pushed closed.

"It's possible that one of your deputies could be responsible for the roadside murders," she said, her voice hushed but firm, intent on showing confidence in her authority.

Sheriff Powell broke eye contact with Wyatt and focused his attention on Ashley.

"What the hell are you talking about? Don't you think I'd know if one of my people was a killer?"

The sheriff in Laurel County had never suspected that Troy Luckadoo, one of his trusted team, had been involved in abduction and murder. Powell was familiar with the case. She shouldn't have to remind him.

"It wouldn't be the first time that a member of law enforcement managed to fool everyone else on the force, including his boss."

"You got some nerve, little lady. Telling me I don't know how to do my job. That I can't read my own deputies."

Ashley knew the derogatory term was designed to put her in her place. But she wasn't going to let the sheriff wreck her confidence.

"Serial killers can be experts at hiding their true nature," she stated, refusing to back down. "Even from the people who spend the most time with them – who seem to know them the best."

Sheriff Powell clenched his fists, his body rigid. "Well, I ain't that blind. So you and your partner can shove your crazy accusations up your ass and get the hell outta my office."

Wyatt took a step closer to the sheriff, a move Ashley assumed was meant to intimidate the older lawman. She hoped the two wouldn't resort to a fistfight.

"You're making a mistake, Powell," Wyatt said, his voice low. "A big mistake."

A ripple of doubt flashed across the sheriff's face. He started to open his mouth as though he had something to say. But seeming to think better of it, he remained silent.

A smile nudged the corner of Wyatt's lips, as if he realized that he'd just gained the upper hand.

"I don't think I need to repeat what we discussed yesterday," he said.

The cryptic statement hung in the air like a thick cloud of dust, making Sheriff Powell appear as though he was about to choke.

Wyatt continued, "It's in your best interest to cooperate. Just give us the name, and we'll be on our way."

Powell swallowed hard. He dropped his gaze toward the floor and let out a sigh. "Tyler Yates," he grumbled. "Now leave."

Ashley glanced at Wyatt and then took the lead, heading back toward the reception desk. She didn't want to spend any more time at the sheriff's department than necessary. The red-haired deputy on duty wore a sheepish grin as she approached the counter. He'd likely heard Powell's shouts blasting from his office.

"Is Deputy Tyler Yates on patrol right now?" she asked him.

"Yates?" He shook his head. "Not today. He's at home today."

Wyatt appeared at her side. "We need the address," he said, his voice calm.

The deputy nodded, seeming to now understand that the TBI outranked the sheriff. He scribbled the address on a piece of note paper and handed it to Wyatt.

"Thanks."

A crystal-clear azure sky greeted Ashley as she stepped out into the parking lot. It was a welcome change from the dense clouds that had marred the previous day. She hoped her relationship with Wyatt would mirror the weather, finally becoming storm free.

The thought of bringing up the misunderstanding they'd had at the Shipley farm tugged at her heart. She wanted Wyatt to know that she had his back. That she'd do everything in her power to ensure his safety. But reminding him of her harsh words might spoil the unusual camaraderie they'd managed to share this morning. For now, she decided it would be best to let the matter lie.

She studied his face as he buckled himself into the driver's seat of the county SUV. Curiosity had nibbled at her since the moment he'd dropped his clandestine bomb on the sheriff. What kind of information had Wyatt used to threaten the seasoned lawman? If Powell's reaction was any indication, it had to be something serious. Something damning enough to strike fear into the sheriff's mind.

"So what kind of dirt do you have on Sheriff Powell?" she asked.

A wry smile danced across Wyatt's face.

She waited for him to answer. He didn't.

"So you're not going to tell me what you're holding over the sheriff's head?"

"Can't give away all my secrets," he finally said.

The information must be privileged. Maybe pertaining to another case the state was building. Since she wasn't a permanent employee of the TBI, she realized there were things Wyatt couldn't divulge to her. Not yet, anyway.

A brood of chickens scattered from the dirt driveway as Wyatt steered the SUV toward the century-old farmhouse belonging to Tyler Yates. Angling in beside a green pickup, he cut the engine. He paused a moment, his gaze wandering over the boundaries of the property.

The truck seemed to be a good sign that the deputy was indeed home. Was Yates alone? Was he planning to ambush them the way Shipley had? From the steeled expression on Wyatt's face, she was almost certain her partner's thoughts included the same questions.

An uneasy feeling hit Ashley as she slid out of the passenger seat, bolstering her apprehension in confronting Yates. On reflex, her hand snapped to the Glock in her waistband. She stopped short of drawing her weapon, but remained on guard as she followed Wyatt up the path leading to the front porch.

Had Powell called Yates and warned him about their suspicions? At this point, she wouldn't put anything past the sheriff.

A hen pecked the dried red clay at the base of the porch steps. It clucked, fleeing on spindly legs as they approached. Ashley wondered whether she should circle around the back of the house to block Yates in case he attempted to escape. She motioned toward the rear of the property.

Wyatt shook his head. It seemed he wasn't worried that the deputy might try to sneak out the back. Or maybe he just wanted Ashley to stay where he could keep an eye on her. The last time they separated, shots were fired.

Was her partner feeling just as unnerved as she was? Was he expecting another gunfight?

Wyatt rapped his knuckles against the wooden front door. Peeling white paint flaked off beneath his touch, the tiny chips swirling to the floor.

"Deputy Yates?" he called out. "Wyatt Clark and Ashley Hope with the TBI."

She held her breath, listening for movement inside the house, hoping they weren't walking into a trap.

A strange scraping noise echoed from the other side of the door.

Wyatt's posture stiffened. He glanced at Ashley and then drew his weapon, nudging her past the side of the doorframe. Out of the direct line of fire from the entrance of the farmhouse.

The hairs on the back of her neck prickled as Ashley pulled her Glock from its holster. Ready to provide cover for Wyatt.

"Deputy Yates?" he called out again.

The tumblers of the deadbolt lock clicked and the door creaked open.

CHAPTER TWENTY FIVE

The hope that she and Wyatt had finally uncovered the identity of the roadside killer drained from Ashley's soul as she eyed the man standing in the doorway of the farmhouse. Mirroring the action of her partner, she lowered the aim of her Glock toward the scuffed wooden floor of the porch. A move that signaled they would fire if the need arose, but at the same time softening the threat toward the seemingly unarmed officer.

With his left hand, Wyatt unclipped the badge from his belt, holding it out for inspection.

"I'm Special Agent Wyatt Clark and my partner is Special Agent Ashley Hope," he stated. "Are you Deputy Tyler Yates?"

The man studied Wyatt's badge for a moment before responding. "That's me," he said, a puzzled look in his brown eyes. "What can I do for y'all?"

With Yates's name verified, Ashley's heart sank.

The dark-haired deputy leaned the weight of his short frame against a single crutch. The toes of his right foot peeked out from a plaster cast that extended half way up his shin. If his injury was legit, it would be next to impossible for Yates to be the murderer. How could he have carried Nick's body, hoisting it on top of the picnic table? It seemed an unlikely feat, unless of course, he had a partner in the crime. Maybe someone else on the force.

"We'd like to talk to you about your patrol route," Wyatt said.

The deputy's quizzical expression deepened. "Sure," he said, shuffling a few steps back from the doorway. "Why don't y'all come inside?"

As Ashley crossed the threshold her eyes scanned the living room. Toy trucks and cars littered the hardwood floor. Water pistols, plastic dinosaurs, and building blocks in various shapes and colors crowded the navy sofa and matching chair. Family pictures featuring Yates, along with a pretty brunette and two young children, lined the eggshell-painted walls.

"Sorry 'bout the mess," Yates said. "Me and the wife have twin sons. Four years old. They're a real handful. Just move that junk out of your way and have a seat."

The quiet stillness of the home led Ashley to believe that the children were either asleep at the moment or possibly out somewhere with their mother or a babysitter. Wyatt moved past her and cleared a space for them on the sofa while the deputy eased himself into a wooden rocking chair.

"What happened to your foot?" Wyatt asked once they were all settled.

"I fell off a ladder. The sheriff told me to replace some burned out flood lights on the corner of the building." He shook his head, as though remembering. "The dang ladder slipped. Fractured my ankle. The doc says I'll be laid up for at least six weeks."

"You fell at the sheriff's department?"

"Yep. Workman's comp."

Sheriff Powell had neglected to tell them about the deputy's injury – on purpose, no doubt.

"When did it happen?"

"Tuesday morning. Right after I clocked in. The sheriff had to drive me to the hospital. And he wasn't too happy about it either."

Wyatt and Ashley exchanged glances, a silent agreement passing between them. If Yates had fractured his ankle three days prior, there was no way he could have abducted and murdered Nick. He might still be involved in the killings, but if so, he wasn't working alone.

"You patrol the valley that includes Linley Pass and Bat Creek Road?" Wyatt asked.

Yates nodded. "Yeah, I sure do. It's the loneliest part of the county. Nothing much happens out that way – well, at least not usually. Not until …" The deputy's expression turned grim.

Ashley knew he was alluding to the recent abductions.

She leaned forward. "Were you on patrol when the vehicles belonging to Ian Driscoll and Megan Archer were found?"

Ashley didn't remember seeing Tyler Yates's name anywhere in the case file.

"My shift was already over when Burt Willard – he owns a farm on Linley Pass – called in to report the first car. The last time I drove past his place that day was around two o'clock. The car wasn't there then."

She recalled reading that Ian's sedan had been located in the early evening hours.

"And what about the second vehicle?" she asked.

"Sam Dobbins and his wife came across it on their way to church Sunday morning. That was my day off."

Megan Archer had left her home in Knoxville on Saturday morning, a full day before her vehicle was found abandoned.

"Did you patrol the area on Saturday?"

"Yes, ma'am. I was on Bat Creek Road around one-thirty in the afternoon. I didn't see the lady's SUV. She must have run into trouble after that."

A pattern was beginning to form in Ashley's mind. Did the killer know Deputy Yates's schedule as well? Were the abductions timed around his patrol hours?

"What time does your shift end?"

"I work a rotating shift, on five days then off two. I come in at seven, do my rounds and anything else the sheriff wants, and then clock out at the station around three-thirty."

Ashley assumed the extra half hour had something to do with Yates's lunch break. The county most likely refused to pay for the time allotted for the officers to eat.

"Does another deputy patrol the valley after your shift is over?"

He shook his head. "Nah, not usually. Like I said, it's pretty quiet in that part of the county. We got evening and night patrols, but they normally stick to the highways. And they hit the hot spots. Places were people like to hang out, drink, and get into trouble. We don't usually hear a peep from the folks out in the valley."

She knew that most break-ins occurred during the day when homeowners were at work or shopping. And as was true in the county where she'd been raised, the properties of the valley residents were most likely protected during the night by the brothers Smith and Wesson and their cousin Remington. A tight patrol during the dark hours would be a waste of resources.

"Have you noticed anything out of the ordinary the past two weeks? Maybe people driving around who shouldn't really have a reason to be there?"

He paused for a moment, as though searching his memory. "Can't say that I have. Those roads don't get much traffic. Mainly just the people who live out there."

Ashley was about to move on to her next question when an afterthought seemed to strike Yates.

"I did see Rex Gentry's cruiser a few times," the deputy stated. "But his mama lives on Fox Fork Road. That's just off of Bat Creek."

Cruiser? Was Yates referring to another deputy with the Bonner County Sheriff's department?

"Who is Rex Gentry?"

A sour look crossed Yates's face. "He's a state trooper."

Ashley wondered whether the deputy's seeming distaste for Gentry was due to the fact that he resented a member of the Tennessee Highway Patrol encroaching on the valley backroads, or if he had a personal problem with the man.

Before she could question his motive, Wyatt cut into the conversation.

"Why does the name Rex Gentry sound familiar to me?" he asked Yates.

The deputy huffed. Shook his head. "I don't like to air people's dirty laundry," he said, "but you probably heard about the trouble Gentry got himself into."

Wyatt's forehead creased, as though he was having difficulty remembering. "What kind of trouble?"

"Gentry was planting evidence in out-of-towners' cars. Small bags of weed and so forth. Then he'd demand a bribe to let the driver go. He pulled over the wrong person one day and got busted."

Ashley couldn't believe what she was hearing.

"Then how is it possible that he's still working as a state trooper?" she asked, infuriated that the man hadn't been stripped of his badge.

"He claimed that he was the one who'd been set up. And he's kin to a big wig with the highway patrol, so everything was swept under the rug. They suspended him for a while, but as far as I know, that was it."

She wondered whether there was an internal investigation into the matter. If it was possible that facts had come to light that placed doubt on the trooper's guilt.

"Do you believe that Gentry really was planting evidence?"

"Hell, yeah," Yates said without hesitation.

The deputy obviously saw no reason to question the accusations against Gentry. Did Yates possess even more information about the state trooper that he hadn't yet shared?

"You seem to know Rex Gentry fairly well," she stated, hoping Yates would expand on the details of their relationship.

"Better than I'd like to. Before he was a trooper, Gentry was a deputy. We worked together at the sheriff's department."

Ashley noticed a flash of disgust in Yates's eyes. "So I'm guessing the two of you didn't get along very well," she said.

"Not at all," the deputy replied. "Gentry's got a temper. A mean streak a mile wide. And he let his badge go to his head. Always throwing his weight around. Trying to intimidate everybody he pulled over. Especially people from out of town."

Ashley glanced at Wyatt. It seemed he was sharing her thoughts. Trooper Gentry had just jumped to number one on the suspect list.

Deputy Yates continued, "It got so bad the sheriff pulled Gentry off of the patrol of the main highway and stuck him in the valley."

Wyatt appeared surprised. "The valley?" he echoed.

"Yeah," Yates replied. "Gentry patrolled the valley until he left the department. That's when I took over."

Wyatt's gaze connected with Ashley's once again. It was as though they had finally tuned into the same wavelength.

"How long has it been since he left?" Wyatt asked.

"A little over two years."

So Gentry had been with the Tennessee Highway Patrol less than three years and had already been involved in a major scandal.

"Did he leave on good terms?"

Yates snorted. "Let me put it this way: when Gentry signed on with the THP, he was at the top of the sheriff's shit list."

Picking up a cue from Wyatt that the interview was finished, Ashley rose from the sofa.

"Thank you for taking the time to speak with us," she said.

"No problem."

Yates attempted to push himself up from the rocker, but his crutch slipped and crashed to the hardwood floor.

Wyatt grabbed the deputy's arm, steadying him. "You should take it easy," he told Yates. "We can show ourselves out."

A sense of accomplishment stirred in Ashley's chest as she stepped out onto the front porch of the farmhouse. Finally, it felt as though they were on the right track. Wyatt followed, a pleased expression lighting his hazel eyes.

"Let's go find Trooper Gentry," he said.

Ashley nodded. But as she made her way down the porch steps, a seed of doubt sprouted in her stomach, killing her initial enthusiasm. Sheriff Powell had thrown as many obstacles in their path as he could find. How much more difficult would it be to convince the THP to cooperate?

CHAPTER TWENTY SIX

The county SUV's tires hummed on the asphalt, the steady whine stoking Ashley's anticipation as Wyatt sped up the two-lane highway that ran from Ormond to the town of Alta Mill, the vehicle's blue lights flashing. She kept her eyes fixed on the horizon ahead, searching for Trooper Rex Gentry's cruiser. According to their contact within the THP, Gentry was on duty. And they were nearing the location of his assigned patrol.

Wyatt whipped around a red sedan traveling at the speed limit, swerving back into the right lane as a pickup truck flew toward them from the opposite direction. He seemed oblivious to the fact that his driving might get them killed.

"You think Gentry's our guy?" he asked.

Although Ashley wasn't yet one-hundred percent certain, the odds that the trooper was responsible for the murders seemed high.

"I believe there's a solid chance that he might be," she said. "He's got the means, the opportunity, and possibly a strong motive."

"Tell me about the motive."

She wondered whether Wyatt had already put the pieces together himself and just wanted confirmation for his line of reasoning, or if he was still unsure of what could have driven Gentry to commit such horrible crimes.

"Well," Ashley began, "we know that Gentry has a hot temper and a mean streak running through him. Along with that, he has a history of harassing people driving through Ormond from outside the county. And the person who nailed him for planting false evidence in order to collect a bribe was also from out of town."

"Just like the three victims."

She nodded. "It could be that he's built up a hatred for out-of-towners and blames them for the trouble he got himself into. That maybe he's seeking some kind of sick, twisted revenge."

Wyatt's fingers drummed the steering wheel. "That's pretty much what I was thinking."

A supposed motive wasn't the only thing pointing to Gentry's guilt.

"Plus," Ashley said, "he worked for the Bonner County Sheriff's department so he knows all the stops on the regular nightly patrol. He'd know exactly where to dump the bodies so that Deputy Medford would be quick to find them."

Ashley tensed in her seat as Wyatt ignored the solid-yellow, no-passing-zone lines and weaved around an eighteen wheeler. She prayed they wouldn't hit an oncoming car.

Once they were back in their lane, she continued, "Gentry used to patrol the valley where Ian and Megan were abducted. He has to be aware that there's no cell service out there and he knows the days and hours of Deputy Yates's shift."

"And Yates spotted Gentry in the valley several times," Wyatt added.

She was thankful that she didn't have to convince him of the probability that Gentry was the roadside killer. Relieved to sense that Wyatt's suspicions were strong as well. As she turned the known details of the crimes over in her mind, she realized that when it came to the first murder, her partner's initial theory may have been correct after all.

"You know how you thought that the killings were crimes of opportunity?" she asked. "Well, I think there may be a good chance that you were right about Ian's murder."

Wyatt glanced at her, a stunned expression covering his face.

Ashley gathered that he never dreamed he'd hear those words coming from her lips.

She continued, "What if Gentry had driven to the valley to visit his mother when he saw Ian having car trouble? Maybe he stopped with good intentions – had planned to help. But then he realized that Ian was from the city. They could have gotten into an argument and, like you theorized earlier, Gentry snapped."

"He took his rage out on Ian."

"Right," she agreed. "And he realized how easy it was for him to get away with the crime. Yates said that Gentry has let his job in law enforcement go to his head. He probably thinks that he's smarter than everyone else and will never get caught. So he decided to keep on killing, prowling the valley, and targeting Megan and Nick."

As Wyatt nodded, another idea struck Ashley. One that seemed to explain the reason the killer had been able to find new victims so quickly.

“You might think this is completely off base,” she stated, “but what if Megan and Nick never really had car trouble at all?”

Wyatt’s gaze swung toward her. “What do you mean?”

“Maybe Gentry was out looking for his next victim and saw Megan driving down Bat Creek Road. He would have known by the SUV’s plates that she was from out of town. So he flashes his blue lights and she pulls off the road, thinking she’s gone over the speed limit or something. He could have knocked her unconscious and then messed with something under the hood, making it look like her car had stalled.”

“Hmm.”

She could tell Wyatt’s mind was racing, as though he was processing the theory.

The SUV crested a hill, and in the distance, Ashley caught sight of the unmistakable figure of a police cruiser parked on the side of the road.

“That’s Gentry,” she said, excitement building in her chest.

Wyatt eased off the gas pedal as they drew closer to the trooper’s vehicle. As they approached, it appeared that the cruiser was empty.

“He’s not in his car,” Ashley said, her eyes scanning the edge of the dense forest that butted the highway.

“He could be in the woods. Taking a leak.”

Wyatt steered the SUV onto the shoulder, parking behind Gentry’s vehicle. As Ashley’s boots hit the gravel, she wondered whether word had leaked out at the THP and whether Gentry had been notified that they were looking to question him. If protocol had somehow been breached, and the trooper had realized he was a suspect, he could be waiting for them in the forest. They could be walking into an ambush.

She glanced at Wyatt. He nodded and drew his weapon, letting her know that he was sharing her thoughts. Ashley pulled her Glock from its holster, her pulse accelerating.

As they crossed the shallow ditch bordering the shoulder, Wyatt motioned for her to stay a few feet behind him.

“Gentry?” he called out, his voice echoing through the pines.

There was no answer.

With their weapons poised, they made their way toward the tree line. They were about to head down what appeared to be a narrow path when, to the far right, a rustling in the underbrush caught their attention. Wyatt held up his hand, signaling Ashley to stop.

“Gentry?” he shouted a second time.

Again, there was no response. The forest had gone silent.

Ignoring the path, Wyatt inched into the forest undergrowth with Ashley close behind. They had only advanced a few yards when they heard it again. Leaves rustling, twigs snapping.

In unison, they froze.

Listening. Waiting.

After a few seconds, with no sign of Gentry, Wyatt pushed forward.

Goosebumps broke out on Ashley's arms as she followed. She couldn't help wondering if this was a trap. Was the trooper purposely leading them deeper into the forest? Was the man planning an execution? There was likely no one around for miles. No one to hear the shots ring out. Gentry could bury them in a shallow grave and their bodies would probably never be found.

Wyatt stopped short.

The thicket of bushes in front of them shook, and Ashley's heart caught in her throat.

Training his weapon on the center of the thicket, Wyatt shouted, "Come out, Gentry. We just want to talk."

They were met by silence.

Icy tension stiffened Ashley's body as she held her breath, anticipating Gentry's reaction. Would the trooper come out shooing?

The bushes split and a buck leapt toward them, its eyes wide with fear. The deer stared at them for an instant, and then bounded to their left, swallowed up by the pines. Ashley let herself breathe again. Relieved they'd been tracking a harmless animal and not the trooper.

"We should get back on the path," Wyatt said, turning around.

She nodded. If Gentry had gone into the forest, it made sense that he would stick to a worn trail rather than cut through the dense underbrush. Keeping their guard up, they retraced their steps. Just as Ashley spotted the path a few feet ahead of them, a loud thump echoed from the direction of the highway.

It sounded like a car door slamming shut.

Wyatt met her gaze.

An engine roared.

"Shit!" her partner yelled, darting toward the path.

Ashley raced after him. As they burst through the tree line, she saw Gentry's cruiser veer onto the highway, heading toward Ormond at a high rate of speed. They couldn't let the trooper get away. He could vanish deep into the mountains like a ghost. There were so many places for a local man with strong family ties to hide that they might never find him again.

"Come on!" Wyatt shouted, jumping the ditch.

She sprinted toward the county SUV, her heart pounding in her chest. Hopping into the passenger seat, she jerked the door closed just as Wyatt gunned the engine.

The tires squealed as he swung the vehicle into a U-turn. Ashley peered through the windshield as her seatbelt clicked into place. Gentry's cruiser had already disappeared over the hill.

The trooper had a head start, but she knew Wyatt was determined to catch him.

CHAPTER TWENTY SEVEN

Ashley clenched the door handle of the county SUV, her knuckles turning white, as Wyatt floored the accelerator and sped down the highway in pursuit of Trooper Gentry. Her eyes scanned the road ahead. In the distance, a few vehicles choked their path, but there was no sign of Gentry's cruiser. He had to be traveling well above the speed limit to have lost them that fast.

"Hang on," Wyatt said, flipping on the siren.

Her pulse raced as she gripped the handle tighter. Ashley hoped the trooper hadn't slipped down a side road. If that was the case, he was likely gone for good.

"Do you think he's still on the highway?" she asked.

A concerned look crossed Wyatt's face. "I don't know."

Her partner pushed the Bonner County SUV to its limits, weaving in and out of traffic on the narrow, two-lane, state route. Ashley noted the startled expressions on the faces of the other drivers as they flew past. Did the drivers all have their earbuds or car speakers turned up so loud that they couldn't hear the siren's wail? Maybe they'd all been too busy texting or browsing social media on their phones to notice the police lights flashing in their review mirrors.

"Don't these people know they're supposed to pull off the road?"

He snorted. "They think slowing down's good enough."

As the SUV topped a hill, she surveyed the line of traffic undulating in front of them. Still no THP cruiser in sight.

Ashley's stomach lurched as Wyatt jerked the wheel to the right, just avoiding a head-on collision with a semi. The driver of the truck laid on his horn, the blaring noise competing with the howl of the police siren.

"I really don't want to die today," Ashley said, her tone sharp.

Her partner shot her a dismayed look. "You think I do?"

Stifling her irritation, she turned her focus back toward the highway. She knew Wyatt was trying his hardest to make up ground, but she just wished he'd be more careful. They could be of no help to the families of the roadside killer's victims if they ended up wrapped around a tree. Even worse, if Wyatt didn't keep his driving in check, they risked taking out a few victims of their own.

Her stomach trembled once again as the SUV rounded a sharp curve. After they zoomed past a motorcycle, to her relief, the traffic cleared. Taking advantage of the straight stretch of unpopulated asphalt, her partner smashed the gas pedal to the floor. Ashley felt her heart skip a beat as the speedometer hit one-hundred.

Going full throttle, the SUV vaulted over the top of a hill. A small dot appeared on the horizon. As they sped closer, the dark blob began to morph into a familiar shape.

Hope stirred in Ashley's chest. "Is that …"

"Yeah," Wyatt confirmed, excitement in his tone. "It's Gentry."

The cruiser was about a half-mile ahead, but at their current rate of speed, they'd close the gap in no time. Ashley kept her eyes fixed on the trooper's vehicle. Her pulse quickened as the SUV ate up the ground between them.

With no cars coming from the opposite direction, Wyatt veered into the left lane. He eased off the gas, bringing the SUV parallel to Gentry's cruiser. He motioned for the trooper to pull off the road.

Through the passenger window, Ashley's gaze locked with Gentry's. The man's expression struck her cold and hard. The hairs on the back of her neck prickled. She was almost certain she caught a flicker of evil in his steely eyes. But in an instant, the look was gone. Replaced with a façade of compliance.

Gentry nodded, letting them know that he understood Wyatt's instructions.

The county SUV dropped back into the right lane and Wyatt cut the siren as the trooper's cruiser slowed. Her partner kept an even distance between the two vehicles, following Gentry onto the gravel shoulder. As Wyatt shifted the SUV's transmission into park, an uneasy feeling swept over Ashley.

"I don't like this," she stated, unbuckling her seatbelt.

Wyatt cast her a sideways glance. "You want to stay in the car?"

There was no way she was going to let Wyatt face the armed trooper alone.

"No, but something about Gentry – about the way he looked right before he pulled over – feels off."

Wyatt hesitated, obviously taking her gut instinct seriously. "You think he'll try something?"

An image of Gentry pulling his service weapon, firing toward them, flashed through her mind. Would the man risk a gunfight? Maybe he'd realize the odds of survival were not in his favor.

She shook her head. "I don't know."

"Just be ready. Keep your guard up."

Her nerves on edge, Ashley slid out of the SUV. Ahead, she noticed Gentry hadn't moved. He remained seated behind the wheel of his vehicle, signaling that if the agents wanted to talk, it would be on his terms.

Wyatt motioned for her to approach the trooper's cruiser on the passenger side, rather than following him to the driver's door. With her hand poised on the grip of her Glock, Ashley nodded. Her heart hammered in her chest as she matched steps with her partner and eased toward Gentry's vehicle. Her eyes stayed glued to the trooper's silhouette, watching for any change in his posture. She realized how fast things could spiral out of control. Knew their lives could shatter in an instant.

With less than a yard separating Wyatt and Ashley from the rear bumper of the cruiser, Gentry finally moved. Panic raced through her as the trooper shifted in his seat. Thinking he might turn on them and open fire, she yanked her Glock from its holster and took aim.

Gentry stomped the gas pedal. The cruiser lurched forward, the tires spraying gravel in their wake.

"What the hell?" Wyatt exclaimed.

But the trooper's actions didn't surprise Ashley. She'd somehow known it would be fight or flight with Gentry. She was just thankful the man had chosen the latter.

"We can't let him get away!" she yelled, racing back to the county SUV.

Wyatt tore past her. "We won't," he called as he ran.

Her partner flipped the siren back on and gunned the SUV's engine, peeling out after the cruiser. Gravel pinged against the undercarriage of the vehicle as they careened onto the paved highway. Ashley cursed under her breath as she fumbled with her seatbelt, not daring to go without it. Finally, the latch clicked into place. She sighed and braced herself for the rollercoaster ride she knew was coming.

Although the trooper had a head start again, this time he was still within their sights. The SUV rocketed down the roadway in hot pursuit.

The hard set of Wyatt's jaw let her know that her partner was determined to stop the man from escaping.

As they soared around a bend, a pickup truck came into view up ahead of Gentry's vehicle. The cruiser swerved into the left lane, passing the truck with ease. But as Gentry whipped back into the right lane, he overcorrected, his tires hitting the gravel at the edge of the shoulder.

Ashley held her breath and watched the cruiser fishtail, terrified that Gentry would lose control, flip the car, and die in a fiery crash. Although it seemed likely the trooper had killed Ian, Megan, and Nick, she didn't want it to end that way. She wanted a judge and jury to stop Gentry, not an accidental death.

To her relief, as Wyatt maneuvered around the pickup, the trooper regained command of the cruiser. He raced onward, obviously hell-bent on outrunning the SUV. Gentry's car appeared to be a few years newer than the Bonner County Ford, but she wasn't sure which vehicle would win in a flat-out sprint. She just hoped Wyatt's driving skills would prove superior.

Without warning, Gentry slammed on his brakes. The cruiser spun around in a one-hundred-and-eighty degree turn, tires squealing on the asphalt. Appearing to smash the accelerator to the floor, the trooper plowed straight toward them, in their lane, threatening to hit them head-on.

"He's trying to kill us!" Ashley screamed.

At the last second, Wyatt swerved to the right and hit the brakes, avoiding a collision. The SUV skidded to a stop on the shoulder.

"You okay?" Wyatt asked, his eyes darting over to Ashley.

With her heart in her throat, she nodded. "Yeah, I'm fine."

The trooper had shown his true colors. His game of chicken had proven that Gentry wouldn't hesitate to kill Wyatt and Ashley in order to evade capture. If they let him get away now, it was possible he would disappear forever. He might hide out in the mountains for a while. Then steal someone else's identity, move to a new town, and launch another murder spree. They couldn't let that happen.

Wyatt jerked the wheel of the SUV, spinning into a U-turn. The engine roared as they flew back down the highway at top speed.

The chase was on.

CHAPTER TWENTY EIGHT

Anxiety flooded Ashley's body as she watched the needle of the county SUV's speedometer inch higher and higher, with Wyatt still leaning on the accelerator. A clear road stretched ahead of them. Gentry's vehicle had vanished. Would they catch up with the trooper? Or had the man already ditched the highway and fled into the mountains?

The answer greeted her sooner than she expected. The SUV rounded a curve and Gentry's cruiser materialized in the distance.

"There he is," she said, wishing they could somehow get the trooper to stop. "What if I radio the Bonner County dispatch? Do you think the sheriff will agree to set up a road block?"

Wyatt cut his eyes at her, which obviously meant *no*.

She had hoped that Wyatt's earlier threats at the sheriff's department were strong enough to get Powell to do their bidding from now on. But most of the deputies on duty were likely at the boat dock. The sheriff could use the crime scene as an excuse not to send help.

"It's at least worth a try," she said.

Getting the aid of Sheriff Powell was a longshot, but she knew the TBI didn't currently have enough boots on the ground in the remote area to erect a barrier on the highway.

Her partner shrugged. "Do it."

As the road straightened, Wyatt pushed on the gas pedal, increasing their speed. Ashley tore her gaze from the windshield just long enough to grab the radio mic.

"Dispatch, this is TBI agent Ashley Hope," she stated, her attention returning to the highway. "My partner and I are in pursuit of a suspect and need assistance."

The airwaves which had hosted sporadic chatter between dispatch and the Bonner County deputies just minutes earlier now fell silent. Ashley counted the seconds, waiting for a response. She glanced at Wyatt and then tried again.

"This is Ashley Hope with the TBI. My partner and I need help on Old Alta Mill Highway."

Still, there was no answer. Rather than deny the agents assistance outright, dispatch must have been instructed to simply ignore any requests from Wyatt and Ashley. The sheriff would probably claim there had been a radio malfunction and the calls couldn't be heard.

"Screw them," Wyatt said, his anger clear on his face.

She shared his sentiment, guessing that the two of them would be fighting this battle alone. Unless they could get support from the Tennessee Highway Patrol.

"Do you think the THP would answer if I called?"

"Only one way to find out."

Ashley switched the radio to the THP's open channel, marked on the dial.

"This is TBI agent, Ashley Hope. Do you copy, dispatch?"

"Loud and clear Agent Hope," a female officer replied.

So far, so good. Maybe they would receive help after all.

"My partner and I are following Trooper Rex Gentry on Old Alta Mill Highway at a high rate of speed. Please instruct him to pull over."

For a moment, silence blanketed the airwaves.

"Can you give me your badge number, Agent Hope?"

Ashley sighed. The dispatch officer obviously doubted her identity. Most likely thought her request was a prank. She recited the number.

"We need to speak to Trooper Gentry regarding an ongoing criminal investigation," she explained, hoping they would take her seriously.

"Understood. But until we can check your creds, I'll have to ask you to clear this channel."

And how long would that take? She might as well face the facts: there'd be no aid from the THP.

Ashley shoved her frustration aside and focused her vision on the tail of Gentry's cruiser. The distance between the SUV and the trooper's vehicle had narrowed, and they continued to gain ground. She no longer dared to look at the instrument panel. She preferred not to know exactly how fast they were traveling.

Ahead, Gentry's brake lights flared. The cruiser fishtailed as the trooper swung off the highway onto a side road that disappeared into a thick stand of trees. Just as Ashley had feared, it looked like Gentry might be headed toward a safe haven hidden deep in the heart of the mountains. She wondered whether the man's relatives would rush from the forest and run interference by blocking their path.

Wyatt hit the brakes. The SUV's tires screeched as he made the turn, following the cruiser. The narrow ribbon of road stretching before them was rough, the pavement worn. Ashley grabbed the door handle as they bounded over a pot hole, jarring her teeth.

"Better hang on tight," Wyatt said, appearing rattled as well.

The trees that flanked the road were close enough to touch, their naked branches forming a canopy overhead. Ashley squinted at the cruiser as they raced through the dappled sunlight. She thought she saw something fly out from the driver's side of the car.

"Did he just –"

"Yeah," Wyatt said, sounding surprised. "He tossed something out the window."

What was Gentry getting rid of? And why? Could it be evidence linking him to the murders?

As they sped from beneath the canopy, another object flew out from the cruiser's window. And then, after rounding a bend, another.

Three victims.

Three items of evidence.

"He must know that we're going to catch him or he wouldn't be throwing things out," Ashley said.

"Like we won't go back and collect it."

"Yeah, but there's a good chance it might not be there when we come back."

Wyatt shot her a quizzical look. She realized the idea that Gentry had called his family, letting them know he was in trouble, hadn't yet occurred to her partner.

"The people in Bonner County seem to be a whole lot like the people in Laurel County," she said, "which means that Gentry probably has a slew of relatives living here. I wouldn't be surprised if an army of them were hiding in the woods right now just waiting to pick up whatever it was he tossed."

Wyatt sighed. She guessed that meant that he agreed with her supposition.

The SUV sprinted onward, the altitude climbing higher. Ashley noticed Wyatt's grip tighten on the steering wheel as he maneuvered around a sharp curve. The road soon snaked into a series of switchbacks, wreaking havoc on her stomach.

In front of them, Gentry's cruiser bounced on the aging pavement. His brake lights flared once again as he careened around a tight bend. A second later, the car disappeared, swallowed up by the trees. It was obvious the trooper knew this road well, which put them at a distinct disadvantage.

"Brace yourself," Wyatt said as he stomped the gas pedal.

Ashley's fingernails dug into the fabric of the passenger seat as she held on. She realized they couldn't afford to lose sight of Gentry. They might come to a fork in the road and not know which way he'd turned. If that happened, she knew the odds were good that they'd never find the trooper again. That the truth about what happened to Ian, Megan, and Nick might never be revealed.

The trees blurred in her peripheral vision as Wyatt struggled to keep the SUV under control, increasing his speed on the winding mountain road. They rounded a hairpin turn and her stomach quivered. As the road swung back in the other direction, Gentry's cruiser popped into view. He was still a few hundred yards ahead of them, but at least they hadn't lost him yet.

To her relief, the road straightened and leveled off a bit. Ashley took a deep breath and released her death grip on the seat.

On her right, the forest thinned. The shoulder fell away, the earth dissolving into a deep canyon. She glimpsed a ribbon of white water rushing along the bottom of the gorge. Her pulse quickened. One wrong move and the SUV could plummet over the edge. Wyatt seemed not to notice, his eyes now glued to the rear of Gentry's car.

Ashley pushed her fears of vaulting over the cliff out of her mind and instead followed Wyatt's lead, focusing on the cruiser. Out of the corner of her eye, she caught a flash of movement up ahead on the left.

A large buck leapt from the forest, bounding into Gentry's path.

The cruiser swerved to the right to avoid the deer. But Gentry was traveling too fast. As the car jerked back to the left, it spun out of control, the tires screaming on the asphalt.

Wyatt slammed on the brakes.

The sudden shift of force propelled Ashley forward, the seatbelt biting into her chest.

Feeling as though everything was happening in slow motion, her heart jumped to her throat as she watched Gentry's car swirling toward the rim of the bluff. At the last moment, the trooper pulled out of the spin. But it was too late.

The moan of metal crunching against wood split the air as Gentry crashed broadside into an oak tree.

The SUV skidded to a stop mere feet from the cliff's edge. Ashley threw off her seatbelt and yanked her Glock from its holster. She raced toward Gentry's crumpled vehicle with Wyatt at her heels. Through the window, she saw the dark-haired trooper slumped over the steering wheel. A bloody gash marred his temple. He was lucky he'd hit the tree on the passenger side.

"Wait," Wyatt said. "Let me."

Ashley stepped back, providing cover for her partner.

His weapon poised for action in his right hand, Wyatt pulled the driver's door open with his left. The trooper didn't move.

"Gentry!" Wyatt yelled above the wail of the SUV's siren.

There was no response.

Wyatt checked Gentry's neck for a pulse.

"He's alive," he said. "Just unconscious. Or pretending to be."

Ashley nodded and then cocked her head, listening. She realized that the police siren she heard bouncing off the mountain wasn't just coming from the Bonner County SUV alone.

"Do you hear that?" she asked, just to make sure her mind wasn't playing tricks on her.

"Yeah. Sounds like it's heading toward us."

Wyatt never took his eyes off the trooper.

"Gentry," he said. "I'm taking your service weapon. If you move even a millimeter, I'll blow your brains out."

Wyatt handed the trooper's pistol to Ashley and then grabbed the cruiser's radio mic. She listened as he identified himself and requested an ambulance. They were out in the middle of nowhere. It would likely take a while for help to arrive. Wyatt eased Gentry's head back against the driver's seat and checked the man's vitals a second time.

"His pulse is strong. I think he'll be okay."

Her partner's assessment gave her a small amount of relief. She didn't want the trooper to die.

Wyatt cuffed Gentry's hands to the steering wheel.

The scream of the police siren grew louder. Whoever it was, they were definitely headed up the mountain road. And it sounded as though they were traveling at break-neck speed. She wondered whether Gentry had radioed the THP on their secure channel. It was possible he had claimed that Wyatt and Ashley were the criminals. That they'd tried to run him off the highway.

After making sure her partner was no longer in danger, Ashley darted back to the SUV and switched off its siren. As she pushed the door shut, flashing lights – red and blue – cut through the trees.

She fixed her eyes on the twisting mountain road.

As the car broke into the clearing, a wave of fear hit Ashley.

Was this a trap?

CHAPTER TWENTY NINE

Ashley's heart pounded in her chest as the car sped toward her into the clearing, its siren blazing. The white Chevy was unmarked. A portable light bar, flashing red and blue, topped its roof. Was the driver a member of law enforcement?

Or had she and Wyatt raced into a trap?

Was one of Gentry's relatives behind the wheel? The trooper's family could have been following them using the siren and lights as a ruse. He could have planned to fool Wyatt and Ashley into believing help – maybe the THP – was on the way. While instead, Gentry penned them in between himself and the people in the Chevy. A setup for an execution.

No one knew they were on the mountain road.

The car had to be here at Gentry's request.

Ashley jerked her Glock from its holster.

"Wyatt, take cover!" she screamed.

Keeping her eyes glued to the Chevy, she sprinted behind the nose of the county SUV and took aim over the hood. How many people were they facing? If Gentry had called in the family cavalry, there would likely be more vehicles on the way. All packed with guns and ammo.

The car roared over the pocked asphalt and then screeched to a halt.

The Chevy had stopped just close enough for Ashley to get a clear look through the windshield at the driver. It was a woman. A woman she'd met before. A dark-haired young man – who she also recognized – sat in the passenger seat.

The wail of the siren died, and Sheriff Powell's daughter, Ramona, nodded at Ashley from behind the wheel. Deputy Cody Medford did the same. At first, Ashley was relieved to see two familiar faces. But why was the sheriff's daughter here? Ramona obviously knew Gentry – she'd worked with him.

Were they working together now?

"Get out of the car!" Ashley yelled. "And keep your hands where we can see them!"

The two deputies exchanged glances, seeming puzzled by Ashley's command.

Wyatt appeared at her side, his weapon drawn. The questions that plagued Ashley had likely run through his mind as well. Sheriff Powell had thwarted them at every turn. Could they really trust his daughter?

The doors of the Chevy pushed open and Ramona and Medford slid out, their hands raised in the air.

"What in tarnation's got into you, Ashley?" Ramona asked. "Pulling your pistol on a fellow cop?"

Ashley met her gaze. "The real question is," she began, "what are you and Medford doing all the way out here? Did you just happen to drive up the mountain with your siren blaring and lights flashing?"

"We heard you radio for help."

"Then why didn't you answer my call?"

"You know why," Ramona said, a sheepish grin tugging at her cheeks. "I didn't want my father to know we were heading to help you."

Ashley studied the woman's face, unsure whether she was telling the truth. But there was a tougher question that needed an answer. Ashley had radioed that she and Wyatt needed assistance on Old Alta Mill Highway, but she'd never pinpointed the exact location. The highway stretched from one end of Bonner County to the other. And if the deputies weren't working with Gentry, then how did they know to turn onto the mountain road?

"How did you find us?"

The look that crossed Ramona's face revealed that she had information she wasn't supposed to divulge. "My father wanted to keep tabs on you," she stated. "He put a GPS tracker on your SUV."

It sounded like the kind of stunt the sheriff would pull.

Ashley glanced at Wyatt. After a moment's hesitation, he lowered his weapon. She guessed that meant that he believed Ramona's explanation. Ashley searched the deputy's eyes once more before holstering her Glock. The woman seemed to be telling the truth.

Both deputies lowered their arms.

"What kind of trouble did y'all get yourselves into?" Ramona asked.

"Well, as you can see, we were chasing a state trooper," Ashley said, motioning toward the cruiser wrapped around the oak tree at the edge of the cliff. "We have good reason to think that he may be the roadside killer."

Ramona shot her a stunned look. She and Medford followed Wyatt and Ashley to Gentry's car.

"I know him," Ramona said, leaning toward the driver's seat. "Name's Rex Gentry. He's a piece of scum all right."

Ashley had purposely failed to mention that she and Wyatt knew Gentry had once worked for the Bonner County Sheriff's Department. She'd wanted to gauge Ramona's reaction to seeing the trooper first.

The deputy felt for Gentry's pulse. "He unconscious? Or just playing possum?" she asked.

Wyatt smiled. "I'm not quite sure."

Ashley knew the trooper was likely listening to everything they were saying. Pretending to be out cold in order to avoid being questioned. She noticed Wyatt had bandaged the gash on Gentry's temple. A first aid kit lay open on the center console.

Ramona nodded toward Medford. "Call for an ambulance," she told him.

"I've already done that," Wyatt said.

"Good. This mountain's right on the dividing line between Bonner and Myrtle counties. It could take a while for them to get out here."

The sheriff's daughter stepped away from the mangled cruiser, motioning for Ashley and Wyatt to follow.

"Y'all got hard evidence?" she asked once they were out of earshot of Gentry.

Wyatt glanced at Ashley. "Good enough to justify chasing him down," he said.

Although they might not yet have physical evidence tying the trooper to the murders, the fact that Gentry had led them on a high-speed chase indicated that the man was guilty of something. And what had he tossed out of his car window? Could he have been disposing of the murder weapon and bloody clothing?

"We saw Gentry throw three bags out of his window a few miles back," Ashley said. "If it's okay with everyone, I'd like to take Medford with me and see if we can find them."

Ashley would have preferred to go alone, but she still didn't trust the sheriff's daughter enough to leave both her and Medford here with Wyatt. With Gentry cuffed to the steering wheel of his cruiser, Wyatt could handle Ramona – she wouldn't be able to get the drop on him – but if Medford stayed … the odds were just too risky.

"That's fine by me," Ramona said.

Medford nodded. "I'm up for it."

Wyatt met her gaze. She could tell that he understood. Shared her thoughts.

The young male deputy followed Ashley to the county SUV. After adjusting the driver's seat, she cranked the engine, swung a U-Turn, and headed back down the mountain road. She pushed the SUV as fast as she dared on the winding stretch of asphalt, but not going anywhere near the speeds Wyatt had reached. Just in case Gentry had called his relatives, she wanted to get to the bags before they did.

She noticed Medford's fingers clenched tight around the door handle. The same way she had held on when Wyatt was driving.

"We need to hurry and get back before the ambulance arrives," she said. Since she still held a fraction of doubt regarding the deputy's allegiance, she chose not to explain the real motive behind her hustle.

Medford nodded and tried to smile, but it looked more like a half grimace.

When they neared the area where the third bag had been tossed, Ashley veered onto the shoulder and cut the SUV's engine. She stuck the key fob in the front pocket of her jeans, just to be safe. If Medford was playing for the wrong team, she didn't want him to take off without her.

"We're looking for light blue duffel bags about a foot and a half long," she told him.

Together, they scoured the ditch where she thought the bag should have landed. Finding nothing, they advanced into the tree line and poked through the underbrush. Going deeper, they searched just past the point where it would have been physically possible for Gentry to fling the evidence. And still, no bag. Ashley paused and looked back toward the road. Maybe they were at the wrong spot.

Or maybe someone else had gotten there first.

"Keep on looking in this general area," she told Medford. "I'm going to walk down the road and see if I can find the second bag."

As she made her way along the hard-packed dirt shoulder, Ashley replayed the car chase in her mind. Scanning the ditch, she matched the vision in her head to the contours of the land. As she rounded a curve, the images aligned. This was the exact location where Gentry had thrown the second duffel. She remembered watching the bag as it hit the ground.

The blue duffel had landed in the middle of the ditch, amidst a sea of dried leaves.

She inched along the side of the road, certain she was in the right spot.

Her heart sank. There was no bag to be found.

Ashley's eyes darted toward the forest. Gentry's relatives – or maybe even a partner in his crimes – had collected the duffels. There was no other plausible explanation for the bags' disappearance. Were the trooper's cohorts still here, camouflaged among the thickets, waiting for the right opportunity to attack?

The hairs on the back of Ashley's neck bristled as she drew her Glock. She held her breath, combing the trees for any sign of movement. Except for a slight breeze skirting the mountainside, the forest remained still. Quiet.

She glanced back up the road, toward the bend. The trees blocked her view of the county SUV – and Medford. The thought of calling out to the deputy crossed her mind, but she didn't want to alert Gentry's relatives in case they were hiding nearby. She needed to hurry back to Medford and warn him.

But what about the first bag Gentry had tossed? Was there still a chance she could find it?

Her attention swerved to the canopy of dormant trees just down the road to her left.

When she'd reviewed Medford's information in the TBI's database, she'd learned the deputy had been born and raised in Bonner County. Which meant he knew the ways of the locals. He was likely at home in the forest. He was a trained member of law enforcement. And he was armed.

It would only take her a couple of minutes to check for the first duffel.

Keeping her guard up, and her Glock at the ready, Ashley trotted down the road's shoulder. When she reached the canopy, she slowed her pace. She recalled that Gentry's cruiser had been midway through the tree tunnel when he'd thrown out the first bag.

The brittle leaves crunched beneath the soles of Ashley's hiking boots as she crossed into the ditch. She stepped with caution, trying to keep as quiet as possible. Remaining alert for any noise or movement around her, she inched forward. Her gaze swept back and forth from the road to the dense line of sleeping hardwoods growing along the ditch's bank. As she closed in on the half-way point beneath the canopy, in the shadow of dappled sunlight, a patch of blue caught her eye.

Wedged between the trunks of two gnarled oaks, she spotted the first duffel bag.

Excitement surged in Ashley's chest as she climbed the bank and crept toward the oaks.

The snap of a twig cracked the silence.

Ashley froze.

The sound seemed to have come from the other side of the tree line. Her Glock poised for action, she focused her gaze straight ahead and pushed her way through the underbrush into the forest. She'd only traversed a few yards when the tree cover broke, revealing a small clearing.

The profile of a man flashed into view on her left. Standing over six feet tall, he possessed broad shoulders and muscular arms that looked as though they could break a person in half.

A blue duffel bag dangled from his left hand.

Ashley's pulse skyrocketed.

"TBI!" she shouted, her Glock trained on the man's chest. "Stop where you are!"

The man paused, as if he planned to comply with the order. He angled his face toward her. His lips curled into a wicked grin.

Ashley's blood ran cold as she locked eyes with the man.

At that moment, she knew she was staring into the face of a demon.

CHAPTER THIRTY

Ashley's breath caught in her throat as the hulking man's dark eyes bored into her own. Without shifting her gaze, she steadied the aim of her Glock, targeting his chest. The man's eyes narrowed, and a wave of pure evil hit her. The invisible force so strong, it threatened to knock her from her feet.

Her brain screamed for her to forget about the duffel bag and run from the forest clearing, yelling for help at the top of her lungs. But fear had frozen her legs, its icy grip refusing to let go. It felt as though the man possessed an otherworldly power. That he could yank her very soul from her body with ease. That he had stolen her ability to flee, hypnotizing her, willing her to stand still.

As though he was the grim reaper, and she was his prey.

The man's lips twisted into a feral snarl, his teeth glistening in the mottled sunlight.

A vision of her lifeless body lying bloody on the forest floor, the malevolent man standing over her, flooded Ashley's mind. Her instincts cried that he wouldn't hesitate to kill her, in an attempt to escape with Gentry's bag.

She wouldn't allow that to happen.

Ashley fought to break free of the sudden paralysis. She forced herself to take one step forward, tightening her grip on the Glock. The man was sure to have friends skulking in the forest. She wondered if their eyes were fixed on her now, watching this scene play out.

Did they have their weapons trained on her? Waiting to fire?

"Drop the duffel bag!" she shouted, intent on keeping her voice firm, showing no fear. "And put your hands up over your head."

A low, guttural laugh rumbled from the man's lips.

The wicked chortle sent a chill racing down Ashley's spine. She realized that she might already be surrounded by a large troop of Gentry's relatives. The man appeared unfazed that a TBI agent was holding him at gunpoint. He seemed almost giddy. As if this was a game he'd already won.

The man's cold gaze raked over her body, as though he was summing her up. The eerie feeling that he possessed the ability to read her thoughts swept through Ashley. Was he anticipating her next move? Planning his counter?

"I said, drop the bag!" she yelled again, struggling to shake off her fright. "Don't make me pull the trigger."

The man snickered.

With a jerk of his shoulder, he turned and sprinted toward the tree line, the blue duffel bag still in his grasp.

Ashley cursed under her breath as the man disappeared into the shadows of the thick forest. He'd known that she wouldn't fire. Although she was certain the man was armed as well, he hadn't attempted to pull his weapon. He'd run away. Therefore, he'd posed no actual physical threat. She'd never shoot someone in cold blood, no matter how evil they seemed.

The urge to give chase gnawed at Ashley's mind.

But she felt positive the man hadn't come to the forest alone. He'd only carried one of the duffel bags, which likely meant that someone else had picked up the other. There could be dozens of armed locals lurking behind the trees, just itching for a fight. Trotting after the man without sufficient backup would be equivalent to committing suicide. And he obviously knew Ashley had realized that fact.

With her Glock at the ready, Ashley left the clearing and picked her way back through the forest underbrush. She moved in silence, her guard up, expecting to be greeted by the muzzle of a shotgun at any moment. As patches of the mountain road popped into view between the trees, she realized the remaining duffel that she'd found earlier was probably gone. While she'd been in the clearing, one of Gentry's cohorts had likely circled behind her and grabbed the bag. The duffel's contents seemed doomed to remain a mystery. At least, to Wyatt and Ashley.

As she squeezed between two hardwood trees lining the canopy, her attention swung to her right, toward the location where she'd spotted the first bag Gentry had tossed. Deputy Medford stood next to the gnarled oaks, his back toward her.

To her surprise, the blue bag remained wedged between the tree trunks.

Medford leaned toward the duffel, his arm outstretched.

"Stop!" she yelled, her Glock poised, ready to take aim if needed. "Move away from the bag."

She still wasn't one-hundred percent sure which side the deputy was on. And she couldn't afford to take any unnecessary chances.

Medford jumped, as though she'd startled him.

He turned toward her, a shocked expression spreading across his face. She didn't want the deputy to realize that she still suspected he might be working with Gentry. Thankfully, she had a good excuse for ordering him to stop.

"I don't want you to touch the bag until I've taken pictures of it," she said, hoping he bought her explanation.

He tapped the phone holstered to his duty belt. "Got some already."

She shook her head. "I still have to take evidence photos of my own. It's standard TBI procedure – I can't break it. And besides, you're not wearing gloves."

Ashley wasn't lying about the TBI protocol.

He grinned and raised his right hand. "I was gonna use this," he said.

With her focus honed on the duffel, she hadn't noticed the two-foot-long stick clasped between Medford's fingers. Although it wasn't perfect, she guessed his plan to slide the branch beneath the dual straps and lift the bag from the trees, would have been acceptable.

"I'll take care of Gentry's duffel bag," she said, motioning toward the radio clipped to Medford's shirt. "I need you to call dispatch and get them to round up as many deputies as they can find and send them out here."

She hoped that Gentry's cohorts weren't aware that she'd found the remaining duffel bag. If they were currently watching Ashley and Medford, the odds were good the trooper's relatives would have already oozed out of the trees and tried to take the bag by force. The fact that they hadn't made their presence known, meant they were probably still searching. Maybe they would stick around in the area long enough for help to arrive.

A puzzled looked crossed Medford's face. "What for?"

"I ran into a man in the woods – probably a relative of Gentry. He was carrying one of the duffel bags, and even though I pulled my firearm and tried to stop him, he got away from me. We need a team to comb the forest and look for him and anyone else who might be helping Gentry."

“So there’s more than one guy?”

“You were raised here in Bonner County,” she stated. “What do you think?”

Medford nodded, letting her know that he agreed. He headed back across the ditch onto the shoulder of the road and keyed his radio mic.

While the deputy called for backup, Ashley climbed the bank of the ditch next to the two gnarled oaks. On a hunch, she circled behind the trees. From the forest side, the way the branches twisted together, it was impossible to see the blue bag. She prayed that meant that Gentry’s crew had no idea where the duffel had landed.

The faint wail of an emergency siren wafted toward the mountain. Ashley assumed it was the ambulance responding to Wyatt’s earlier call. Would the siren spook Gentry’s relatives and send them running? She guessed it depended on the value of the duffel’s contents, and what they were willing to risk for it.

Ashley plucked her phone from her jacket pocket and moved back around the trees, snapping photos of the blue bag from various angles. Satisfied that she’d captured enough images, she glanced toward the road. Medford was speaking with Ramona over the radio. The sheriff’s daughter had heard him call for backup and wanted to make sure everything was okay.

Hoping Ramona would keep Medford occupied for a minute or two longer, Ashley slipped on a pair of latex gloves. With the howl of the ambulance growing louder, she slid her fingers beneath the duffel’s straps and eased the bag upward, pulling it free from the grip of the oaks. As the duffel swung around, she caught a glimpse of the side that had been butted against the trunk of one of the trees.

Ashley’s pulse quickened.

A large reddish-brown stain marred the light blue fabric.

It looked just like dried blood.

Medford appeared at her side, a grim expression on his face. “Do you think that’s –”

“It could be.”

Based on the duffel’s outward appearance, she feared what they would find inside. Pulling a wad of plastic evidence bags from her jacket pocket, she motioned toward the road.

“Spread these out on the pavement and I’ll put the duffel on top.”

The deputy grabbed the evidence bags and laid them on the rough asphalt, side-by-side, overlapping the ends. Ashley knelt next to the road and eased the duffel down onto the plastic. She met the deputy's gaze.

"Are you ready?" she asked, her heart thumping.

He nodded.

Ashley held her breath and zipped open the duffel.

Medford's eyes widened. "Oh, shit," he said.

CHAPTER THIRTY ONE

Ashley slammed her fist against the lighted button on the soda machine in the snack room of Myrtle County Medical Center, anger seething in her bones. She should have known that Gentry would invoke his right to an attorney the minute he arrived at the hospital. Now, the TBI was forced to play a waiting game.

The odds ranked high that the trooper had woken within a short time after the crash. That he'd feigned unconsciousness, picked up bits and pieces of the police chatter over the radio, Ashley was sure that he'd figured out one of the duffels had been seized. He'd had plenty of time to plan his strategy.

And it seemed clear that Gentry's relative near the top of the Tennessee Highway Patrol's food chain had run interference. The agency had their own guard stationed outside the trooper's room. There was no way Ashley or Wyatt could get anywhere near Gentry. She wondered whether the decision to transport the trooper to Myrtle County was really due to the proximity of the hospital, or whether the THP had instructed the ambulance driver to get their man out of Bonner County, just to create more red tape.

With a sigh, Ashley banged the button a second time.

Still, no soda.

Wyatt appeared at her side. "Here, let me."

A confident look on his face, Wyatt pressed both of his palms against the side of the machine and gave it a sharp jolt. With a *plunk*, the soda fell into the dispenser tray.

"Thank you," Ashley said, retrieving the can.

"I've had some practice."

She guessed that vending machines weren't the only things he'd wrestled during his years as an agent. With many investigations under his belt, this likely wasn't the first time he'd butted heads with the THP.

"Have you ever built a case against a state trooper before?"

He shook his head. "This is a first."

“How many hoops do you think we’ll have to jump through before we can get an interview with Gentry?”

Of course, she realized that once the interrogation procedure was approved, the trooper’s attorney would be present. Which meant that it was doubtful they’d get any straight answers.

Wyatt shrugged. “The TBI has a pretty good working relationship with the THP. But in this case … I’m not sure what to expect. And there’s no physical evidence tying Gentry to the murders. So the DID will probably get to grill him first.”

Ashley popped the top of her soda can. When she’d seen the reddish-brown stain covering the bottom of Gentry’s blue bag, she’d thought for sure there was bloody clothing stuffed inside.

She’d been wrong.

Gentry had been hiding another secret.

“I can’t tell you how shocked I was to zip open that duffel and find it filled with crystal meth,” she said, recalling that the look on Deputy Medford’s face had mirrored her own.

Under the circumstances, it made sense for the TBI’s drug investigation division to take precedence in interrogating Gentry. If the blue duffel had contained a bloody murder weapon, things would be different.

“Brenda said they’d suspected a state cop was transporting meth from the Alabama line to the Kentucky line,” Wyatt stated. “They just didn’t know who.”

A weak smile tugged at Ashley’s lips. She hoped that busting Gentry’s drug courier service would earn Wyatt and Ashley points with the TBI’s deputy director.

“Well, I’m glad we were able to give Brenda her answer.”

Wyatt motioned toward the door of the snack room.

“You ready to hit the road?”

Ashley nodded. She led the way as they strode down the wide hallway to the lobby, through the automatic doors, and into the parking lot of the medical center. With Gentry off limits for the moment, their only choice was to head back to Bonner County. Maybe the deputies had found something – or someone – during their search of the forest surrounding the mountain road that would help to advance the murder case. As usual, Sheriff Powell had failed to notify them of any progress. But the DID team was on the way. Ready to take over from Powell.

Wyatt steered the county SUV onto the highway that led back to Ormond. A minimart popped into view on their right, and he tapped the brakes.

"We need gas," he said.

As the SUV veered toward the fuel pumps, a flash of red caught Ashley's attention.

A late-model convertible whipped past them, driven by a young sandy-haired man wearing a flannel jacket. Although the afternoon temperature hovered in the mid-fifties, the sports car's top was down. A twangy county tune blared from the radio. The man parked in a space near the end of the building.

"That car looks just like the pictures of the one Nick owned," Ashley said, excitement fluttering in her chest.

Wyatt craned his neck. After spotting the convertible, he bypassed the pumps and swerved to the side of the parking lot. He brought the SUV to a stop next to an idling eighteen-wheeler. They still had a clear view of the sports car from around the end of the semi's trailer, but Wyatt had angled the SUV in such a way that Ashley hoped the young man wouldn't notice them.

"Let me run the plate," Wyatt said.

The convertible bore a Myrtle County license tag. Ashley watched the tall, sandy-haired man leap from the driver's seat of the sports car, strut past a pair of ice machines, and then disappear through the glass door of the convenience store.

What were the odds that someone living in the mountain town of Alta Mill would own a convertible the same model, year, and color as Nick's car? Although she was certain a countless number of these cars had been sold across the nation, the pricy vehicles tended to be a rare sight in the rural counties running along the Cumberland Plateau.

Wyatt's fingers flew across the keys of the small laptop mounted to a swivel base between the front seats of the SUV. After a few moments, he shifted his eyes from the screen and met Ashley's gaze.

"Those plates were issued to a pickup truck."

Hope swelled in Ashley's heart. Had they finally found Nick's missing car?

"I'll head into the store and keep an eye on the driver while you check the convertible's VIN number," she said, sliding out of her seatbelt.

Rounding the cab of the semi, Ashley scanned the windows of the minimart. The store's display racks butted against the glass, making it impossible for her to see the customers inside. She had no way of knowing whether the man in the flannel jacket was browsing the aisles, or if he was already in the check-out line. Maybe she would start up a conversation with the man – pretend to accidentally bump into him – anything to keep him occupied long enough for Wyatt to compare the VIN numbers.

Even if the car proved not to belong to Nick, the young man still had some explaining to do. Why had he switched the plates with a pickup? Was the convertible stolen?

And if the VIN number did match Nick's …

Had the driver been paid to ditch the car, but decided to have a little fun first?

Or was he in on the murders?

As Ashley strode toward the entrance of the minimart, the glass door pushed open. Her heart leapt to her throat. The tall, sandy-haired driver shouldered through the door and met her gaze, his arms laden with bags of chips and a six-pack of beer.

Ashley rushed forward, blocking the man's path.

"Hey, don't I know you?" she asked, forcing a cheerful note into her voice.

He shot her an odd look.

"No."

She touched his arm and swiveled to her left, trying to draw the man's attention to the other end of the parking lot, away from the direction of the convertible.

"Yeah, you were at that party a few weeks ago, remember?"

Dressed like a local in her jeans, hiking boots, and fleece jacket, she hoped the man would buy the ruse and stop to talk with her for a while. He struck her as the partying type. She figured it was likely he'd attended some kind of gathering recently.

But the man didn't hesitate long enough to search his memory banks.

"Wasn't me," he said.

She flashed him a wide smile. "I'm sure that we've met each other before, somewhere."

The man shook his head. His eyes cut to the side and his body stiffened.

Ashley's heart rate spiked as she followed the man's line of sight, realizing that he'd spotted Wyatt leaning over the convertible, jotting down the VIN number.

The color drained from the man's face. His purchases slipped from his fingers as he shoved Ashley aside.

"Get outta my way!" he yelled.

The bottles of beer exploded on the asphalt.

The man sprinted across the parking lot, heading toward a pawn shop.

Ashley raced after him.

CHAPTER THIRTY TWO

Adrenaline surged through Ashley's body as she ran across the parking lot of the minimart, chasing the tall, sandy-haired man. As soon as he'd spotted Wyatt studying the red convertible, he'd dropped his beer and snacks on the pavement and had fled in a panic. Was the car's young driver a cold-blooded killer? Did he commit the roadside murders? Or did the convertible belong to someone other than Nick?

Wyatt's back had been toward her as he checked the car's VIN number. She couldn't see her partner's expression. Had no idea whether the number matched Nick's.

Either way, the convertible was obviously stolen. Why else would the car's plates have been switched with tags issued to a pickup truck?

The man raced into the parking lot of the adjacent pawn shop with Ashley not far behind.

"Stop!" she yelled. "TBI!"

The man ignored her shouts. He flew past the shop's letter-board sign advertising guns, ammo, and hunting equipment for sale. Was the man carrying a weapon? She hadn't noticed the bulge of a firearm beneath his jacket, but that didn't mean he wasn't armed. That he wouldn't shoot if cornered.

Angling to the right, he darted between an SUV and an old station wagon, clearing the closely-parked vehicles in a split second, never brushing against either of them. Then he wound around a teen pedaling through the lot on a bicycle. The man seemed to possess an innate agility – almost a graceful quality. He chanced a quick glance over his shoulder, as though gauging the distance between himself and Ashley. Then he burst forward, gaining speed.

Ashley cursed under her breath as the man disappeared around the corner of the aging brick building. She was still in top physical shape from her time spent training at the police academy. But with his long legs, the young, sandy-haired man ran like a gazelle.

Pushing harder, she barreled toward the end of the pawn shop. The arm of her jacket scraped the brick as she cut the corner too sharp. Ahead, she caught sight of the man as he leapt over a pothole filled with murky water. He sailed across the fissure with ease, as though he was accustomed to maneuvering through obstacle courses. Or maybe, he had practice running from the police.

Veering to the right, Ashley skirted the edge of the pothole. She struggled to keep her balance on the uneven asphalt. The gap between herself and the man widened. He zipped across a side street, heading toward some type of industrial building.

The realization that the man was just too fast, that he would likely escape, ripped through her mind. But she refused to allow herself to give up. Determined to do everything in her power to stop him, she propelled herself forward. Her leg muscles screamed as she drove them to their limits.

Just as her right foot touched the side road, a black sedan popped into view on her left – seemingly out of nowhere. Ashley's heart thundered in her chest, her gaze darting toward the nose of the car.

The woman behind the wheel opened her mouth in a silent scream, her eyes wide with terror.

The horn blared as the sedan screeched to a halt, missing Ashley by mere inches.

With no time to apologize, or to let herself think about what had almost happened, Ashley soared across the road. The man was now several yards ahead of her and she was still losing ground. The gray industrial building loomed ahead, and she feared that if he made it inside, he would vanish, and she'd never find him.

Gathering strength from deep within her soul, Ashley rocketed after the man, her eyes laser-focused on the back of his flannel jacket. He was nearing the loading dock of the building. Three rolling metal doors dotted the concrete block wall. Two of the doors were shut tight. A gap less than a foot tall separated the third door from the concrete slab below it. Not enough space for the man to squeeze through. If he planned to hide inside, he'd be forced to stop. To take time to raise the door. Time to allow her to catch up.

At the last instant, the man swerved to the right, bypassing the doors. He bolted past the loading dock and sped toward the street adjacent to the building's parking lot. Ashley's heart sank. Her hope of catching the man dwindled. She was no match for him on the open road.

The howl of a train whistle split the air, and Ashley pried her eyes from the man's running form. In the distance, she spotted a railroad bridge stretched across a deep gorge surrounded by rocky bluffs. The train's wheels hummed along the tracks as it headed into the small town of Alta Mill.

Her lungs burning, Ashley swung a left around the end of the industrial building and charged onward. She noticed a pile of stones on the ground up ahead. She might not be able to run fast enough to catch the man, but maybe she could hit him with one of the rocks and knock him off balance. Cause him to fall. Ashley slowed just enough to scoop one of the rocks into her hand.

The man jetted down the street ahead of her, his feet seeming to barely touch the pavement. He showed no signs of fatigue. Nothing to indicate that he might slow his pace.

The train wailed again.

Ashley watched as red lights flashed at the railway crossing bisecting the road. The warning bell dinged in a rapid cadence as the orange and white striped signal arms lowered. The man veered onto the right shoulder of the road, his stride almost appearing to accelerate.

He made a beeline for the tracks.

In that instance, she felt certain she understood the man's plan. If he could make it to the railroad tracks in time to zoom across, he would be home free. He likely thought that Ashley was too far away to cover that much ground in so little time. That the train would cut her off, and she'd be forced to abandon the chase.

But Ashley wasn't ready to give up just yet. The man still had a few yards left to go before he reached the tracks. Ignoring the stitch in her side, she channeled every smidgen of her energy, focusing on her ultimate goal. She blasted forward at top speed.

As the man flew along the side of the road, he risked another glance over his shoulder.

His lips curved into a smile.

The expression covering his face let Ashley know that the man thought he was about to make the escape of a lifetime. That he felt confident there was no way she could stop him.

Ashley chose that moment to strike. Mustering every ounce of her strength, she hurled the stone straight toward the man.

He cried out in pain as the rock made contact with the center of his back. The man stumbled, his feet almost betraying him. But he failed to go down. Getting his legs back under control, he lunged forward.

The train's whistle shrieked its final warning as the engine bore down on the crossing.

With a seemingly new burst of energy, the man raced toward the tracks.

He was fast. But not fast enough.

He'd lost precious seconds when Ashley had hit him with the rock. His stumbling proved to be his downfall. Fewer than five feet separated the man from the tracks when he obviously realized his fate.

As the man skidded to a stop on the gravel shoulder, the train plowed through the crossing with a deafening roar.

Triumph flooded Ashley's heart as she closed in on her quarry.

She yanked her Glock from its holster as another sound hit her ears. The squawk of a police siren. Out of the corner of her eye, she caught sight of the Bonner County SUV barreling down the road, lights flashing.

The sandy-haired man swirled around, facing her.

Ashley snapped into a firing stance, her aim square on the man's chest.

"TBI!" she shouted. "Get your hands up!"

CHAPTER THIRTY THREE

Ashley sighted the aim of her Glock on the sandy-haired man's chest, her breathing ragged and her thigh and calf muscles tingling from the foot chase. For a split second, she feared the man would keep running. That he would blaze ahead, attempting to jump over the railroad tracks, and be hit by the oncoming train. Fortunately, he'd had the sense to slide to a quick stop on the road's gravel shoulder.

"Put your hands in the air!" she shouted.

As the locomotive zoomed behind him in a blur of motion, the man glanced at Ashley, his face now masked with fright instead of the pride he'd shown earlier. He swiveled his head, his eyes darting from side to side.

It seemed he was trying to make a decision.

Ashley held her weapon steady, her body language indicating an intent to shoot. She wouldn't kill a suspect who posed no threat to her. But the sandy-haired man didn't know that.

Wyatt stood on the road a few yards away, his Glock trained over the hood of the Bonner County SUV. Her partner's decision in pulling the trigger would likely mirror Ashley's.

What thoughts were racing through the sandy-haired man's mind?

Was he armed? Would he pull a weapon of his own?

Under the circumstances, he had to realize the action would be equivalent to suicide. Ashley could fire several rounds – bringing him down – before he even had time to take aim.

Would he try to flee?

The shear drop-off into the gorge blocked his left path. Wyatt, and the county SUV blocked his right. There was nowhere left for him to run.

He was trapped. It was either surrender, plunge to his death over the side of the bluff, or attempt to fight.

"I said, get your hands up!" Ashley yelled.

The man settled his gaze on Ashley's Glock. With a resigned sigh, he raised his arms.

She was glad he'd made the right choice. She didn't want him to end up dead at the bottom of the gorge.

"Now, get on your knees!"

A defeated look spreading across his face, the man dropped to the ground.

Wyatt circled around the county SUV, dangling a pair of handcuffs. Glancing at Ashley, he holstered his Glock. He angled in behind the young man – obviously making sure Ashley maintained a clear shot – and then slapped the cuffs on the man's wrists.

"Do you have any weapons on you?" Wyatt asked.

The man shook his head. "No, sir."

"Any drugs or needles?"

"No."

Wyatt pulled the man to his feet and then proceeded to pat him down while Ashley held her aim. Her partner retrieved a wallet from the back pocket of the man's jeans and tossed it onto the ground before searching the man's lower legs. Finding no weapons, Wyatt picked up the wallet and shoved the sandy-haired man toward the SUV.

Ashley followed.

"What's your name?" Wyatt asked.

The man hesitated. "Do I have to tell you?"

Tennessee didn't currently have a stop-and-identify law, so technically, the man had a right to refuse to answer.

"Things will go a lot easier for you if you do."

Ashley yanked open the rear passenger door of the SUV and then stepped to the side.

"Doug," the man finally stated. "Doug Putnam."

"How old are you?"

"Twenty-two."

Ashley had pegged the man for twenty. She hadn't been far off.

"Well, Doug, you're under arrest," Wyatt said.

"Why?"

"For starters, the car you're driving has stolen plates."

The man's face reddened. "That's not my fault," he said. "It's not my car. I just borrowed it."

"Who loaned it to you?"

Doug didn't answer.

Wyatt leaned into the SUV and strapped the seatbelt around the man. Then he grabbed a metal cable out of a pocket in the SUV's cab and clipped one end to Doug's handcuffs and the other end to a metal loop built into the floorboard. Once the man was secure, Wyatt pulled a piece of paper from his pocket and handed it to Ashley.

As Wyatt began reciting Doug's Miranda rights, she unfolded the slip of paper.

Ashley's pulse quickened as she read the words scrawled in her partner's familiar handwriting. Wyatt had printed the VIN number for Nick Weaver's sports car at the top. Below, he had written the VIN for the red convertible driven by Doug Putnam.

The numbers matched.

Her gaze jerked toward the sandy-haired man who now appeared so harmless.

Was Doug Putnam the roadside killer?

She studied his face, his eyes. Doug didn't have the look or body language of a cold-blooded killer. At that moment, he didn't set off any of her instinctive alarms.

The attacks on Ian, Megan, and Nick had been brutal. Revealing a motivation of rage and extreme bloodlust. She didn't pick up that type of energy from Doug. But then she reminded herself how trustworthy Ted Bundy had seemed to the people who thought they knew him well, who worked with the murderer on a daily basis.

Was the heart of a madman hiding behind Doug's seemingly innocent outward façade?

She directed her attention toward the man's hands, cuffed in his lap. The image of Nick's battered skull popped into her mind. Considering the severity of Nick's wounds, she would expect the killer's hands to have sustained at least a few minor injuries during the beating. Small cuts or bruises.

Doug's hands appeared smooth. The skin unbroken.

The man might not be the one who'd wielded the blows, who'd actually killed the three victims. But it was possible he knew the identity of the murderer.

After receiving Doug's answer – confirming that the man understood his Miranda rights – Wyatt continued his line of questioning.

"Why'd you run, Doug?"

The man's gaze shifted to the floorboard. "I don't know. I was scared."

"You weren't carrying any drugs or weapons. If you hadn't done anything wrong, then what were you scared of?"

The man shrugged.

Doug's story of borrowing the convertible didn't ring true. He'd obviously known the plates were stolen. Did he know the car he'd been driving belonged to a dead man?

Wyatt shifted gears, taking the questioning in a different direction. "Where do you live?"

"My folks have a farm over on Turtle Hill Road."

"Is that in Alta Mill?"

"Not really. It's out in the county."

"Myrtle County?"

Doug nodded. "Yeah."

Nick had been abducted in Bonner County. Ashley wondered whether Doug had family members living near Ormond. Placing her hand on the SUV's open door, she stepped closer to the man.

"So what were you doing over in Bonner County?" she asked.

The question was designed to catch him off guard. To make Doug believe that they already knew for a fact that he'd been in the area where Nick had most likely had car trouble.

"I've got kin there."

The statement came out easy, as though Doug's visit to Bonner County was no secret.

Wyatt shot Ashley a look that said he approved of her tactic.

She pressed further. "Did you borrow the red convertible from one of your relatives?"

This time, Doug wasn't so forthcoming. Instead of answering, he stared at his feet.

Wyatt took over.

"Listen, Doug," he began. "I'm going to level with you. Right now, you're in a lot of trouble. The only way out is to tell the truth."

Doug lifted his head, his gaze shifting from Wyatt to Ashley, and then back to Wyatt.

"Am I gonna go to jail?" he asked, his voice low.

At that moment Doug looked more like a scared child than a serial killer.

Wyatt sighed. "That all depends. You need to tell us how you got the car."

Doug pressed his eyes closed. When he opened them again, Ashley could see his fear.

"Okay, I lied," he said. "I didn't borrow the car. I stole it."

"In Bonner County?"

"Yeah. I switched the plates with a pickup. I was just gonna keep it a few days, just long enough to have a little fun. And then I was gonna take it back where I found it."

Doug's choice of words sparked a question in Ashley's mind. "*Found it*" implied that the convertible was somewhere it shouldn't have been. Had he stolen the car before or after Nick was abducted?

"Where exactly was the car when you decided to steal it?" she asked.

"Out by my grandma's place. I was checking her cattle fences and seen it parked on the side of the road."

Ashley exchanged glances with Wyatt.

"Do you happen to know the name of the road?"

"Nell's Glade."

Nell's Glade Road ran through the same valley where the vehicles belonging to Ian and Megan had been found.

"Did you see – or speak with – the owner of the car?"

Doug shook his head. "Naw. There wasn't nobody around. The hood was up. I figured the owner went to get help. And at first, I was just gonna look at the engine. See if I could tell what was wrong with it."

"Are you a mechanic?"

"Not really, but I tinker a bit now and then."

Ashley guessed he knew more about automobiles than most, since it seemed he'd managed to repair the high-priced convertible.

"So are you the person who got the car running again?"

He nodded. "It was an easy fix. Just about anybody could've done it."

A pang of sadness hit Ashley. Nick hadn't been familiar enough with the engine to do the repair. And it had cost him his life.

"What was wrong with the engine that caused it to stall?"

"Wasn't the engine. It was the petcock. That's the plug on the bottom of the radiator. It got loose and all the coolant drained out."

Having spent countless hours at her family's auto repair shop when she was growing up, Ashley was well acquainted with the term.

After seeming to realize that she understood what he was referring to, Doug continued.

"I just tightened the plug. Put in some water and anti-freeze, and she was good to go. After that, I waited around for a while. I was sure the owner would show back up. But they never did. So … I decided to borrow the car."

Doug's explanation seemed more than plausible. And he'd pinpointed the same location where Ian and Megan had gone missing. If he was somehow involved in the murders, he was doing an excellent job at hiding it.

Wyatt stared at Doug for a moment. Ashley could see the wheels of her partner's mind turning, as though he was pondering his next question.

"How did you meet Nick Weaver?" he asked, obviously trying a sneaky tactic of his own.

Doug's brows furrowed, a puzzled expression covering his face. "Who?"

There was no recognition in the young man's eyes. Nothing to lead Ashley to believe that he'd ever heard Nick's name before.

"The owner of the car." Wyatt stated.

"Like I said, I didn't see nobody. But you'll tell him I'm sorry, won't you? That I didn't mean no harm."

Wyatt sighed. "Nick Weaver is dead."

Doug's complexion paled. He leaned his head back against the SUV's seat and closed his eyes. Ashley knew the young man had a lot to think about.

Wyatt nodded, letting her know that they were finished. At least for now.

"Let's get him back to Bonner County," he said.

As she climbed into the passenger seat, a memory flashed in Ashley's mind. She grabbed the case file and rifled through the pages. When she found what she was looking for, her heart skipped a beat.

"You're not going to believe this," she said, turning to Wyatt.

"What?"

"I just figured out what happened to Ian, Megan, and Nick."

CHAPTER THIRTY FOUR

The killer squinted at the woman on the other side of the counter as she wrote her personal information on the customer form. Her hair reminded him of a movie star, whose name he couldn't remember. All shiny and red and glued into place with a bucket of hairspray. As she moved the pen along the page, her fingernails sparkled with silver glitter in their paint. Long and shaped into a point, he knew they had to be fake.

Just as fake as the woman's smile.

"There's no need to be formal," she had said when he'd addressed her as ma'am. "Just call me Veronica."

Such a snooty name. It fit her.

Although she put on an air of friendliness, he could tell it was all an act. He knew that inside, she was laughing at him. Thinking that he was stupid – a worthless hillbilly. And looking down her nose at him because he chose to use good manners, rather than calling her by her given name.

The city folk were all the same. They had no morals. No concern for the welfare of the people living in Bonner County. With their fancy clothes and expensive cars, they only cared about money. And what they could trick other people into doing for them.

But he wasn't fooled.

He could read the woman's thoughts just by looking at her face. Knew that her soul was as dark as a moonless mountain night.

He'd seen a similar darkness in his father's eyes. And in his own when he looked in the mirror. But like righteous indignation, the malice that burned deep within him was justified. Someone had to rid Bonner County of the urban filth. And he finally realized that he'd been chosen.

It was his job to teach the haughty city dwellers a lesson.

They had to learn to respect the mountain way of life. To stay out of places they didn't belong. His efforts thus far had proved to be a good start, but like a cancer, the depraved city slickers just kept coming back.

They invaded the booths at the diner, cheating the servers out of a fair tip. They spoiled the beauty of the scenic overlooks, leaving their trash strewn across the picnic tables. And they insulted the locals at every turn, making fun of the mountain traditions, of the way the native folks talked, and of how they dressed. But once news of his work spread, all that would change.

He'd make sure his message was received, loud and clear.

Then soon, the people living in the cities would drive miles out of their way in order to avoid Bonner County. And when his work here was finished, he'd consider branching out to one of the neighboring counties that needed his help.

Veronica pulled a credit card from her dark-brown leather wallet.

"You'll really be able to take care of me today?" she asked, her tone saccharine sweet.

Her lips glistened from a heavy layer of gloss.

"That's right," he said, smiling to himself.

The woman had no idea of how well he planned to take care of her.

He picked up the credit card she'd placed on the counter, although he had no intention of running the charge through. He'd been lucky to meet two of the vermin he'd disposed of before her at South Bend Grill, and the third at the diner. They'd never stepped foot on his home turf prior to their abductions. There had been nothing to link him to the killings. And now, he'd make sure there would be no paper trail in Veronica's financial history that would suggest he'd ever met the woman. The police wouldn't find a receipt for his services.

Nothing that could tie him to Veronica's murder.

He turned away from the woman and pretended to swipe her card through the machine resting on the opposite counter.

Excitement flooded his chest as he thought about the lessons he would teach her.

CHAPTER THIRTY FIVE

Ashley's stomach knotted as she watched Wyatt pace back and forth down the back hallway at the Bonner County Sheriff's Department, his cell phone glued to his ear. She had only caught snippets of his conversation with Brenda, but judging by the shrill tone of the deputy director's voice, the news wasn't good.

He ended the call, pocketed his cell, and glanced at Ashley.

"Gentry's lawyer says he's not guilty," Wyatt stated.

She wasn't surprised. In fact, the denial was expected.

"Don't all attorneys claim that their clients are innocent of the charges?"

Wyatt cut his eyes at her, as if that was a given, that there was more to it this time.

"The lawyer has proof Gentry didn't commit the murders," he said.

"What kind of proof?"

"Dash cam footage. When Megan went missing, there was a big pile-up on the main highway in Myrtle County. Took them all day to clear the wreckage. Gentry's on the video. They've also got footage of him on the days Ian and Nick disappeared."

Ashley's heart sank. The state trooper had seemed like the ideal suspect. But the fact that Gentry had been ruled out as the killer gave more credence to her latest theory. A theory she hadn't yet had the opportunity to share with her partner.

"Well, at least we've got Gentry dead to rights on the drug trafficking."

Wyatt shook his head. "No. We don't," he said, his tone sounding almost defeated.

Ashley couldn't believe what she was hearing.

"How is that possible? You and I both saw him throw that blue duffel full of meth out of his car window."

"His lawyer claims it was a setup. That we planted the evidence. And that we ran Gentry off the road on purpose."

Trooper Gentry was a stranger to Wyatt and Ashley. They worked homicide cases, not drug investigations. They had no motive to frame the man for meth trafficking.

"That doesn't even make any sense."

"The guy's a lawyer. It doesn't have to."

A gust of wind hit Ashley as the rear door of the sheriff's department pushed open. Deputy Medford strode into the hallway, nodding at Wyatt and Ashley as he passed.

Once Medford had disappeared around the corner, out of earshot, Wyatt continued.

"Brenda's on her way here now," he said. "We're meeting with the lawyer and a rep from the THP."

The last thing Ashley wanted was to be stuck in a small conference room with Gentry's attorney and a member of the THP's brass.

"Will we get to see the footage from Gentry's dash cam?"

Wyatt looked at her. There was a message in his eyes that she couldn't read.

"Your name's not on the invitation," he said. "Since you're working on a trial basis, Brenda though it would be best to keep you off the THP's radar."

Ashley wasn't quite sure what that meant in regard to her future with the bureau. Was Brenda trying to protect her? Or had the deputy director already decided that Ashley wasn't the right fit for the job?

The expression that had haunted Wyatt's gaze made her fear the latter.

At least Brenda hadn't yet pulled her off of the murder investigation. Ashley wanted to be allowed to see it through. Wanted to help secure justice for the families of Ian, Megan, and Nick.

"What do think about Doug Putnam's story of how he found Nick's convertible?" she asked.

"It's probably true."

She agreed with Wyatt's assessment. Everything that Doug had told them seemed to line up with what they already knew. And the young man didn't give off the vibes of someone who was capable of murder. They hadn't yet received confirmation for the alibis the sandy-haired man had given them, pinpointing his location at the time of the victims' disappearances. But deep in her gut, Ashley knew Doug's story would check out.

Ashley jumped at the sudden ring of her cell phone.

She glanced at the screen. The caller had blocked their number. Could it be Daniel calling again from a burner phone? As far as she knew, the agent was still working undercover.

"I need to take this," she told Wyatt.

He nodded as she headed around the corner of the hallway. She shouldered through the swinging door into the ladies' room for a bit of privacy.

"Hello?"

Static hissed on the line.

And then she heard the moan of a low-pitched, electronically-altered voice.

"Your days are numbered!"

The warning echoed over the airwaves, as though the voice had come from a dank underground tunnel.

A chill raced down Ashley's spine as the line went dead.

Was the caller the same person who had stolen her scrunchie and then left it on the passenger seat of the Bonner County SUV? Was it one of Troy Luckadoo's relatives?

The person who had helped Troy commit several murders?

Ashley's hands shook as she stuffed her phone back into her pocket. Should she tell Wyatt about the call, or should she keep it to herself? He already knew that she believed she was being stalked. And he had the meeting with Brenda, Gentry's attorney, and the THP to worry about. Now didn't seem like the right time.

Grabbing a paper towel from the dispenser on the wall, she switched on the faucet of the chipped porcelain sink, letting the water run cold. As she dabbed her face with the wet towel, she stared at her reflection in the mirror. This case, and the fact that she was being taunted by an unknown enemy – perhaps a killer – were taking a larger toll on her than she'd realized.

But she knew where she had to focus her priorities. She had to shake off her fear of the person who'd called her and channel all of her energy into solving the roadside murders. Since Gentry was no longer a viable suspect, that meant the killer was still running free. He could already have a fourth victim in his sights.

They had to find him before he could kill again.

Gathering her wits, Ashley forced a smile onto her face and pushed through the bathroom door into the hallway. As she rounded the corner, the theory that had struck her on the way back from Myrtle County popped into her mind. With Doug riding in the rear seat of the SUV, she hadn't been able to discuss her suspicion with Wyatt. And since they'd arrived at the sheriff's department, they'd had no real time alone to talk. She was anxious to get her partner's reaction.

In her heart, Ashley felt certain she now knew how the abductions had been carried out.

Wyatt was no longer in the hallway. She cast her gaze through the rear door of the sheriff's department and saw him standing outside, a plastic soda bottle in his hand. He must have wanted to make sure she had all the privacy she'd needed for her phone call.

A light breeze rustled through her hair as she headed down the sidewalk. She glanced to her left and then to her right, making sure there was no one within hearing distance.

"I think I've figured out how the killer was able to kidnap Ian, Megan, and Nick," she told Wyatt.

A smile played across his lips. "How?"

"The timing of the abductions has bothered me since the start of this investigation. How could the killer stumble onto three people – all out-of-towners – who'd had car trouble in such a short amount of time? Is that normal? And what are the odds that their vehicles would all be found in the same valley?"

"It's bothered me too. That's why I thought it was Gentry."

"Right. It would make more sense if he'd been pulling the victims over and then making it look like their car had stalled, after the fact. But now we know there's no way Gentry could have kidnapped them."

"So who did?"

Although she wasn't one-hundred percent positive, Ashley had a pretty good idea of who the killer would turn out to be. Of course, she didn't yet know his name, but she felt certain she knew his profession.

"When Doug told me how easily he was able to fix Nick's car, I remembered something I'd read in the case file. The police mechanic who looked at Megan's SUV found the very same thing wrong with her car. There was no water or coolant in Megan's radiator. Usually when that happens it's because of a broken hose. And I guess I just assumed that was the problem with Megan's car. But I double-checked the mechanic's notes and he didn't mention anything about the hoses. And he didn't find any punctures in the radiator."

"You think she also had a leaky petcock."

Ashley nodded.

"And I think the plug had been loosened on purpose," she stated, her tone confident.

Wyatt chewed his bottom lip as though he was considering the rationality of her theory.

"It sounds plausible," he said. "But we still don't know who did it. Or how he got them all out into the valley."

Her partner might not have put the pieces together yet, but Ashley felt certain she had.

"I think we do know," she said. "Megan's husband said that she'd been having trouble with her SUV before she ever left home, but that she wanted to wait to have it checked out. What if she decided to stop at an auto repair shop here in Bonner County? A shop she passed on the highway."

Wyatt stared at her. "You think a mechanic sabotaged their cars?"

It wasn't just a thought. Her gut screamed that she'd found the right answer.

"It makes more sense that the killer would work at an auto shop than anywhere else," she said. "Megan probably did or said something to make the mechanic angry. While he was repairing whatever was really wrong with her car he could have loosened the petcock. Someone with experience draining radiators would know how long it would take for enough fluid to leak out to cause problems. He would know how far the victims would be able to travel."

"Okay. That all adds up, but why did the victims drive to the valley?"

"I didn't have a solid lead on that until you told me about Gentry's alibi. You said that there was a huge wreck on the main highway running through Myrtle County on the day Megan disappeared. What if the killer used that information to steer Megan where he wanted her to go? He could have given her directions to bypass the traffic."

Wyatt nodded in agreement. "Right into a valley with no cell service," he said.

Ashley smiled, glad to see that her partner felt the theory was valid.

"I pulled up a list of the auto repair shops on the highways while you were talking to Brenda," she told him. "I'm going to go check them out."

"No."

Wyatt's voice was firm. His mouth set in a thin line.

Her partner's quick denial surprised her. Was it because he wanted to go with her in case she found hard evidence that could convict the killer? Or did he know something about her employment status that he hadn't yet told her?

She remembered the look he'd given her when he'd said she wouldn't be allowed to attend the meeting with Brenda.

Her stomach dropped. She stared at him, not sure what to say.

"You don't need to go alone," Wyatt finally stated. "Take Medford with you."

Ashley felt the color return to her face. She nodded and headed back inside the sheriff's department. She wondered whether this would be her last task as a TBI agent.

She found the deputy in the break room, wrangling a pack of cupcakes from the vending machine.

"Come on, Medford," she said, tapping him on the arm. "You and I are going for a ride."

CHAPTER THIRTY SIX

A surge of adrenaline hit Ashley as she climbed into the driver's seat of the county SUV, anxious to check out the area's automotive repair shops. Were they finally on the right path? All the facts they had gathered on the case pointed to a mechanic being the roadside killer.

Everything fit.

Although she was under strict orders from Wyatt not to raise anyone's suspicions – to gather preliminary information only – she hoped she'd run across some type of evidence that would help identify the murderer.

Deputy Medford hopped into the passenger seat next to her.

"Why are we scoping out auto shops?" he asked.

Ashley hesitated. She drummed her fingers on the steering wheel as she tried to figure out the best way to phrase her answer to the young deputy's question. She wouldn't lie to Medford, but she also knew better than to give up pertinent information on a lead to a member of the Bonner County Sheriff's Department.

"There's a good chance that one of the murder victims stopped by a repair shop before she was abducted," Ashley said, keeping her eyes focused on the road. "We just want to know if they remember seeing her. If she told them where she was going … things like that."

"That would be Megan Archer," Medford stated, seeming satisfied with her answer.

"Right."

Although Ashley had previously suspected that Medford might be working with Trooper Gentry behind the scenes, she no longer considered that idea to be a possibility. The deputy's actions since they'd found the duffel of meth seemed to indicate that he was an honest cop, trying his best to learn the ropes and do a good job. But still, Sheriff Powell was his boss, and he was bound to do Powell's bidding. Which made the deputy a quasi-enemy.

Ashley merged onto the highway that connected with the main street running through the town of Ormond. There were three auto repair shops near the small town. One in the city limits and two out in the county. Megan would have likely passed all three on her trip from Knoxville to Murfreesboro. It made sense for them to visit the one located inside the city limits first.

The sun had dipped into the horizon, painting the sky orange as she piloted the SUV into the parking lot of Sommer's Tire and Auto. The interior of the building appeared dark. The sign out front unlit.

"I thought I read online that they stayed open until six," Ashley said.

"They usually do."

She glanced at Medford as the SUV rolled into a parking space near the front door of the business.

"Do you know the owners of the shop?"

"Yeah. My step-father brings his car here."

Ormond was a small town. It made sense that everyone knew each other. She thought about quizzing Medford about the Sommer family, but she realized her questions would likely make the deputy suspicious.

She grabbed her cell and tapped in the phone number painted on the window of the auto shop. After the fifth ring, the call was transferred to a voice mail message. It was clear the business had closed early. She'd have to come back the following day.

Checking her list for the location of the next shop, she pulled back onto the highway and headed east. She hadn't been able to uncover much information regarding Hatcher's Total Auto. The company didn't have a webpage, and from what she could garner, it seemed to be a small family-run shop. She couldn't even find any reviews online.

A loud boom ricocheted through the cab of the SUV, striking fear in Ashley's heart.

The back end of the vehicle jerked to the right, her seat vibrating like a jackhammer.

She clenched her fingers around the steering wheel in a death grip, struggling to keep the SUV traveling in a straight line.

"We've blown a tire!" she shouted, her panic clear.

As soon as she'd learned how to drive, Ashley's father had nailed into her mind all the things that could go wrong on the roadway. And how to survive them. She knew not to slam on the brakes, or to even let off the accelerator. Either action could send the SUV spinning out of control. Although it seemed to go against every impulse in her brain, the only way to avoid a crash was to maintain the vehicle's forward momentum. She had to speed up.

The rear end of the SUV fishtailed.

Ashley pressed down on the gas pedal.

She held her breath, fighting to keep the vehicle on the road.

As the SUV accelerated, she felt the wheels whip back under her control. Once she was confident they wouldn't spin out, she let off the gas. The deflated tire moaned, *flap*, *flap*, *flap*, as she eased onto the shoulder of the highway.

Shifting the transmission into park, she looked at Medford. All the color had drained from the deputy's face.

"Are you okay?" she asked him, hoping that he couldn't tell that her heart was thumping as well.

He nodded. "At least we don't have far to walk," he said, pointing through the windshield.

The sign for Hatcher's Total Auto glowed up ahead on their right, appearing to be a little more than a tenth of a mile away.

"We don't need to walk," she said, surprised that he would even suggest it. "I learned how to change a tire even before I learned how to drive."

She hit the button for the cargo door, slid out of the driver's seat, and circled around the back of the SUV. The vehicle slumped to the right, the rear tire on the passenger side shredded. She leaned into the cargo area and released the latch beneath the storage drawer. The drawer popped up, out of the way.

Anger flooded Ashley's heart.

The spare tire well was empty.

Sheriff Powell had attached a GPS device to the SUV in order to keep tabs on Wyatt and Ashley. Had he sabotaged the tire? Had he taken the spare so the agents would be left stranded on the roadway?

If so, Powell was even more despicable than she'd ever imagined. Both she and Deputy Medford could have been killed when the tire blew. She was certain that maintaining the spare would be a regular part of the sheriff department's safety protocol. It had to be missing on purpose.

"I guess we'll be walking after all," she told Medford, her tone tinged with ire.

Ashley grabbed her cell phone from her pocket.

"I'm going to let Wyatt know where we are."

She tapped out a text telling her partner about the blow out and the missing spare tire. He was sure to be just as angry as she was, if not more.

Medford fell in beside her as they trod down the gravel shoulder of the highway toward the auto shop. They'd only traveled a few yards when the deputy's cell phone rang.

He checked the screen and then met Ashley's gaze.

"It's my wife," he said, with an apologetic edge to his voice.

The feeling that the deputy somehow thought she'd become his boss hit Ashley. But her department wasn't the one paying for his time.

"Stay here and take the call," she said. "Then meet me at Hatcher's."

A gust of wind whipped up, tousling her hair. Ashley pulled her fleece jacket tight around her torso and continued down the road's shoulder. She'd noticed the time when she'd texted Wyatt. 5:27 pm. She hoped the shop was still open. The hours weren't posted anywhere on the internet.

The main entrance of the old, concrete block building sat back about fifty feet from the road. Ashley didn't see any customers' cars parked in the gravel lot. The garage bay doors had been pulled shut, but the interior lights still glowed through the front window. She thought that might be a good indicator that someone was still inside.

A door alarm buzzed – high pitched and loud – as she shouldered her way into the lobby. Empty waiting chairs, upholstered in avocado-green vinyl, greeted her. There was no one behind the cashier's counter. A radio – tuned to a country station – rested on a separate counter next to a landline telephone and an ashtray filled with cigarette butts.

"Be with ya in a minute," a voice called from somewhere in the back of the building.

There were three partially-open doors leading out of the lobby area and she wasn't quite sure from which direction the voice had come. She wandered toward a display rack filled with air fresheners while a song about drinking whiskey, heavy on the fiddle, accosted her ears.

Ashley jumped when she felt something slide over her foot.

A white cat wound itself between her ankles. The fluffy animal purred and mewed as she knelt down to pet it.

"Well, aren't you a sweet little thing?" she said, running her fingers over the cat's back.

The cat pushed its pink nose against her hand.

Fear cut through Ashley's heart as she noticed the sleeve of her fleece jacket.

Long white hairs clung to the navy blue fabric.

The same type of hairs found on the bodies of the murder victims.

Bolting to her feet, her eyes darted back to the butt-filled ashtray. She made a beeline toward the counter. Picking up one of the crushed cigarettes, she realized that it had no filter. The name Black Panther inked the side of the white paper.

Just like the cigarette butt she'd found on Bat Creek Road.

As she reached for her Glock, she felt movement behind her. She started to spin around.

Pain sliced through Ashley's skull.

She fell to the floor, her vision blurry.

Just before she lost consciousness, she saw the face of a man. A man with narrow eyes as dark as night.

It was the man from the forest.

CHAPTER THIRTY SEVEN

Lloyd Hatcher ripped off a length of duct tape from the hefty roll and wound it around the head of the pretty, blonde TBI agent, covering her full lips. How had the woman managed to track him down? She'd only seen him for a brief moment in the forest, and he hadn't left any clues behind. No trail for her to follow.

He should have known not to answer his stupid cousin's call.

Should never have agreed to try and help Rex Gentry clean up his latest mess.

He'd heard his cousin was going down hard this time. That the cops had found one of the bags of meth on the mountain road. They were likely putting the screws to Gentry. And state troopers didn't last long in prison. But Lloyd knew his cousin was no rat.

Men in Bonner County who squealed always died. It was the mountain way.

The police were probably checking out all of Gentry's kin.

Dammit!

This meant Lloyd would have to lay low for a while. After he finished with Veronica – and the blonde TBI agent – he'd have to put his life's mission on hold. But just long enough to make sure the cops didn't come sniffing around.

There were no drugs here.

Lloyd had never taken part in Gentry's schemes.

And there was no way anyone could know about Lloyd's work. He'd been careful. His calling too important to risk making a mistake.

He ripped off another ribbon of tape and wrapped it tight around the agent's shins. Hiking boots covered her ankles, and he didn't have the time to try and yank them off of her feet. But it was okay. The woman wouldn't be going anywhere.

Flipping her over onto her stomach, he bound her hands behind her back. He shoved her pistol into his pants pocket and dragged her across the floor of the lobby, into the adjacent hallway. He'd made it halfway to the rear garage when the high-pitched alarm buzzed.

Somebody had come through the front door of the shop.

He let go of the woman.

"Be with ya in a minute!" he shouted.

He raced into the office tucked at the end of the hallway and glared at the screen connected to the lobby's security camera. A seed of worry sprouted in his stomach. A sheriff's deputy stood at the front counter. He had to get rid of the man. Lloyd checked the clock hanging on the wall above the desk. He would have to hurry.

He was running out of time.

He pulled the hallway door closed as he stepped into the lobby.

"What can I do for ya?" he asked the deputy.

The man offered his hand. "I'm Deputy Cody Medford," he stated. "I came here with TBI Agent Ashley Hope."

Lloyd plastered a wide smiled onto his face and accepted the handshake. He should have known that the pretty agent wouldn't have barged into the shop alone. Cops always worked in pairs. Double the trouble. But he could handle it.

"Oh, right," Lloyd said, his voice cheerful. "Real nice lady. She wanted to get herself a look at the place. She's right back this a way."

Lloyd led Medford to the other side of the lobby. He opened the door to the storage room and stepped inside. His heart pounded in his chest as he slipped his hand into his pocket. His fingers curled around the grip of the agent's pistol. As the deputy crossed the threshold, Lloyd took aim.

He fired a single shot into Medford's brain.

The deputy fell at Lloyd's feet.

With his ears ringing from the blast, Lloyd tossed the agent's gun onto a metal shelf, closed the door of the storage room, and locked the keyed deadbolt. There was no time to clean up the mess now.

Veronica was waiting for him.

His pulse raced as he darted into the lobby and locked the shop's front door. He couldn't afford to be interrupted again. Rushing back to the hallway, he hoisted Ashley over his shoulder. Like the city slickers who'd invaded the county, the agent needed to be taught a lesson.

He'd teach her that she never should have pulled a gun on him in the forest.

That she should have stayed away from his shop.

That she should have minded her own business.

Anticipation fluttered in his chest as he thought about the fun they would have together. He hauled Ashley into the rear garage, the oldest part of the building. The area was no longer used to service cars – that type of work was done in the newer bays, with lifts installed, built onto the side of the shop.

This particular garage had a much more noble purpose.

He carried Ashley down the aluminum ladder into the cold, dank inspection pit.

The plastic shower curtain that covered a section of the oil-stained floor had been meant for Veronica. The two women would be temporary roommates in the pit, but they wouldn't need to share a curtain. He had a large supply in the storage room.

He dropped Ashley onto the plastic.

A rush of excitement hit him as he stared at her sleeping form.

She would be awake when he returned.

Before heading back through the hallway, he checked the time again. He cursed under his breath. Veronica would already be in the valley by now, her radiator spewing steam. Would the haughty city woman wait for him? Or would she get out of her car and walk to a farmhouse?

He could only hope that she'd be too afraid to venture out into the darkness.

That she'd sit tight in the comfort of her leather seats.

As he neared the lobby, three rapid booms echoed down the hallway. Somebody was pounding on the shop's front door. Probably another cop. He swung back into the office. A man dressed in a sports jacket stood in view of the exterior front security camera, a badge clipped to his belt.

A TBI agent.

If he ignored the cop, would the man go away?

Anxiety swelled in Lloyd's stomach.

Ignoring the man seemed like a risky move. What if the agent gathered a swarm of cops together and then busted into the shop. They'd tear the place apart. Lloyd couldn't let that happen.

Just as he made the decision to let the man in, he heard an electronic melody play. He'd tossed Ashley's cell phone on top of the desk. On the security monitor, he saw that the agent had a phone stuck to his ear. Lloyd switched off the power button on Ashley's cell, hid it in the bottom drawer of the desk, and then hurried toward the lobby. He smiled at the cop through the glass as he unlocked the shop's front door.

“How can I help you, sir?” he asked in the politest voice he could muster.

The man flashed his badge.

“My name is Agent Wyatt Clark,” he said. “My partner, Ashley Hope, and Bonner County deputy, Cody Medford, arrived here a little while ago. I just need to speak with them.”

Lloyd scanned the parking lot. He only saw one vehicle. Had the other two cops arrived on foot? No car, no proof the cops were ever here.

He shook his head. “There ain’t nobody here but me,” he said.

The agent stared at him. “You’re sure about that?”

“Yes, sir. My last customer left over an hour ago. I ain’t seen nobody else since.”

If the agent pushed it, he would claim that he’d locked the door at five. That he’d been busy in the garage until just now, and wouldn’t have been able to hear it if someone had knocked.

“You don’t mind if I come in, look around a little bit, do you?”

A pang of dread knifed through Lloyd’s chest.

He forced the smile back onto his face.

“Why, sure. You just come on in. Make yourself at home.”

Lloyd stepped back, pulling the glass door wide open.

He gritted his teeth behind a mask of cheer as the agent circled the lobby.

“The real show’s out in the garage,” he said motioning toward the side of the building.

The agent nodded, a condescending look on his face.

The man was from the city. Lloyd could tell. The city scum seemed drawn to his shop like a magnet. Guided by an unseen hand.

A light flicked on inside Lloyd’s mind.

This time, a genuine smile lifted his lips.

He realized what he was supposed to do. The visions he’d seen in his dreams were real. He truly had been chosen by a higher power. And the agent had been sent to him as proof. He’d allow the man to strut around for a minute or two. Make him feel comfortable. Welcome.

And then at the first opportunity, he’d knock the agent out.

He’d have a little fun. Teach a few lessons.

Then Lloyd would kill Wyatt Clark.

CHAPTER THIRTY EIGHT

Ashley's head throbbed with pain as she forced her eyelids open. For a second, she wasn't sure whether she was awake or dreaming. Deep shadows obscured the area around her. A dank chill hung in the air, carrying the familiar scent of motor oil. And the faint odor of something else. Something she'd smelled before. Ammonia?

She lay on her left side, the floor hard and cold beneath her.

Was she at her family's auto repair shop?

As she tried to sit up, a bout of vertigo hit her, as though she'd been spun like a top. She pressed her eyes closed, waiting for the dizziness to pass. Her eyes flew open again as she realized her arms had been twisted behind her back, and her wrists bound together.

A memory flashed through her mind.

An image of a man who possessed the dark soulless eyes of a demon.

The man from the forest.

The roadside killer.

Her heart hammered in her chest as she jerked her arms, testing her bindings. What she thought was duct tape stretched from her wrists down the backs of her legs and had been secured to her calves. The way she'd been hogtied, she'd never be able to get up onto her feet.

The sharp taste of glue swirled around her tongue. The killer had stuffed a thick wad of duct tape into her mouth before wrapping the tape around her head.

Ashley screamed.

As she'd feared, although she'd shrieked with every ounce of energy she could muster, the sound came out as little more than a whimper. No one would be able to hear her cry for help.

Where had the killer taken her?

Fighting the dizziness, she lifted her head. Out of the shadows, a dirty concrete wall rose in front of her. She remembered walking into the repair shop – Hatcher's Total Auto. She'd pet the white cat, the source of the long hairs found on the victims' bodies. She'd seen the unfiltered cigarette butts in the ashtray. The same brand she'd discovered at the spot Megan had been abducted. And then, the killer had surprised her. But she'd seen his face.

Was the killer one of Gentry's relatives? Was the state trooper in on the murders after all?

The killer had hit her with something heavy.

A wrench maybe?

The same wrench he'd used to beat Ian, Megan, and Nick? The thought shot a bolt of nausea through her stomach.

And then she remembered something else.

Medford.

The deputy had ridden to the auto repair shop with her. He'd lagged behind to talk to his wife on the phone. Where was he now? He didn't know that Wyatt and Ashley had pegged the roadside killer to be a mechanic. Medford hadn't seen the man in the forest. And she'd never told the deputy what the man looked like. She prayed that meant Medford was safe. That the killer would leave him alone.

But Medford was sure to come looking for her. He'd ask questions. Questions that could get him killed.

Ashley had to break free. She had to find Medford before it was too late.

Taking a deep breath of the noxious air, she rocked her body back and forth, trying to propel herself up onto her knees. The bindings fought her, making the task seem impossible.

One ... two ... three ...

With a final push, she gained the momentum she needed. A feeling of triumph raced through Ashley's chest as she swung herself into a semi-sitting position. Her back curled forward, her wrists tied to her calves, there was no way she could walk. But at least she could now see the space around her.

A shaft of light cut through the gloom to her far left. A hole gaped in the ceiling, the source of the light. An aluminum ladder hugged the wall beneath the hole. The images and odors clicked. Ashley knew exactly where the killer had dumped her.

A partially-covered vehicle inspection pit.

She was still at Hatcher's Total Auto. In the not-too-distant past, the same type of pits had once dotted the floors of her own family's auto repair shop. The mechanics would climb down into the concrete-walled pits and work underneath vehicles parked on top. But due to a lack of natural ventilation – trapping harmful fumes, drainage problems, and accidental falls into the concrete wells, the pits posed a dangerous hazard. In modern times, the pits had become obsolete, replaced by safer hydraulic lifts.

Ashley had to figure out a way to rip off the tape that encircled her legs. The adhesive clung to the fabric of her jeans, not her skin. She had to break the bonds enough that she could climb that ladder.

Voices drifted toward her from the ceiling.

She strained her ears, listening.

Did the man have a helper? For all she knew, Gentry's entire family could be cold-blooded killers. Plotting the murders together.

She couldn't make out the muffled words of the people above her, but Ashley recognized a voice. Not just the voice of the man who'd called out to her when she'd first entered the lobby of the auto repair shop.

She heard Wyatt's voice!

Hope surged within her chest. Ashley screamed again, this time with more force than she'd realized she possessed. But her cry died in the air almost as soon as it left her lips. Tears sprang to her eyes. There was no way to get Wyatt's attention.

Or was there?

The voices above her faded. Was Wyatt leaving? She had to hurry.

Ashley swerved her body to the left and then scooted forward on her knees. A sheet of plastic covered the floor beneath her. A shower curtain. She shuddered when she realized the purpose of the plastic. But she didn't have time to think about that now. She had to keep going.

The rough concrete snagged her jeans as she edged off the curtain. She thrust her right leg forward and then her left. A dull pain radiated through her thighs as the hard surface grated against her kneecaps. Gritting her teeth, she shoved the pain aside and pushed onward. Directed all of her focus on reaching her goal.

The aluminum ladder.

Right ... left ... right ... left ...

She repeated the mantra in her mind as she shuffled across the floor. The grip of the tape on her jeans restricted her movement, only allowing her to advance inches at a time. The seconds seemed to stretch into an eternity.

Please don't leave, Wyatt!

With only a few feet left to go, Ashley lunged forward. She flipped onto her side. Pivoting her body around, she slammed her heels against the bottom rung of the ladder.

The ladder wobbled, and then crashed to the floor.

The clank of aluminum on concrete echoed in the narrow pit.

If Wyatt was still in the room above her, he definitely would have heard it. So would the killer. But Wyatt was armed. And she knew he was a fast draw.

She lay on the cold concrete, listening. Waiting to hear Wyatt's voice again. This time, calling out her name.

The seconds ticked by. There was no movement above her. No voices. No sounds of any kind. Just the thumping of her own heart.

The tears that she'd blinked back earlier welled in her eyes once again.

Was Wyatt safe? Or had the mechanic killed him?

Sighing, Ashley glanced to her right. Something glinted at her from the corner, reflecting a dot of light. She squinted her eyes, but in the gloom, she couldn't identify the object. She had to get back onto her knees.

Rocking her body from left to right, as she had before, Ashley soon had her legs under her again. She inched toward the corner. The object began to take shape. Tall and skinny and rod-like with metal ends, leaning against the wall.

It was an old-school florescent tube lightbulb.

She recalled that the ancient inspection pits at her family's auto shop – now filled in with concrete – had contained florescent lighting fixtures mounted to the walls. The same was likely true here.

Adrenaline rushed through Ashley's body as an idea struck her.

Swiveling around, she backed toward the lightbulb, inch by inch. She moved at an angle, careful to keep her feet from knocking against the glass tube. Her plan had to be executed with precision in order for it to work. And even then, she knew it might fail.

Holding her breath, Ashley stretched out her fingers. The tips touched the glass. She scooted one final inch. The glass melded with her palm, firmly in her grasp.

Yes!

She slid her fingers down the tube, mindful of the top-heavy weight. If she allowed the tube to tip over, it would hit the concrete floor and shatter. She needed a large piece of the bulb. A specific piece.

Ashley cupped the metal end of the tube in her right palm, steadying the bulb with the fingers of her left hand. She twirled around again, this time backing toward the aluminum ladder that lay on the floor.

When she felt she was close enough, she breathed in deep and concentrated. Tightening her grip around the metal end of the bulb, she closed her eyes.

This had to work. It was her only way out.

Ashley whacked the glass against the side rail of the ladder.

The tube vibrated in her fingers as the blub splintered in pieces.

Opening her eyes, she looked back over her shoulder. Her heart soared. The shard of glass that remained crimped in the metal contact was just the right size. Exactly what she needed.

Her fingers out of the way, protected by the metal end of the bulb, she sawed the broken glass against the duct tape wrapped around her legs. She focused her efforts on the area between her two calves. She pushed against the tape as hard as she dared, the fabric of her jeans shielding her skin.

After a full minute of sawing, she felt the tape give way.

Ashley's legs were free.

CHAPTER THIRTY NINE

Ashley's pulse raced as she jerked her legs free of the duct tape that had bound them. Breaking the florescent light bulb had worked. She'd been able to saw through the tape with a shard of glass. Now, she had to free her hands, still bound behind her back. Then she could climb out of her prison – the dank vehicle inspection pit.

She had to find Wyatt and Deputy Medford before it was too late. Were they both still here at Hatcher's Total Auto? She couldn't imagine either of them leaving without her. She just prayed they were both still safe.

With her wrists no longer hog-tied to her calves, Ashley possessed a much wider range of motion. She slid her arms past her behind, down her legs, and finally over her feet, bringing her hands in front of her body.

The cold seeping from the rough concrete floor permeated the seat of her jeans as she pulled her knees up to her chest. Her feet together, she wedged the metal end of the broken florescent tube between the toes of hiking her boots. Her heart pounded as she sawed the tape binding her wrists against the jagged glass.

Careful not to scrape her skin, she counted off the strokes in her mind. The killer had looped the tape several times, creating a thick layer. One that wasn't easy to pierce. But she knew she had to hurry. The lives of Wyatt and Medford might be at stake.

A wave of relief washed over her as the shard split through the tape.

She ripped the bindings from her wrists. The adhesive chapped the skin of her cheeks and refused to let go of several strands of her hair as she peeled the tape from her mouth and head. But finally, she was free.

Ashley grabbed the aluminum ladder and propped it against the concrete wall of the pit, beneath the hole in the ceiling. As her boot landed on the first rung, her pulse quickened. The killer could be at the top, waiting for her.

Holding her breath, she eased her head out of the hole. Her eyes scanned the room. Stained cardboard boxes filled the garage. An old refrigerator – its door removed – sat in the corner. A dusty metal filing cabinet and a beat-up wooden chest of drawers blocked the rolling bay door. It appeared the area was now used for storing unwanted items, not for working on motor vehicles.

Maybe that was how the roadside killer had been able to hide his victims. The customers – and the other mechanics working here – likely had no reason to venture into this area of the shop. It was the perfect spot for a torture chamber.

Still on alert, she continued up the ladder.

The mechanic was nowhere to be seen.

There were no tools lying about. Nothing she could see that could be used as a weapon.

Ashley crept toward a swinging door on the far side of the garage. She kept her ears perked, listening for voices or movement. Silence filled the shop. She pressed her palm against the cool metal door, pushing it open a crack. She peered into the adjoining room. An empty hallway stretched before her with three doors, all on the left.

Without making a sound, she slipped into the hallway.

The first door to her left gaped open. As she tiptoed toward the room, she heard noises coming from inside. Ashley froze. She held her breath and waited, ready to dart back into the garage.

The noises continued. A faint squeak. Rattling. Wheels rolling on a hard floor.

She inched toward the room and peeked through the crack between the open door and the frame. Panic flooded her heart.

Wyatt!

Her partner sat slumped in an office chair, unconscious. A bloody gash striped his temple. The mechanic's back faced her. He held a large roll of duct tape. She could hear the man chuckle as he wrapped the tape around Wyatt's right wrist, binding it to the chair's armrest.

Slightly behind the man, to his right, she noticed a large video monitor mounted on the wall. Four sections divided the screen. A view of the cashier's counter in the lobby, an exterior view of the front entrance, and exterior views of the two garage bay doors that faced the parking lot.

She had to save Wyatt. Had to find something she could use as a weapon. And she needed to call for help. She remembered seeing a landline phone on top of one of the counters in the lobby.

Could she get to the phone without the mechanic seeing her on the video monitor?

With her heart hammering in her chest, she eased past the office. She kept her back to the wall as she skulked toward the next room. The light inside the room was switched off, but in the glow from the hallway she could see a porcelain sink and toilet. She scurried toward the final door.

Praying the mechanic wouldn't hear her, that the door wouldn't creak, she put her hand on the knob and twisted. The door opened into the lobby. The room sat quiet. No one in sight. Crossing the threshold, she inched the door closed behind her.

She scanned the wall, searching for the surveillance camera. She spotted it perched high in a corner, angled toward the cashier's counter. The phone rested on top of the counter lining the opposite wall. If she skirted the edge of the room, she should be able to reach the phone without being caught on the surveillance video.

On the tips of her toes, she flew around the perimeter of the lobby toward the counter with the landline. She grabbed the entire phone – a push-button model that looked like a relic from the nineties – and ducked down beside the counter. She put the receiver to her ear.

A shrill, rapid *beep, beep, beep, beep* blared from the speaker.

Somewhere in the shop, another phone was off the hook. Probably in the office. She had no way to call for help. Then she realized Wyatt must have driven himself to the auto repair shop. The county SUV sat on the shoulder, down the road. But her partner's vehicle was likely parked in the gravel lot.

Wyatt's SUV was equipped with a police radio.

And a rifle.

The extra key fob was still in the front pocket of her jeans. The auto shop's door alarm would buzz when she ran out, alerting the killer. But she'd be inside the SUV before the mechanic could make it down the hallway to the lobby. She'd grab the rifle. And then …

Ashley peeked over the top of the counter. She was still alone. The lobby silent. She raced toward the door of the business and yanked the metal handle. The door didn't budge.

Locked!

The door featured a deadbolt. It could only be unlocked with a key. She realized the other shop doors were likely locked tight as well. Fear gnawed at her heart. But she wouldn't let the mechanic kill Wyatt. She had to find something she could use as a weapon. There was only one choice left.

Ashley needed to attack the killer.

And she was running out of time. How long would it be before the mechanic realized that she had escaped from the inspection pit?

Two additional doors led out of the lobby, both located to the right of the counter area. She rushed toward the first door. It stood open, but only just a crack. She paused and listened. She didn't hear anything. Opening the door a bit wider, she squeezed inside. Free-standing metal shelves, stocked with automotive parts, stood to her left. She turned to the right.

Terror sliced through Ashley's heart.

A six-foot-long bundle lay on the floor, wrapped with a shower curtain. Deputy Medford's lifeless face stared at her through the clear plastic. Ashley fought the urge to vomit as bile rose in her throat.

The young man had just started his career. He'd been honest, dedicated. He'd had his whole life ahead of him. A world of possibilities. And he had a wife.

Tears sprang to Ashley's eyes and rolled down her cheeks.

The mechanic had murdered the young deputy, and Wyatt was his next target. She had to get to the garage area and find a heavy wrench – a crowbar – something – that she could use as a weapon.

And she had to go now.

As she swerved back around, the glint of silver metal caught Ashley's eye. A large pneumatic hammer rested on a shelf located behind the door. A quick-change chisel retainer had been mounted onto the tool. Fresh blood coated the retainer's steel end.

Was it Wyatt's blood?

Was the steel air hammer the weapon that had killed Ian, Megan, and Nick?

A tremor of fear and disgust shook Ashley's body. Filling her lungs with a deep breath of air, she counted to ten and forced herself to calm down. She knew what she had to do. And she couldn't let her nerves interfere.

Ashley grabbed the air hammer.

CHAPTER FORTY

Revulsion flooded Ashley's body, chilling her to the core and spewing bile into the back of her throat, as she gripped the handle of the pneumatic hammer. The tool felt heavier than she'd imagined. Perhaps weighted down by the terror and pain its blows had inflicted. The memory of the lives the roadside killer had stolen ingrained into the cold steel.

An image of the grief-stricken face of Megan's husband, Jay, flashed into her mind. Her heart ached for their two children, whose mother would never come home. Ian had a child as well, a son. And Nick had been engaged to be married. She knew the loss of the three souls would impact the lives of the people who loved them for decades and beyond.

Fastened onto the end of the tool, the quick-change chisel retainer glistened with fresh blood.

Wyatt's blood.

She wouldn't allow the mechanic to end her partner's life. She'd kill the man first. She only wished she'd been able to break out of the vehicle inspection pit in time to save Medford.

Ashley's pulse quickened as she peeked around the storage room door into the auto shop's lobby. Her eyes scanned the room. It was still empty. She raced around the perimeter of the lobby, careful to stay out of view of the security camera mounted on the wall in the corner.

As she skidded to a silent halt next to the closed hallway door, something snagged the bottom right leg of her jeans. Startled, her gaze jerked toward the floor. The long-haired, white cat pawed at the laces of her hiking boot. A loud *meow* sprang from its lips.

Please be quiet! Ashley's eyes screamed at the cat, but she didn't dare voice the words.

Nudging the cat to the side, she pressed her ear to the closed door and listened.

Had the mechanic finished taping Wyatt to the office chair? Was he lurking in the hallway? Or was he on his way to the inspection pit?

What would the man do when he found out she'd escaped?

Ashley's heart hammered in her chest as she eased the door open and peered into the hallway. It was clear. The man nowhere in sight.

The cat squeezed around her feet, darting toward the bathroom.

Shit!

Would the mechanic wonder how the cat had managed to get into the hallway? Should she grab the ball of fur and carry it back to the lobby?

With no time to think it through, Ashley crept into the hallway. She followed in the cat's tracks and headed to the bathroom. The overhead light inside the room was switched off. But when she reached the doorway, in the shadows, she caught site of the animal perched on top of the ancient porcelain sink.

Before she could grab the cat, a white paw shot out and swatted a bottle of liquid soap hovering on the sink's edge.

The bottle hit the tile floor with a loud *thud*.

Ashley's heart skipped a beat. She jumped behind the bathroom door. Her breathing shallow, she waited. A second later, she heard movement in the hallway.

Through the crack between the door and the frame, she saw a shadow approach the bathroom. Panic bubbled in her stomach as the shadow froze. She could feel evil radiating from the dark soul of the mechanic. Depraved and malignant.

Did he sense her presence?

She tightened her grip on the air hammer in her raised right hand.

The shadow moved. The man's footsteps echoed on the tile floor. She heard him pick up the bottle of liquid soap and place it back on top of the sink.

"You best behave, now," he said, his voice gruff.

The cat's feet issued a soft plunk as the man dropped the animal onto the floor of the hall.

For a moment, the man stood still in the doorway, as though he was listening.

Could he hear her breathing? Hear her heart pounding in her chest?

The shadow moved again and then disappeared down the hallway.

Ashley pressed her eyes closed and allowed her breathing to settle back to normal. It sounded as though the man had returned to the office. She hadn't heard the swinging door to the rear garage open. The cat was likely in the office with him.

And Wyatt.

Ashley inched out from behind the bathroom door. She peeked into the hallway. Noises emanated from the office, but she couldn't tell what the man was doing. She prayed Wyatt was okay.

With her back brushing against the wall of the hallway, she edged toward the office door.

Her stomach jumped at the sound of a cell phone ringing.

Not just any phone. She recognized the tune. It was Wyatt's cell. Was it Brenda checking in? When he failed to answer, would the deputy director search for him? All of the TBI agents' phones were equipped with a GPS app. Brenda would know how to locate them.

Unless someone switched off the phone.

The tune stopped – cut short in the middle of a ring.

Ashley's hopes sank. No one would find them. At least, not until it was too late.

She slid closer to the office. Her back pressed to the wall, she stopped right beside the doorway. Her pulse raced as she stood still, straining her ears, trying to figure out what the mechanic was up to.

A shadow fell across the hall floor and Ashley felt movement just inside the office door.

Her heart in her throat, she raised the air hammer above her head.

Would the man turn right, toward the rear garage when he passed through the doorway, or would he turn toward Ashley? If he caught sight of her, there was a good chance he would dodge the blow.

And she knew the man was armed. A bullet had killed Medford – fired into the side of his head – not the air hammer.

The seconds ticked by as she waited, the steel air hammer growing heavier with each shallow breath she took. The shadow finally retreated. She heard a low rumbling noise like wheels rolling across a hard floor. The man had pushed Wyatt's chair across the room.

The shadow popped back into view, moving fast. Footsteps reverberated toward the hallway.

She held her breath, the air hammer poised high.

As the man stepped across the office threshold, his body veered to the right.

Ashley slammed the end of the air hammer into the back of the mechanic's skull.

The man shrieked, the cry bouncing off the hallway walls. He staggered a few feet, and then turned around and lunged toward Ashley.

His muscular arms snapped around her waist, knocking her off balance. The air hammer slipped from her fingers as Ashley crashed to the floor. The man's towering frame landed on top of her legs, trapping her.

Kicking her feet, Ashley scooted backwards, trying to twist out from under the mechanic's weight. She looked back over her shoulder. The air hammer rested on the hallway floor, just a few inches away.

The man grabbed her left wrist.

"I'm gonna kill you!" he shouted, his demonic eyes locking onto hers.

Terror flooded her soul. She had to get away. Had to save Wyatt.

Ashley jerked her arm, but the man's grip was as strong as a vise.

She swiveled her hips and kicked upward as hard as she could. The mechanic howled in pain as her foot smashed against his groin.

The man let go of her wrist and Ashley thrust herself backwards. She swung her right hand behind her. Her fingertips brushed against the cold steel of the air hammer. The tool was just beyond her grasp.

The man cried out again, though not from pain this time. It was a low guttural cry signaling an attack. As he hurled his body forward, Ashley pushed her left heel against the floor, scooting herself back the final inch.

The man cinched his hands around Ashley's neck. His lips twisted into a wicked smile as he began to squeeze.

Her breathing cut off, Ashley's lungs burned as she fought to remain conscious. Her fingers curled around the grip of the air hammer. With every bit of strength she could summon, she swung the tool toward the man's head.

The end of the chisel retainer bashed against the mechanic's skull with a loud crack.

A moan escaped the man's lips. But instead of loosening his grip on her neck, the man's fingers tightened. His determination to kill her clear.

As blood trickled down the man's forehead, Ashley pummeled the air hammer into his skull a second time, and then a third.

Finally, the mechanic's hands fell from her neck and he slumped to the side, his shoulder hitting the floor. The man was still very much alive, but he was out cold.

Ashley struggled to catch her breath. She wriggled her way out from under the man's body and dashed from the hallway into the office.

Wyatt was still unconscious, his wrists, torso, and ankles bound to the rolling chair. A gash, covered with dried blood, marred his temple. She felt his neck for a pulse. She let out a sigh of relief as she confirmed that he was still alive.

She had to cut him loose. Get him to wake up.

Rifling through the drawers of the metal office desk, she found a letter opener. She sliced through the duct tape wrapped around Wyatt's wrists first, then moved to his chest, and finally his ankles. She picked at the end of the tape covering her partner's mouth, careful not to tear his skin as she ripped away the adhesive.

"Wyatt, can you hear me?" she said, shaking his shoulders. "It's Ashley. You're going to be okay."

His eyelids fluttered.

He spit out a wad of duct tape and then grunted. As he pushed his eyes open, he met her gaze.

Wyatt smiled at her.

Ashley's heart soared.

In that moment, she knew that her partner really would be all right.

Grabbing Wyatt's phone from the top of a filing cabinet in the corner, she switched it back on and dialed 9-1-1. His Glock rested on top of the cabinet as well. She chambered a round and headed back to the hallway.

Ashley trained the weapon on the center of the mechanic's chest and waited for reinforcements to arrive.

CHAPTER FORTY ONE

Two Weeks Later

Ashley waved goodbye to her father and brothers as Kyle backed the moving truck out of the driveway of her new garage apartment in Briarwood. With all the furniture – what little she owned – now tucked inside the one-bedroom, second-story space, she could turn her attention to unpacking her clothes and other personal belongings. Soon, she knew it would feel like home.

It was a bittersweet moment. Although excitement filled her heart when she considered all the possibilities her new life in the Nashville suburb could bring, she realized she would miss her family, the peacefulness of her father's sprawling acreage, and the colorful mountains of Laurel County. She'd even miss her father's old hound dog, Ace.

But there was a key advantage to her being out of her hometown of Mettler Ridge. She wouldn't be running into Troy Luckadoo's relatives. Since she'd been back from Ormond, there'd been no more strange phone calls. And she had no longer experienced the eerie feeling of being watched. She hoped that meant the Luckadoos had decided to leave her alone. That she wasn't worth their trouble.

As she pivoted toward the wooden staircase that stretched along the side of the garage, Daniel met her gaze, his blue eyes sparkling.

"Thank you for helping me get settled in," she said. "I really appreciate it."

The offer had come as a bit of a surprise. But not because she thought he'd run from the prospect of heavy lifting. Ever since she'd partnered with Wyatt, her relationship – friendship – whatever it was – with Daniel had felt a bit off. Strained.

"No problem." He patted his stomach. "Moving furniture is a good way to work up an appetite."

"Well, I hope you're not expecting home cooking because I haven't had time to go to the grocery store yet."

"How about we order a pizza?"

"Yes," she said with a smile.

Pizza delivery ranked at the top of her list of things that Laurel County lacked.

Ashley bounded up the stairs with Daniel at her heels. It felt really nice to have him here. She hoped he planned to visit on a regular basis.

As they headed inside, she noticed Daniel glance at the envelope she'd tossed on top of the small dining table next to the galley kitchen. The TBI logo emblazoned on the upper left corner was hard to miss. She hesitated a moment, waiting to see if he would ask about the letter.

Although his expression looked as though he'd stolen it right off the face of the Cheshire cat, he didn't say a word. She realized he already knew what the envelope contained, but he was obviously going to wait until she was ready to discuss it.

"That's my official job offer from Brenda Huddleston," she finally stated.

The offer had come in at a higher salary than she'd expected. Brenda had praised the work Ashley and Wyatt had done in Bonner County. The deputy director had remarked that capturing the roadside killer proved Ashley possessed the skills necessary to be one of the TBI's top agents. And the letter stated that Wyatt had specifically requested that she remain his partner. Which had hit her as a bit of a shock.

"Is that what that is?" Daniel said, his voice playful. "And what's your answer?"

She chewed her bottom lip.

"I'm going to think it over for a few days," she heard herself say.

He looked stunned. As though he didn't know how to respond.

The answer had come as a surprise to Ashley as well. Her hesitancy wasn't due to the fact that she didn't enjoy the work – she loved it. But there were other things she wanted to consider.

Like her personal life.

If she took the position, Wyatt would be assigned as her permanent partner. At least for the foreseeable future. In one aspect, that was good. She wouldn't technically be working with Daniel, so there'd be no conflict of interest if their relationship evolved into something more personal.

But Daniel clearly had issues when it came to Wyatt.

If she agreed to accept the job, would her work end up pushing her and Daniel further apart?

As if reading her mind, Daniel's expression turned serious, his gaze locking onto hers.

"There's something I've been meaning to tell you," he stated. "When you were in Bonner County, I acted like a jerk. And I'm sorry."

She never would have accused him of being a jerk, but he'd definitely made her feel uncomfortable. As though he thought that she was hiding something from him. That he believed she wanted to pursue a romantic relationship with Wyatt.

"Okay."

"The truth is – I was jealous."

The admission hung in the air, stealing Ashley's breath. She was afraid to speak. Afraid she'd misunderstood the true meaning of his words and would say something to embarrass herself.

Daniel caressed her hand, entwining his fingers with hers.

Ashley's stomach fluttered.

"For a while now, I've had feelings for you," he said. "Feelings that go beyond friendship. I'm not sure where they'll lead. Or if you even care. But if you're willing, I'd like to find out."

Ashley smiled as her heart soared. Should she admit that she had strong feelings for him as well? Or should she play it cool? She didn't want to appear overeager and scare him away.

"So what exactly are you suggesting?" she asked, struggling to keep the giddiness out of her tone.

"Can I take you to dinner tomorrow night?"

She nodded. "It's a date."

"Good," he said, his Cheshire cat grin returning. "Now, what about that pizza?"

She laughed. "I guess I need to place the order."

"Don't worry. I've got it."

He held up his cell phone.

Ashley realized she'd left her own phone downstairs in her car. She darted toward the door.

"I'll be right back," she told Daniel, over her shoulder.

A feeling of contentment settled over her as she skipped down the wooden steps. She had a new apartment, most likely a new job, and best of all: a new *almost* boyfriend. Her world seemed full of promise.

She hopped off the last step and circled around to the front of the garage. The bay door was up, her sedan nestled inside. The vehicle's lights blinked as she tapped the unlock button on her key fob.

As she drew even with the side of the car, she noticed a piece of paper wedged beneath the windshield wiper on the driver's side. Had Shane left her a silly goodbye note? It seemed like something her younger brother would do. Her grin widened.

She snatched up the paper.

Ashley's blood ran cold as she read the printed block-style words.

YOU WILL DIE SOON

Jerking her gaze toward the driveway, she scanned the street and the lawns adjacent to her own. The hairs on the back of her neck prickled.

Was the message a warning? Or a threat?

NOW AVAILABLE!

LET ME BREATHE
(An Ashley Hope Suspense Thriller—Book 4)

Ashley Hope is an average Southern woman, happily engaged—until dark secrets from her past tear her life apart. Now a member of Tennessee's State Police's Violent Crimes Division, Ashley must enter a murderer's mind and follow a serial killer's mysterious trail of victims through toxic waste sites. But could Ashley be next?

"Phenomenal debut with a huge creep factor… So many twists and turns, you'll have no idea who the next victim will be. If you love a thriller that will keep you awake well into the night, this book is for you."
—Reader review for Let Me Go

LET ME BREATHE is book #4 in a new series from #1 bestselling mystery and suspense author Kate Bold, which begins with LET ME GO (Book #1).

A dark crime thriller full of mystery and suspense, the ASHLEY HOPE mystery series is rife with twists and jaw-dropping secrets as it unfolds into a riveting psychological thriller. Join this brilliant new female protagonist as she hunts down a serial killer, keeping you spellbound and turning pages late into the night. Fans of Rachel Caine, Teresa Driscoll and Robert Dugoni are sure to fall in love.

Books #5 and #6 in the series—LET ME FORGET and LET ME ESCAPE—are now also available.

"I really enjoyed this book… It draws you in right away and keeps you turning the pages right up to the end. I am really anticipating the next book."
—Reader review for Let Me Go

“A really good read. The story went quickly and the characters were interesting. I'm looking forward to the next book in this series!”
—Reader review for Let Me Go

“Good read with good plot, plenty of action, and great character development. A thriller that will keep you awake into the night.”
—Reader review for Let Me Go

“Excellent start to a new series… Get this book and read it, you will love it!”
—Reader review for Let Me Go

Kate Bold

Bestselling author Kate Bold is author of the ALEXA CHASE SUSPENSE THRILLER series, comprising six books (and counting); the ASHLEY HOPE SUSPENSE THRILLER series, comprising six books (and counting); the CAMILLE GRACE FBI SUSPENSE THRILLER series, comprising five books (and counting); and the HARLEY COLE FBI SUSPENSE THRILLER series, comprising three books (and counting).

An avid reader and lifelong fan of the mystery and thriller genres, Kate loves to hear from you, so please feel free to visit www.kateboldauthor.com to learn more and stay in touch.

BOOKS BY KATE BOLD

ALEXA CHASE SUSPENSE THRILLER
THE KILLING GAME (Book #1)
THE KILLING TIDE (Book #2)
THE KILLING HOUR (Book #3)
THE KILLING POINT (Book #4)
THE KILLING FOG (Book #5)
THE KILLING PLACE (Book #6)

ASHLEY HOPE SUSPENSE THRILLER
LET ME GO (Book #1)
LET ME OUT (Book #2)
LET ME LIVE (Book #3)
LET ME BREATHE (Book #4)
LET ME FORGET (Book #5)
LET ME ESCAPE (Book #6)

CAMILLE GRACE FBI SUSPENSE THRILLER
NOT ME (Book #1)
NOT NOW (Book #2)
NOT WELL (Book #3)
NOT HER (Book #4)
NOT NORMAL (Book #5)

HARLEY COLE FBI SUSPENSE THRILLER
NOWHERE SAFE (Book #1)
NOWHERE LEFT (Book #2)
NOWHERE TO RUN (Book #3)